Biggest Little
Girl

Biggest Little Girl

Jodi Angel

LAKE DALLAS, TEXAS

FIRST EDITION

Requests for permission to reprint or reuse material
from this work should be sent to:

Permissions
Madville Publishing
PO Box 358
Lake Dallas, TX 75065

Cover Design: Jacqueline Davis

ISBN: 978-1-956440-41-6 paper; 978-1-956440-42-3 ebook
Library of Congress Control Number: 2022944365

For Shelby

PART I

Chapter 1
The Grooming

Underneath me the Greyhound rolled from side-to-side, like the waterbed reeling on the wood frame in my bedroom when my mom was at work and a neighbor boy had dug his toes into the rubber mattress with his cutoffs tangled around his ankles and held me down by my wrists so that he could grind some compliance into me, and I could hear the tires slap the wet asphalt, and with each shudder I knew that I was getting farther from home. I was fourteen years old and tall for my age and I had been on the bus for twenty minutes and nothing mattered anyway because I had watched my mom sleeping before I left—in the same way that she had been sleeping since I had been born—and if she had woken up while I stood there, ready to run, and asked me what I was doing, I would have told her, *nothing*, and she would have made one of those noises in her throat and rolled over and gone slack and back to sleep, but she didn't wake up and I didn't wake her, and I was gone in the click of a screen door and Converse on pavement. The bus was crowded—so many people getting gone before the long weekend—and I was lucky to get one of the last window seats that I had spent $5.50 for the privilege of sitting in, and outside the window the rain streaked the glass and everything was one long blur of wet and no color, and the woman beside me had her purse on her lap, carefully protected by both of her arms, and she was slowly chewing on an apricot as the bus spit back the miles moving us north.

"This is some kind of travel weather, isn't it?" she said. She was wearing a dress and dark nylon stockings, and her heavy black shoes were braced against the footrest in front of her. She was maybe as old as my Grandma Mavis, but it was hard to guess, and I could tell that her hair was a wig because there were white hairs curling out from underneath in the places where it didn't quite sit snug to her head. For a little while I wondered why she disguised herself with a wig—what she was covering

1

up underneath?—and I had to swallow the urge to pull on it and see what was true.

"It's really raining," I said.

"It never rains this time of year," she said. "Not around here. One of those strange years, I guess. Has been all summer." She took another bite of her apricot and chewed slowly, moving her mouthful from side to side like the bus shifting beneath the thin metal floor separating us from the asphalt. "You going to Portland?"

"Redding," I said. The bus smelled like bleach and wet dog and sour food and Lysol and a toilet that hadn't been flushed in a while.

"Seeing family?"

I cleared my throat. "My dad," I said. "He's ummm," I paused for a second. "He's a doctor there." My father had skipped town after my fifth birthday, but he was divorced from my mom by then, and I used to have a picture of him where we were standing beside a creek, both squinting into the sun and holding a stringer of trout between us, but I had lost the picture a long time ago—about the same time I lost the memory of what his voice had sounded like.

"Oh, a doctor? That's something. I'm going to Portland. Visiting my daughter. She's a bartender. I go there at the end of every summer so I can see my grandkids before school starts. End of summer and Christmas. That's our routine." She shifted her feet around. "She might go back to school in the spring. Finish her degree."

I really didn't know what to say to the woman, and the bus was too warm, and there was a lot of noise between the tires, the pavement, the talking, and some kids up front screaming back and forth while their mom tried to wrangle them back into seats. It was only a 45-minute ride to Redding, and then I would have to figure out the next thing to do. I wasn't ready to go to Portland, but maybe I would. Maybe when I got off the bus, I would just buy a ticket for the next stop and keep going.

"You want an apricot? I have another one in my purse." She unclasped the bag on her lap and began digging around, and I could see her wallet and a scarf and her hand digging deeper as she searched.

"No, no thank you," I said. "I'm not hungry."

She kept digging for a second and then stopped. "Are you sure? I have to eat on these trips. Makes the time pass."

Outside the window, I could see trees and grass and long fields of yellow grass, but mostly all I could see was rain and the run of drops as they streaked the glass. I closed my eyes for a second and just felt the wheels turning beneath me. When I opened my eyes, there was a man holding onto the headrests as he swayed, coming up the aisle toward the bathroom in the back, and he was wearing a big coat and holding a bottle wrapped in a paper bag as he steadied himself against the rows of seats, and the old woman beside me opened her purse and took out a small spray bottle of perfume and squirted it on her neck, and I was misted with Avon and the smell of something sweet.

"So many people on this bus," she said. "It's always so crowded. Everybody going somewhere, I guess."

After what felt like an hour, but was probably fifteen minutes, the bus slowed down and the sound of the wheels changed from their steady slap, and then the bus shifted into a lower gear and groaned and we left the freeway, took an offramp that I did not see the name of, and then rolled down a smaller road.

"Is your dad picking you up?" the old woman asked.

I looked out the fogging window. "He'll be here," I said.

"You're lucky you have such a good dad. My daughter's boyfriend left the day after Caleb was born—that's my grandson—he's starting kindergarten. Her boyfriend decided he wanted to join a band in Seattle and that was that. He just up and left. Hasn't ever come back. Being a dad didn't cost him a thing." The bus made a left turn into a wide parking lot. There was the sound of gravel crunching underneath us, and then we shuddered to a stop and there was a hiss of air, and the bus went quiet except for people standing up to leave their seats.

"Redding station," the driver said. "Ten minutes."

I stood up, awkwardly, and the old woman beside me did, too. "I'm going to stretch my legs," she said. "That's one thing I've learned on these trips. You have to get out and walk when you can." She moved into the aisle and I stepped beside her and reached up and took my backpack off the metal rack above the seats.

"Well," the old woman said, "you have a good time. Enjoy your dad," she said. I thought she was going to hug me for a second, but then she just turned and made her way slowly down the aisle, holding onto the seats as she went, swallowed up by the crowd of other people.

I stepped into the fresh air and took a deep breath. The rain had stopped for now, and there was a group of people lighting up cigarettes, and the driver was stretching his back, and nobody looked at me like I was up to anything. I walked toward the building. The old woman who had been sitting beside me was wandering to the edge of the parking lot, walking slowly, with her purse slung over her shoulder.

The station was just a one-room building with a long wooden ticket counter fronted by screened windows with rows of plastic chairs without armrests, and all the chairs faced a small TV that was mounted from the ceiling and the Showcase Showdown was on *The Price Is Right*. There was a blue sign with an arrow that pointed toward the bathrooms, and there was already a line forming, and a group of teenagers were crowded around a vending machine that was spitting out Butterfingers. The only person in the seats was a man in a sweatshirt and a coat, who was asleep, his hood pulled up and his head thrown back despite all the noise of my bus emptying. I sat down in one of the plastic chairs and pretended to stare at the TV.

Behind the counter, a woman shuffled papers and stamped some things, and then she put the papers into different boxes in a tray behind her. She didn't look at me at all, and it was as if I was just another plastic chair in the row, and then the station started emptying out, and then it was empty, and it was only me and the sleeping man, and the woman behind the window kept moving papers around and ignoring me, and then she looked up at the empty room and looked out the window and saw the bus loading up outside, and she said, "You'd better hurry up if you're going to Portland," and I just shook my head and said, "My dad is picking me up." She looked at me for a second and then went back to the papers and the stamping, and then she put a sign in the window, "CLOSED," and she walked toward another door behind the rows and opened it and was gone. The man in the corner kept sleeping, and on TV, Bob Barker was reading the actual prices of the showcases while the audience groaned in the background at how the contestants had come so close to the actual prices but had overshot and got nothing.

I should have bought a ticket to Portland. I heard the engine on the bus outside roll to life, and I looked out and saw the doors close, and all the windows were full of faces, staring out at the parking lot, and I was cold suddenly and wished I had a jacket. I wondered how long I could sit there in the station, staring at the TV, buying candy bars from the machine, and at the thought of a candy bar, my stomach made a low growl, and I wished that I had eaten a bowl of cereal before I had slipped out of the house in the still dark before dawn.

I stood up and tested my knees, and it was as though my feet had been planted in cement, because suddenly I wasn't sure just exactly what I should do, but *The Guiding Light* was coming on, and it reminded me too much of things that I didn't like—the end to morning television, the reality of daytime coming on, the fear of switching the TV off and worrying that it was time to do something else, and I could feel adrenaline pumping through me as I stood there, and it made me feel too hot, and I was scared for a second because I knew that I had to do something else.

I pulled open the door to the station, and a little bell above the door went off and the door from behind the ticket windows opened and the woman who had been stamping papers stuck her head out, saw it was me, and then closed the door again. Outside, the sky was dark and even though there was no rain at the moment, I could feel that it was coming, and the asphalt smelled wet and the cars on the road went by with their headlights on, slowing down to take the corner where the long street beside the bus station split into the city. I slung my backpack over my shoulder and started walking, moving in the opposite direction than we had come, and my stomach growled, and the wind picked up my hair and lifted it off of my neck, and everything was damp and covered in small puddles that were waiting for the sun, and it was August and there should have been some.

Beyond the bus station there were people pushing shopping carts, hunched over against the wind, and there were bag-wrapped bottles and clouds of cigarettes, and a woman on the corner was walking in circles on the sidewalk, raising her hands toward the clouds and yelling for somebody named Mike. I could feel my clothes drying out, my backpack getting lighter, and I picked up my pace and walked past them all—the homeless people shouting and drinking and smoking, trying to get my attention, calling me over to look at something that they held, and I could feel myself loosening up as I went, my feet falling into rhythm, and I looked down at my tennis shoes and watched my stride. When I reached Tehama Street, I went right, and then Tehama became Market Street, and the cars passing me picked up speed and the shopping carts thinned, and then there was no one on the sidewalk in front of me, and in the distance I could hear the freeway and I kept walking that direction, and above me the clouds bunched together, crowded out the sky, and they got thicker, darkened until it felt like there was no more light behind them that was straining to come out, and their bottoms were swollen and I tried to walk faster because I knew that it was just a matter of time before they split apart underneath, like a stuffed animal at the seams, and they let loose everything that was building inside of them.

I passed by busy storefronts, people going in and coming out, and a restaurant and a cart that was selling hotdogs on a corner, the steam rising from metal pans, and my stomach growled, and I felt a cramp down low, and maybe it was the baby that I was carrying telling me that I was depriving her of food, and I was sure it was a girl by now—and I thought about the old woman on the Greyhound and her daughter in Portland that she was going to visit, and Caleb, the boy who had no father, and I wondered if my mom would take a bus to come and see me, to take a baby out in the stroller in some park where the trees blocked the clouds, and I tried to imagine us walking together, laughing at squirrels chasing each other under those trees, but the harder that I tried to focus, the less that I could see my mom, and I kept following the sound of my shoes on the sidewalk, chewing up cement, and then the sky burst with a flash of light and the thunder came right behind it, hollow and loud, and in the distance I could see the neon of a truck stop, all parking lot and big wheelers, and there was a diner lit up bright, and I kept walking toward it as the rain came down in small drops and then bigger drops, and then sideways, and I ducked my head and gripped the strap on my backpack, and I walked as fast as I could toward the distant lights.

The diner was warm and bright and smelled like bacon that had just gone to crisp, and there were a lot of men inside, talking loud, and the waitresses walked from table to table, filling cups with hot coffee and carrying plates loaded down with eggs and hashbrowns and all the things that I wanted, but I sat at the counter near the register and ordered a cup of soup, and I ate it slowly, filling the bowl with all the packets of crackers that came on the saucer beside the cup. I was soaking wet and so were most of the things in my backpack, and I had gone to the bathroom and tried to dry off with the little rough, brown paper towels from the dispenser, but all I had managed to do was move the water around. I spooned more crackers into my mouth and chewed carefully, trying to taste the last of the soup, and I sipped at my coke, and when no one was looking, I put my hand into the front pocket of my jeans and tried to feel the wad of money I had left. I knew how much was in there—$94. That was everything I had to get me somewhere else.

There was a clock on the wall behind the register and above the window where the hot plates of food sat and waited to go to their tables, and I watched the food and the clock and tried not to think about the fact that I had only made a plan to leave town and hadn't thought much about what I'd do once I left. I wasn't far away from home, but it felt like a thousand miles, and I didn't know how much motel rooms cost, or how far $94 would carry me, and I wished again that I'd bought another ticket and just stayed on the bus all the way to Portland, next to the old lady who would feed me apricots and mist me with Avon and tell me about her daughter and her grandson, and maybe when we got off the bus, I would just end up going along with her and she'd take me in and me and her daughter would become best friends, but somehow it felt safer to be gone but not far—run away but not lost.

"Can I get you something else?" A waitress stood in front of me and I looked up at her from under my wet bangs, and she gave me a look that I thought might be sympathy, but I wasn't sure what that might look like from her, and for all I knew she was impatient and angry at me for dripping water onto the floor underneath the stool.

"No, thank you," I said. She kept looking at me, and then looked down at my cup full of crackers that were no longer sticking to soup, and turned slowly back toward the row of coffee pots behind her, and she was probably already expecting that I wouldn't tip, and I wished I could tell her that I wouldn't do that to her. "Wait," I said. "Do you think I could get more crackers?"

She turned back to me, and she took another bowl from the shelf and walked down the counter, and bent down, and when she came back the bowl was full of packs of saltines and oyster crackers, and I thanked her.

"Really coming down out there," she said. We both turned and looked out the big windows that faced the parking lot and the big trucks lined up to refuel, and even though the windows were fogged with steam, we could see the rain bouncing off the pavement and all of the men were walking with their heads bent and their hats pulled low.

"Not a good day for driving," a man said. He was standing at the register, his ticket in his hand and a wad of money tucked into it. He was wearing a brown suit and tie, and he had a big gold watch on his wrist that caught the overhead lights.

"You hitting the road today, Jerry?" The waitress asked him, and she moved over to the register.

He nodded at the waitress and handed her the check. "Soup. Breakfast of champions, huh?" he said, and I realized he was talking to me, and I looked at him and then went back to staring into my bowl.

"Actually, it's lunchtime," I said, and pointed to the clock on the wall. It was almost one, and I knew I only had a matter of hours to make a decision on the next thing I was going to do before the day failed me and I would be left to figure out the night.

"Ahh, yes it is," he said. He stepped back from the register and sat down in the empty seat beside me at the counter. "You mind if I sit here?"

I looked at him. His suit was dry and there were diamonds on his tie—brown and gold—and unlike the truckers who came through the door, stamping water off their boots and shaking out their hats, he wasn't wet at all.

"You want something else, Jerry?" The waitress asked, and she took the empty cup from in front of him and flipped it right-side-up and turned toward the row of pots behind her. "Another cup?"

"Sure, Holly, why not?" he said. "And why don't you tell Mickey to put together a burger. Hot fries. You like cheese?" He looked at me.

"I'm okay. Really. Thank you, though."

"You can't just eat crackers."

"It was soup."

"You can't just eat soup."

I opened a package of oyster crackers and shook some into my hand. "I'm full," I said. "But thank you."

"She looks like she likes cheese, Holly. Make it a cheeseburger. And why don't you get that shake machine going and get her a chocolate one."

The waitress was writing down things on her order pad, and I wanted to reach out and stop her hand. "I don't have the money for that. I'm fine, really. I appreciate it. Thank you."

"I've got this one. I'm Jerry." He stuck his hand out and I noticed that his nails were clean and they shone like his watch under the lights.

"Thank you, Jerry. But I can't eat that food." I said.

"You won't? Or you can't?"

"I won't. I don't want you paying for it." I cleared my throat and I thought about a cheeseburger dripping juice onto my plate, and my stomach made a low growl that I hoped he didn't hear.

"Never turn down a free meal, kid," he said. "My momma taught me that rule." He picked up the sugar and poured it into his coffee, and then stirred it around and tapped the spoon on the rim. "She also taught me not to talk to strangers, but that one didn't stick." The waitress had moved down the counter and was refilling coffees, and then she walked over to the milkshake machine and started scooping ice cream into a tall metal cup.

I didn't speak for a while, and Jerry drank his coffee and he asked me what my name was, and I told him, and then he didn't say anything for a few minutes. I watched the window where the food came up, and I watched the eggs and bacon and stacks of pancakes make room for sandwiches and burgers and chicken fried steak, and I could smell everything.

"You live around here?" he asked.

I shook my head. "Not exactly," I said.

"Ahhh, traveling. Going to grandma's?"

I pulled my red sweatshirt tighter against me and shook my head.

"So, you're not exactly from here, and you're not going to grandma's. Just seeing what the day brings, I guess?"

I nodded my head. "Something like that."

"You ever been to Reno? Great place for traveling. Biggest little city in the world."

I shook my head. "No," I said. "I've never been."

"I think you'd like it," he said. "All kinds of people there—but nobody from around there. Like you." He took another drink of coffee. "Lots of fresh ground. Room to stretch."

I had seen pictures of Reno, and I knew some friends who'd been there with their parents, and nobody had really said anything about it that had stuck with me, except that there was a rodeo and nothing else good to do. All I could picture was a casino, like I had seen on TV.

"It's just a bunch of gambling, isn't it?" I asked. "Sounds boring."

Jerry laughed and took another drink from his coffee. "Sure, sure. Lots of gambling. Lots of things going on. What are you? About 16?"

I didn't want to smile, but I couldn't help it. "Not quite," I said. "But close." I was stuck in the gap between fourteen and fifteen and ready to skip ahead.

Jerry nodded. "Ahhh. But still a great age for traveling. See the world a little bit."

The waitress put a plate in front of me, heaped with hot french fries and a burger I would have to struggle to get my mouth around, and there was a milkshake glass sweating in front of me with a straw stuck deep in thick chocolate, and for a second I was afraid to touch anything, but my stomach was throwing a fit, so I dug in and crammed my mouth full, poured ketchup over the fries, shoveled them in as fast as I could move my hand.

Jerry watched me from the corner of his eye, and when my mouth was as full as I could get it, he leaned his head in close to me so that I could smell him—cologne, coffee, bacon, heat—and said, "So, you look like you might want to make some money."

Outside the diner, a big wheeler cut loose on the air horn and it blew long and sharp so that I had to jerk my head to look, but some of the men at other tables just laughed and pumped their fists toward the windows and the parking lot, and I could tell that the rain had slowed, maybe even stopped, and there were more trucks crawling out of the parking lot with their running lights turned low. I chewed slowly, trying not to swallow too hard, and I took a sip from the milkshake straw to help grease my throat, and I just looked at him for a minute with my mouth full of food, and he was smiling, and he was clean shaven, his cheeks as shiny as the counter in front of him, and he didn't look old even though he had long sideburns, and his eyes were green, and he had a dimple in his chin that reminded me of the picture of my dad, and I could feel all the money I had to my name burning against my thigh through the dampness of my jeans—more than I had ever had in my life and not enough to last, and I thought about it for a minute and then I nodded slowly, took another sip, swallowed.

"Yeah," I said. "I want to make some money."

Chapter 2
The One

The clouds clenched up and the rain stopped somewhere along Highway 44 East toward Reno, and Jerry drove with one hand, turning the volume up on the radio with the other, and I stared out my window and watched the pine trees blur by as the car picked up speed on the straightaways.

There are some people who wouldn't understand why I got into a car with a man who had just bought me a burger at a diner in a town that I didn't live in—and most of those people are the girls at school whose biggest regret in their lives was that they got bangs, but I had been in a strange man's car before, and I had been in the cars of men who were almost like family, and I had been promised trips to the carnival that ended up at a dirty trailer in the back of an almond orchard, and I knew better than to talk to strangers, but there sometimes wasn't much difference between the man I didn't know and the one that I did, and there is a trust that still rests in the cells before adulthood takes it out of you, and it's almost like I could forget the bad things that had ever happened—except the ones that happened with my stepdad Dale—and where I should have been afraid, I just wasn't, as though that switch in my mind couldn't be flipped, and I had lost my virginity on a scrap of cardboard over a patch of dirt down by the muddy slough while my best friend stood with his back to me and kept watch while two neighbor boys took turns, and all I wanted out of it was a bag of Black Cat firecrackers that the neighbor boys had stolen, and sometimes that's what life was like—closing my eyes and thinking about something else and hoping for the best until whatever was happening just got up and walked off and I wasn't afraid of Jerry, and maybe I should have been.

"I like your car," I said, and I did—it was warm and smooth and fast and it felt like I was sitting in the cockpit of an airplane as Jerry popped in an 8-track and turned the knob. Freddy Fender came over the speakers, sad and loud and lamenting the time he wasn't spending right. It was my stepdad Dale's music, and I knew all of the words.

"Yeah?" Jerry said. He smiled and I could tell that he was pleased with the compliment. "You know much about cars?"

"A little," I said.

"So if I tell you that this is a Ford LTD with a 351 Windsor V8, that would mean something to you?"

I watched another mile marker tick by, and even though it had a number on it, I didn't know what it meant any more than I knew what Jerry was talking about, and maybe I could have told him that—that all I knew was that his car was taking me farther away from home and I didn't know him at all, and this car was just a big blue machine with a low humming engine and soft seats and it wasn't holding me any more hostage than the gravity that was keeping me pulled to the earth.

"No," I said.

Jerry lit a cigarette and cracked the driver's side window, and I could smell wet pavement and clean air, and I thought about hitting the button to lower my window, too, but I wasn't sure if I could. Everything in the car was electric—windows, locks, the seat that held me, and the heater spit out a warm breath of air from the vents. The windshield was a wide expanse that kept me in my seat so that I watched the world slide by in a shiny smear of wet droplets and sunlight that came out in a burst and bounced off of everything that was standing still.

"It's a good car," Jerry said. "One of my favorites."

As he drove, he smoked and changed the music, skipped a track and then back to replay, then forward again, and back, and he told me about his job, that he was just a salesman, and what he could offer me was a delivery position, and as he called it "easy money" and all I had to do was follow directions and be fast—did I think I could do that?—and I said yes, I thought I could do that, even though I had no idea what exactly *that* was, and he said that it was better if I didn't ask questions, because questions implied a certain misunderstanding, and he didn't have the time to sort that kind of thing out. I stayed quiet and listened to him explain things in general nothingness, but mostly I just watched the trees and the sun and the grass and the mile markers, ticking back a distance that I didn't really understand.

"I've gotta make a stop," Jerry said, and then the LTD slowed and Jerry took an exit, and we were on the outskirts of Susanville, to the east of the town, and there were few cars on the road and fewer houses, and the only thing that marked the hillsides were mailboxes and dirt offshoots of road.

I should have been nervous, I guess, but I wasn't. I was curious about where we were going, and what I would do, and everything felt new and fresh and like an adventure, and Red Bluff felt like a memory I had, or a dream, or something that I had made up, and it didn't matter anyway because I didn't live there anymore, and even if I had stayed, it would never be my home again, and I knew that there would come a time when my mom's new boyfriend would probably kill me, so it was best to get gone now in a way that I could choose, and Jerry had a soft voice, and his eyes were sharp but not mean, and when he smiled just right his whole face changed, and he had paid for my burger at the diner, walked me to the car, opened the door for me, and not once did I feel like he was going to hurt me, and even a dog can sense when an open hand is going to clench into a fist, and maybe that's how it is with the men that will hurt you most—they have a way of making you never see it coming—but even as I stood by the register with him and he paid the bill, pulling the money off a roll of bills that was pulled tight and clipped in a gold band—a stack so thick that the clip could barely hold it together—nobody looked at me like I should be afraid—not the waitresses or the truckers in their greasy hats, or the men with newspapers, or the few women who sat with coffee—nobody looked at me as if what I was doing was wrong, or bad, or might get me hurt—not like in the movies when a man leaves a place with a girl that doesn't belong to him and somebody says to the girl, *are you sure you're okay*—and the waitress just added up the bill and gave Jerry back the change, and the door to the diner swung open with the chime of a bell and I walked behind Jerry as he led the way to the parking lot and the LTD that I had never been in before, and when I looked over my shoulder at all of the people sitting there in the dry warmth of the fluorescent lights, nobody even lifted their eyes from their plates of burgers and fries and gravy and meat to look at me, to raise an eyebrow, to give me a sign that I was in danger and all I had to do was signal back and they would come running, ask a question, take me by the arm and put me back where I was safe.

I wanted to fall asleep in the warmth of the car—I had no idea what time it was, but I was exhausted and felt like I hadn't slept in days, but the truth was that I had only been up since early this morning, had barely slept the night before, and I shouldn't have been tired at all, but there was something about riding in a car with the sound of the tires on the pavement, the gentle roll, that made me sleepy, and my stomach was full of food, and I was probably pregnant and carrying a baby was all about exhaustion—that's what I had learned from TV—and if I licked my lips carefully, I could still taste the salt from the hot french fries, and if I had been somewhere else, in some other car, I probably would have let my head fall back just like it wanted to. Instead, I watched the sun get brighter, and I could smell the wet trees through Jerry's open window, and that woke me up a little bit.

"So what do I have to do?" I asked. I cleared my throat. "I mean, what kind of job are you paying me for?"

Jerry pulled the visor down on his side and a pair of gold-rimmed sunglasses fell into his lap, and he put them on and then he turned down the volume on the radio and Freddy Fender's voice faded into a whisper from the back seat. My backpack was between my feet on the floorboard in front of me and my jeans were still damp, and I wanted to open my backpack and start drying out the few things that I had brought with me.

"I'll explain it later," Jerry said. "But it's not a hard job." He lit another cigarette and the smoke caught the wind and whipped its way outside of the car.

"But like, is it washing cars or mowing lawns, or babysitting? Or something like that?" I couldn't think of any other jobs I might be qualified to do.

"It's deliveries," Jerry said. "I told you. You just deliver."

The only deliveries I knew of involved a truck and a uniform and I could imagine a UPS man or a post office worker in blue carrying a package up the sidewalk. "Like what kind of deliveries? Like packages?"

"I'll explain it later," Jerry said. "That's what I said, right?"

I was quiet for a minute and stared out the windshield that was streaked with mist still rising from the road. "But like what kind of deliveries?" I asked again.

"Jesus, kid. You don't give up, do you?"

"No."

"Okay, let's say you deliver sandwiches."

"Sandwiches?" I knew he wasn't the kind of man who ran a deli, and I knew that I wouldn't be delivering tuna on rye wrapped in wax paper, but I wanted to keep pushing at him until I could find the soft spot. "But like what kind of sandwiches?"

"Are you fucking kidding me?"

My feet were still wet, and I knew it would take a long time for my shoes to dry out, so I slipped my feet out of them and tried to tuck them closer to the heater vent that was blowing underneath the dash.

Jerry flicked his cigarette out the window and turned the knob on the heater so that it suddenly cut off. "It's getting hot in here," he said.

My feet retreated back toward my shoes. I ran my fingers through my hair and could feel that it was dry, and my head felt tingly. I was thirsty, and I wondered how much longer we were going to be in the car.

"How long until we get to Reno?' I asked. I had seen the signs on the side of the road—but I hadn't been paying close enough attention to know just how many miles were left until we got to where Jerry said we were going, and I didn't know how miles connected to time—how many hours there were in the numbers that I had seen, and it all seemed like a word problem from math class that I would struggle to answer: *If an LTD traveling from Redding at 60 mph . . .*

"I gotta make a stop first," Jerry said, and then he signaled and the LTD cruised off of the narrow two-lane road and we were shaded in trees, and went up a short hill where there was a stop sign at the top and we crossed back over the highway and we climbed even higher, following a winding road, and the highway disappeared behind us and the trees closed in, and we wound around and higher until we dropped again and then the car slowed and Jerry pulled onto a gravel road that was uneven and pocked with puddles of standing water, and the LTD rose and dipped, and Jerry slowed down to a crawl, and I could hear the gravel spin up from the road and pelt the side of the car like hail.

"This road is shit for my paint job," he said, but we kept creeping along, and Jerry swung wide around the bigger washouts, and the trees crowded in until the sun that had been drying the road disappeared and there was nothing but shade.

"Where are we going?" I asked.

"Again with the questions." He turned the volume back up on the radio, paused for a second, ejected the tape, and popped in another one that he pulled from the dash. The Eagles came on loud through the speakers, and it was one of my mom's albums, and for a second I thought that I missed her, but then we went over a small rise, and I could see a clearing in the distance where the trees pulled back from the narrow road, and there was a muddy circle of bare ground and a little house sitting in the middle of it, and as we got closer, I could see that the front of the house was covered with a blue tarp, and the front steps were falling down, and there were other small buildings around it, what looked like sheds and chicken coops, and there were some cars in the clearing, some of them without wheels, sitting on chunks of wood, and there were motorcycles with long curved handlebars, shiny and naked and throwing back the sun that finally had a small chance to break through.

"Who lives here?"

Jerry just looked at me, and then we were in the clearing, and he pulled the LTD to a stop and the car went quiet except for the sound of the engine ticking as it cooled. The windows on the house were covered from the inside, and I couldn't see anything, and if I would have come here by myself, I would have guessed that nobody lived here.

"Sit tight," Jerry said, and he threw his door open and I was surprised at how warm the air was, and I could hear birds and the sound of the wind blowing way up high so that the trees whispered that language that only has a voice in the middle of nowhere.

Jerry got out of the car and stretched his back, and I waited for somebody to come out of the house, but no one did, and Jerry stood beside the car for a minute, looking up at the empty porch and the tarp that lifted in the slight wind.

"Can I listen to the radio?" I asked.

"No," he said, and he reached down and pulled the keys from the ignition and dropped them into his front pocket. "Don't get out of the car. If you get bored, there's a book in the back seat. Read something."

I settled back and put my feet up on the dashboard.

"Get your feet off the dash," he said. "This isn't that kind of car." He pushed his door closed and the feel of the outdoors was reduced to just a small puff of air lifting through his partially open window, and then he took a few steps towards the house, and I could see the front door open, but I couldn't see anyone in the shadow, and Jerry raised his hand and went up the front steps that were rotted and broken, and I saw the gap in the door closed, and that was it—I was alone in the car.

I looked around in the front of the car for something to do, but everything was clean except for a few tapes, and I tried to open the glove compartment, but it was locked. I looked through the tapes for a second—Peter Frampton, more Eagles, some names I didn't recognize. It didn't matter anyway because I couldn't listen to them without the keys. I moved my backpack around on the floor in front of me and pulled

16

the visor down, but there was nothing—not even an empty wrapper or paper cup. I pulled the ashtray open and there was a book of matches advertising a towing place in Anderson. Through Jerry's open window, I could feel the warmth of the sun when it blew in on the short breeze, and I realized that it was almost September and after the long weekend, school would be starting and I guessed I wouldn't be there.

From around the corner of the house, two little kids came into the clearing, both of them in sagging diapers with shaggy hair, and they weren't wearing any clothes, and the blonder of the two had a puppy draped over his arm, and they were followed by a hound-looking dog, skinny with long ears, and she was swinging milk underneath her, and I figured it must be the mother of the puppies, and then another dog came from behind the house, and this one was barking, and the two kids in diapers just stood in the dirt, barefoot, and staring at me.

I raised my hand and waved. The one with the puppy could barely hold it, and he had a grip on its back leg to keep it from falling out of his arms. The one without the puppy shoved a finger up his nose and stared, and I noticed that they were both dirty and the one with the puppy had a smear of mud across his face. I waved again. This time the one with the puppy lifted his hand and I thought he was going to wave back, and I smiled at them, and then he flipped me off, and they both started laughing and ran back around the house, through the mud that they had come from, and the dogs followed, barking as they went.

The other buildings looked empty, as though they were just there to store things, probably full of spider webs and rats, and the cars looked the same way—as though they had been forgotten and were just there to hold what they could. One had a bumper that had been balanced through the open front windows, sticking out on either side. I sat up and turned around so that I could look at what was in the backseat of Jerry's car, but it was clean like the front, except for a book on the driver's side, and I reached over and picked it up. There was a man on a horse on the front cover, and he had his hand resting on the holster of a gun against his hip. *Shane.* I flipped the book over and read the back: ... *a man named Shane rides out of the great glowing West and up to their farm in 1889 ... young Bob Starrett is entranced by the stoic stranger ... entangled in the deadly feud ... a profoundly moving story of the influence of a singular character on one boy's life.* A Western. Boring. I tossed the book onto the seat and turned around. I sat back and closed my eyes.

I was almost asleep when I heard voices coming from the porch, and maybe I was asleep and had been dreaming them, but when I looked up, I could see Jerry coming down the broken steps with another man, and Jerry was carrying a black duffle bag in his hand and they were talking, laughing about something, and then the man looked toward the car, and he could see me through the windshield, and I sank lower in the seat. He was a big man, in a pair of jeans and a leather vest with no shirt underneath, and he was wearing sunglasses, the mirrored kind that reflected everything, and he had long shaggy hair and a beard, and he slapped Jerry on the back as Jerry stepped into the clearing, and I figured he would stop there, stay close to the house, but he didn't, and Jerry opened the trunk and dropped the bag inside, and the man came around to my side of the car and signaled to Jerry to drop the window. All I could see was his stomach covered in hair, and I didn't want to look up at him.

Jerry put the keys in the ignition and my window slid down, and then the hairy stomach was next to me, and the man bent down and I could smell him—wet leather and sweat and spilled beer, and he looked at me through his sunglasses with his eyes that I couldn't see.

"How you doing?" he asked.

Jerry stood outside the car and lit a cigarette, but it didn't do anything to erase the smell that was coming in through my open window. The air was hotter now, with the sun realizing it was still August, and the clouds that had been confused and dumped their loads over us had broken up and dissolved.

"I'm fine," I said.

The man leaned his arms on the roof of the car. He had a gold cross hanging from his neck and I watched it bounce in his dark chest hair.

"I'm Lalo." He stuck his hand through the window and I shook it slowly.

"Hi," I said.

Jerry was leaning over the roof on his side, and I couldn't see his face—just his tie and his white shirt, and the brown belt with the gold buckle dividing my view.

"So, you know when Chuck's getting back?" Jerry asked, and I could hear him exhale a long lung of smoke.

"Nah, he's up at the cabin with Wendy. He thought you'd be here yesterday, but you weren't. He waited."

"Yeah, well I got hung up."

Lalo bent down so that his face filled my window and I could see his teeth that were flecked with black. "You hang him up?"

I didn't know what he meant, but I shook my head. "No, sir," I said.

He laughed. "Sir. I like that." He smiled, but it didn't reach his eyes. "Polite, huh? Not like the last one."

"You tell Chuck that I'll give him a call in a week," Jerry said.

"Yeah, Chuck ain't too happy with you," Lalo said.

"Well shit happens."

"It shouldn't, Jerry," Lalo said. "Not around here, you know? It's thin ice, man. Chuck ain't got a lot of patience anymore, and my hands are tied. You gotta make it right."

"I'm gonna hit the road," Jerry said, and I was relieved suddenly. I just wanted to get away from the hair and the smell coming through my window, and there was something about Lalo that felt as if it was coiled tight and ready to break loose at any moment.

"So this is the one, huh?" Lalo asked. He dropped his head down toward me even though the sunglasses didn't move. He stretched his arms out over the roof and I could see drops of sweat clinging to the hair in his armpits, and my stomach rolled a little bit, and for a little while I had forgotten that I was probably pregnant, but in the slow roll, I remembered that I probably was.

"For now," Jerry said. "We'll be in Reno before sundown. Like I said. Tell Chuck I'll call him in a week."

"You got one week, Jerry. Chuck says stay out of the Cal Neva," Lalo said.

"Yeah, well, since when does Chuck make the rules?"

"Hey, I'm just the fucking messenger, Jerry. Just telling you." He stepped back from the car and held up both of his hands. "Like I said, this is the last chance, Jerry. No room on this one."

"Well maybe you need to remind Chuck just who carries the fucking bag."

Lalo turned and spit on the ground. "Wait up a minute," he said.

Jerry stood outside the car and Lalo walked toward the house and I could hear a dog barking and a puppy start yelping, and then Lalo yelled something that I couldn't hear and Jerry got in and pulled his door shut. He didn't say anything, and we both looked toward the house and waited.

After a few minutes, Lalo reappeared and came down the steps, and he was drinking a can of Budweiser and had something in his other hand, something that I couldn't see, and instead of coming around to Jerry's side of the car, he came around to mine, and he leaned down and filled the open window with his face. He reached across me, and for a second the smell was so strong that I couldn't breathe, and his gold cross dangled against my shoulder, and then I saw something flash in his hand, catch the sunlight for a second, and Jerry took it from him and Lalo pulled back from the window.

"You're gonna need these," he said, and then he smiled down at me. "You believe in Jesus?" He asked me.

I had only been to church three times in my life, and two of them had been for Easter and all of them had been with Grandma Mavis, and my sister and I had had to wear dresses, and it had been the worst two hours of my life every time.

"Yes," I said.

"I believe in Judas," Lalo said. "You know what I'm talking about?"

"Yes," I lied.

"It's not the one at the head of the table that has all the power," Lalo said. "It's the one next to him. The one who watches when nobody else is paying attention."

I looked over at Jerry and he was holding a pair of scissors in his hand—the kind with the black handles, like the ones my mom kept in her sewing kit next to the fabric bean bag tomato covered in stick pins.

"You're gonna need those," Lalo said again, and then Jerry turned the key and the radio came on loud again and Lalo stepped back from the car and took a long drink from his beer.

"Tell Chuck," Jerry said, and Lalo nodded, and I watched the reflection of the car get smaller in his sunglasses.

"One fucking week, Jerry," Lalo said, and Jerry lifted up his hand and gave a small wave, and then the car crept backwards in the clearing and Jerry swung the wheel around, and the little house left my view and was replaced with the gravel road climbing back toward the trees, and we climbed with it, and for a long time I could still smell Lalo on me, as if he was still clinging to the car and leaning in, and I could remember my stepdad's friends, the ones who didn't shower, the ones who wanted me to sit on their laps, the ones who had thick fingers and big hands and a long reach and who liked to pull at my hems, raise them up, and my stomach got tight for a second, but I didn't look back to make sure that Lalo wasn't following us even if his smell was in the car and as if he was still clinging to the seat.

Chapter 3
It'll Always Grow Back

We got back on the highway and then Jerry took a cutoff to Highway 395 South, and there were signs that said *Reno* and I knew that we were finally on the road. There were fewer trees to block the sun and Jerry loosened his tie and rolled up his sleeves, and he drove with the windows down so that the wind blew through the car and lifted my hair but didn't touch Jerry's—slicked back and glossy—and he exchanged one tape for another in the stereo, and turned the volume up or down as the songs bled together.

"Who's Chuck?" I asked. I was getting bored with the music and the road and the silence, and there was nothing to look at that caught my attention, and usually I didn't mind riding in silence with nothing but the sound of the wheels on the pavement, but I was restless and awake and I knew at some point we were going to cross into a different state, and every time I thought I about it, I felt an electric jolt climb up my spine.

"A friend," Jerry said. "Chuck's a friend."

"That guy smelled bad," I said. "That Lalo guy."

Jerry smiled. His sunglasses were dark and I couldn't see his eyes, but they weren't mirrored like Lalo's had been and it was nice to not have to see myself looking back at me.

"They don't shower a lot up there," he said.

"You're telling me." My clothes had dried out and I wanted to stretch my legs. "So, what's in the bag?" I asked. "And why did he give you scissors?"

"You know, kid, we're gonna get along a lot better if you don't ask so many questions." He lit another cigarette with the lighter from the dash, and the car filled with the smell of Merits.

"Well you don't tell me anything," I said. "I mean, I thought I was going to make some money—that's what you said. And now we've just been stopping and talking to people. And I thought we were going to Reno. So I could deliver … "I paused for a second. "Deliver sandwiches."

"See, you got all the information you need," Jerry said. "So no more questions. I ask questions. You answer. How about that?"

"Whatever. Maybe I don't want to do this. That's all."

"You had your chance to punch out. Fair and square. If you're gonna keep fucking with me, maybe I don't want you. You think about that scenario?"

I watched the desert scrub roll by in muted color, and when I looked in the outside mirror, I could see the mountains behind us—a jagged peak of sliding rock and tired trees—and there was nothing in front of us except more asphalt and I didn't want to get dumped out yet so I got quiet and stared at the road.

Jerry got in the fast lane and the car picked up speed, and I could hear the engine in front of me, loud and low, and we passed a Volkswagen full of teenagers who waved as we blew by.

"Where's your parents?" he asked.

"They're dead," I said.

Jerry laughed. "You think that's gonna work? That answer?"

I looked out the window and we drifted back into the slow lane and the car came back down to cruising speed and I saw a dead deer on the side of the road, its legs twisted around, its head thrown back toward where we had already been, and I looked away so that I didn't have to see it, but I couldn't get the image of it out of my mind.

"My mom is moving," I said. "My dad is dead." It wasn't exactly the truth, and it wasn't exactly a lie.

"So why aren't you home?"

"I don't have a home," I said, and that was the truth. My mom had been with a guy named Chris for a while, and I had spent enough time around that sort of thing to know that things were going to get bad, and he had already started looking at me all of the time in ways that I didn't like, and the other night at dinner, I had mouthed off to my mom, said something about the shit on the plate, and Chris had stood up from his chair before I even saw him flinch and he had picked me up by the neck and put me against the wall so that my feet didn't touch the floor, and he had told me to apologize—apologize right goddamn now—and my mom had just sat there, with her fork held in that open space between her mouth and her plate, and I waited for her to tell him to stop, to put me down, to let me go, but she just sat there, saying nothing, and then she finished her bite and washed it down and dug her fork back in and dropped her eyes to her plate.

"You have brothers? Sisters?"

"No," I said. I did have a sister, and she had just turned eleven, and I couldn't think about her because I had left her behind, and I felt guilty that I had abandoned her, but I had promised myself that I would bring her to me when I found a place to land, and I knew it had to be soon that Chris started looking at her in the same way that he had been looking at me.

"Yeah?" Jerry said. "Me neither. And both my parents are dead."

"Really?"

Jerry smiled. "Sure," he said. He tucked the car behind a big wheeler that was taking its time in the slow lane.

"How old are you?" I asked.

He turned his head and looked at me. "How old do you think I am?"

I studied him for a second. I could see dark stubble on his cheeks, but his face was covered by his sunglasses. "I think you're like thirty-five," I said.

"Thirty-five, huh? Good guess."

"So you're thirty-five?"

"No," he said. He hit the turn signal and the right blinker came on, and then he slid the car over into the exit lane and we left the highway.

"Where are we going?"

"Gotta get gas," he said. He guided the car down a short strip of frontage road, and I could see a 76 station ahead.

"I'm thirsty," I said. "Can I get a Coke?"

He pulled up to a pump and shut off the engine, and then he opened his door and the sound of the adjacent highway was loud beside us, but the air was warm and with the car stopped, I could feel the heat rising around us. I watched him walk around to my side of the LTD and open the gas cap, and then he stood for a while, pumping gas, and I thought about just opening my door and going into the store and getting something to drink, but I could see Jerry's reflection in the outside mirror and I could tell that he was watching me. When he was finished, he paid the guy who was standing on the small cement island between the lanes, and then he got back into the car and started it up.

"I'm really thirsty," I said.

Jerry pulled the car forward and instead of getting back onto the road toward the exit and the highway, he swung around to the side of the gas station and turned off the car again.

"Come with me," he said.

I opened my door and it was good to finally stand up again, to feel the blood moving in my legs, and a gust of wind picked up and blew some trash out into the weeds that crept up to the back of the station, and there was nothing behind the building but a dumpster and more weeds and more trash, and beyond that there were just the low bunches of plants and sand and nothing for as far as I could see. I thought we were going to go inside the store and I started to walk that direction, but Jerry stopped at the back of the car and took a key and unlocked the trunk instead.

"Come here," he said. I looked past him at the few cars at the pumps and the attendant he'd paid, but nobody was paying attention to us. The trunk was wide and dark inside, and I could see the black duffle bag he'd picked up from Lalo, and there were a couple of other bags and Jerry moved them around, and even though I wasn't great at math, I could tell that there was enough space inside for me to fit. I hung back for a second, but Jerry waved me closer, until I was staring inside, and I waited for him to shove me in.

"Here," he said. He reached into one of the bags and pulled out some clothes—jeans and a T-shirt, then a plaid long-sleeve with buttons, and he handed them over to me.

"What's this?" I asked. My clothes weren't wet anymore, and I had more clothes in the backpack that was still on the floorboards in the front.

"Go in there and put these on." He handed them to me, and I took them from him and held them up.

"I have clothes," I said. "These are boys' clothes."

"They should work," he said.

From behind us, the pump lanes emptied and a line of trucks went by, and I could smell diesel fuel and dirt, and for a second it was hard to hear anything.

"I'm not putting these on," I said. I held them out toward Jerry.

He straightened up from the trunk and looked at me, and I could almost see his eyes through the tint in his glasses. He smoothed his hair back from his forehead and shoved his keys back in his front pocket.

"Look, kid, here's the deal, okay? This is the uniform. You wanted the job, now here's part of it." He pulled a pack of Merits out of his shirt pocket and shook one out, and then he searched through his pants until he found a lighter, and I watched him. He exhaled and the smoke caught under the trunk lid and lingered for a second before the wind whipped it away.

"No way," I said.

"You're smart," he said. "So look at it this way—I can't be a guy by myself driving around with a what, fifteen-year-old girl? It doesn't look right." He took a long drag from his cigarette. "And I can't have people looking at me wrong."

I was still holding the clothes in my hands, and I could smell them now, even over the fuel and the cigarette and the dirt and heat. They smelled clean, like good laundry detergent.

"It's just jeans and some shirts," I said. "I don't think they're gonna change much."

"Just go put them on."

I hesitated and then turned and walked to the side of the building, toward the doors labeled Men and Women, and I pushed open the Women door and went in, and the door closed behind me and it smelled like bleach and pee, and there was something black in the sink on the wall, and the mirror was covered in graffiti—almost too many words to make out an image, but the stalls were empty, and I went into the first one, where the toilet was flushed but there was paper all over the floor, and I shut the door and hung the clothes over it. I undressed slowly, and I put on the T-shirt, and it was too big, but the jeans fit okay despite being about two inches too long, and then I put on the other shirt, and it had long sleeves that I rolled up, and I already felt too hot with it on. I stood in the stall for a little while, looking down at the clothes on my body, and there was nothing about me that looked any different than when I'd come in, other than now I was wearing some shirt that said Kawasaki on the front, and a plaid shirt over it, and a pair of jeans that I'd have to roll up to walk in. The door to the bathroom opened, and I went quiet for a minute, and then I saw black shoes from under the stall door—black men's shoes, and I knew that Jerry was inside.

"You dressed?" he asked. He knocked softly on the stall door and part of me was scared to open it. "Come on."

I unlocked the door and opened it, and Jerry was standing there with his sunglasses off, and they were hanging by a stem in the front of his unbuttoned shirt, next to his tie. His eyes were blue, and I watched them graze me.

"Not bad," he said. He moved away from the door so that I could come out of the stall and then he walked over to the sink and stood facing me.

"These shirts are hot," I said. "It's too hot to wear two shirts."

Jerry examined me closely. "Button the shirt," he said.

"It's hot. C'mon." I pulled at the buttons but did not fasten them.

"You don't have much up top, but it's enough," he said. "You need to look flat."

I wrapped my arms around my chest. I wore a cotton sports bra just so I could have something for show in the locker room when we dressed down for P.E.

"It's a good thing," Jerry said. "Otherwise you wear two T-shirts underneath."

I started buttoning the shirt. Jerry looked me up and down, then put his hand on my shoulder and turned me a little bit under the stuttering fluorescent light.

"That'll work," he said. "For now. You can roll up your sleeves. But the shirt stays buttoned."

I pushed at the long sleeves and cuffed them as high on my arm as they would go.

"Now, one last thing," he said. He pulled his hand from his pocket and he was holding black-handled scissors, and he held them up and snapped them open and closed, and I could see the flickering fluorescent light reflect off the blades.

"What?" I asked.

"The hair. It's gotta go."

I reached up and put both of my hands over my head to cover it. "No," I said. "No way."

"It's not up for negotiation," Jerry said.

"Forget it. You're not cutting my hair." I had been growing my hair out for two years, and it was long enough to pull back now. I was proud of it. "I'll put it in a ponytail."

"No," he said. "It goes."

"Forget it," I said. "Then I don't want this job. You can have your clothes back and we can forget the whole thing."

Jerry dropped the scissors back to his side, and he reached over and turned the lock on the bathroom door. He looked at me as if I were a small child who was too dumb to understand just what he was going through. I'd seen that kind of look before.

"Forget it," I said. I stepped back into the stall.

"You've got two choices, kid, and I'm gonna be really clear about them, okay? You can lose the hair and we can get back in the car and keep going to

Reno and you can make more money than you've ever seen before. That's a promise. Or I can walk out of here and get back in the car and go to Reno alone, and you can figure out your way out of here. Take your chances."

I thought about what it would be like to have to hitchhike from this gas station, to get into someone else's car, to ask a stranger for a ride, to go backwards, however many miles it was, to Susanville, to Redding, to towns I'd never lived in, to be standing on some empty road in the dark with nothing but my backpack and the small wad of cash I still had in the front pocket of my own jeans, holding out my thumb.

Jerry looked at the gold watch on his wrist, shook it slowly. "You have one minute to make the decision," he said. He stared down at the hands on his watch. "You've come all this way," he said. "Be a shame to quit now for something that will always grow back. But hey, it's your deal. Lots of truckers out there. Gets lonely on the road. I'm sure there'd be a few who didn't mind getting a girl up in the cab, all alone."

"How come I'm the one doing all this stuff and you keep talking about a job, and so far I haven't seen any job or money. Maybe I should quit."

"You wanna quit?" He stepped back and laughed at me. "You seriously want to quit? I tell you what—here's severance pay." He reached into his front pocket and pulled out a wad of bills that were held together by a wide rubber band. He peeled off the top twenty-dollar bill and handed it to me. "Here. You can call it severance. Or you can call it your first bonus. It's up to you." I took the money out of his hand and the wad disappeared back into his suit pants.

The money was slick in my fingers. It felt good.

"Fine," I said. "But my hair is worth sixty bucks. Not fucking twenty." I stepped all the way out from the stall and stood in front of the sink, and I could see both of our reflections in the mirror, and I could read some of the words—names, phone numbers, "Fuk," and "Diane is a bitch," and "M + L Forever."

Jerry peeled off two more twenties and handed them to me and then shoved the wad back into his pocket, and I wondered how much was there and what it would feel like in my own front pocket, and I didn't have much of a plan about what came next for me, but I knew that I needed money because nothing that I wanted was going to be free.

"Okay," I said. "Do it."

Jerry stepped behind me, and I felt him lift my hair with the blades of the scissors, and then I could hear them cut through, and I felt the inches fall off and slide down my back, and the blades kept on moving and I held my breath, and the only sounds were the blades coming together, metal on metal, and water that slowly dripped from the sink. Jerry moved me around as he worked, turning me slowly by the shoulders, and I watched the hair go, felt it fall, and he went slowly around my ears, and he kept cutting, and I wanted to tell him that it was short enough, but even when I thought that he would stop, he kept going, and I could feel air on my head in places that I hadn't felt it in a long time, and someone knocked on the door for a second and then quit, and Jerry didn't flinch—he just kept cutting, and I closed my eyes and stopped watching. After what seemed like a long time, he stepped back from me and said, "Yeah, that's good," and then he wiped the scissors clean on his pants. He reached into his back pocket and took out a little black plastic comb, like the kind they gave you at school on picture day, and Jerry handed it to me.

"Here," he said. "You can wet it down and fix it." I took the comb from him. In the reflection in the mirror, there didn't seem like there was even enough hair left to comb.

"It's terrible," I said. I reached up and touched it, but there wasn't enough left to touch unless I flattened my hand and ran it across my head.

"Clean up this hair, and I'll meet you back in the car," Jerry said. He stepped back and looked at me. "Now you're ready," he said. "Welcome to the team."

He turned the lock on the bathroom door and pulled it open and the bathroom filled with light, and the person looking back at me from the mirror wasn't me anymore. When Jerry was gone, I ran water into the sink, and wetted the comb, careful not to touch what was black and growing along the porcelain, and after I had tried to comb my hair in ways it would not go, I took some stiff, brown paper towels and began wiping the hair up off the floor. I got most of it into a pile that I could scoop, and then I got some more towels wet and wiped the floor, and the door to the bathroom opened and I expected it to be Jerry, but instead it was a woman in a wrinkled skirt, and she looked down at me squatting on the floor with the paper towels, and she gave me a funny look.

"The men's room is next door," she said, and I just looked up at her and then I nodded and shoved the paper towels into the overflowing trash can in the corner and grabbed my old clothes and pushed my way past her, and I could feel her still looking at me as the door swung shut and I walked back toward the car. Jerry was already waiting inside, his sunglasses back on, the engine running. I pulled the passenger door open, and I could see a can of Coke on my side of the seat, and a bag of barbecue potato chips, and when I looked down at my shadow, it didn't belong to me anymore—it belonged to somebody else.

Chapter 4
Shambala

When I was nine years old, my stepdad Dale, took us on a road trip out of state, up the coast to Oregon, where he decided we were going to camp at Crater Lake, and my sister and I rode in the back of Dale's pickup, with the camper shell on, and when we needed something, we knocked on the sliding window that separated the cab from the bed, and my sister and I stretched out on a pile of blankets and sleeping bags that had been spread out over the carpeted liner Dale had built for the back of the truck. My sister colored while we wound along the edge of California, flipping through the blank pages of a sketch book and starting one project before getting bored and moving onto another, and I buried my head in a pillow and cried as we climbed and hair-pinned along the ocean because I had the worst earache I'd ever had—so bad that I could not chew or open my mouth wide enough to speak, and I was burning up with a fever and couldn't lift my head to look out the tiny windows lining the camper shell to see the view.

Every hour I knocked on the window and cried to my mother that I couldn't take the pain anymore, and she would pass me back a couple of baby aspirin to chew on, but they were nothing but pink-tasting sugar chalk, and they didn't do anything to stop my suffering, and finally Dale said to keep the window closed unless it was an emergency. I cried harder and begged my mom to do something, but Dale just reached over his shoulder and slid the window shut so that I had to pull my head back to keep my neck from getting caught between the panes.

"I drew this for you," my sister said.

She held up a picture from her sketch book and I opened one eye to look at it. It was a girl with brown hair and a striped shirt on, like the one that I was wearing, and her stick legs were stretched out and punching through the bottom of what I guessed were some cutoffs. There were large circles popping out of the back of the shirt, and she had colored them in with yellow.

"What are those?" I asked, trying to point at the stick girl's back.

"Wings," she said.

"Why do I have wings?" I asked.

"Because you're dying, and when you do, you'll be an angel."

I turned my head back into the pillow, but the pain was radiating all the way from one side to the other now and it hurt no matter what side I tried to lay on.

"I'm not dying," I said into the pillow.

"Yes you are," she said.

She took a sip from a root beer she had opened without asking.

"Let me have some of your soda," I said.

"No. You'll give me germs."

"I'll tell mom," I said.

"Go ahead. Dale won't let you open the window anymore."

I didn't even have the energy to fight with her and couldn't make the effort. I had bad ears—that's what the doctor had told my mom the first time this had happened. He had put the scope inside and pulled on them a bit to get a better look, and I had cried then, too, and he said that I was prone to swimmer's ear, that I had a tendency to get water trapped inside, and I'd have to be careful every time that I put my head under. He had cleaned my ears out then, shooting hot water in with a syringe and making me tip my head so that it drained back out again, and it pulled a canal full of dark wax that pooled in a shallow dish he placed under the side of my head. It was one of the most disgusting things that I had ever seen, but afterward, I felt a lot better—almost lighter in a way, as though my head had lost weight—and he gave me some pills to stop the pain, and after that I was careful about getting my head wet, always swimming with a dog paddle so my head wouldn't go under, and I swam that way for a long time after, even when my cousins made fun of me.

I fell in and out of sleep, dreaming in a fever delirium, something about chickens and blue tarps, and there was a stray kitten that I had seen months before that I had wanted to catch but could never get close enough to it. Whenever I opened my eyes, my sister was still coloring—horses, a princess, a group of trees, a handful of flowers, my mother. At one point, I fell asleep during a long stretch of flat highway, and when I woke up again, we were in another state—we'd crossed over into Oregon—and there were tall pine trees outside the windows and I wanted to slide one open and smell the air and see if it was any different than what was in California. I had never been out of the state before, and we had been traveling for so long that I thought California would stretch forever, but in reality, we had been in Oregon for a little over an hour, and the only thing to mark the change had been a little sign on the side of the road that I would have probably missed anyway. I did not know that a change of state could be so easy like that—just a stretch of road that didn't change and a sign on the side and then you could be someplace completely different. In the end, we had to cut our camping trip short because of my ear infection and the fact that I couldn't eat, and there was blood and pus on my pillow one morning when I woke up, and Dale wouldn't speak to me for days, except to call me a pussy, a wimp, a whiner, a mama's girl, a knucklehead, a crybaby, a loser for not being tough enough to handle a little bit of pain and ruining our vacation for everybody.

Jerry drove with both front windows down, and the wind whipped through and blew his cigarette smoke around, and I kept expecting my hair to get into my eyes but there wasn't anything left to lift. He drove with one hand on the wheel and cigarette in the other, and he turned the volume up on the radio so that I could feel it in the seat. Even though the sun was setting, the air outside was hot, and there was nothing much to look at except for sand and scrub and low plants, and occasionally in the distance I could see a single house with a small postage stamp of green lawn to separate it from the desert closing in all around. I didn't want to fall asleep, but my eyes felt gritty and I closed them, and I felt the car underneath me, vibrating over the asphalt, and then I felt myself slide past that thin curtain between sleep and being awake, and my head fell forward for a moment, and I was back at home in my bed, listening for the sound of Chris to get out of bed and cross the small living room and come into my room. He *had* been coming in, sometimes, and I would lock the blankets around myself and I could feel him standing in the doorway, looking at me, and he had closed my door behind him once, and he had slapped me, quietly, telling me that I needed to clean my plate at dinner, that I was a fuckup and needed to get right in my ways, and with each statement, he hit me on the side of my head, and I remembered it as I slept on the seat, and then I could hear Jerry's voice, and I pulled myself back to the surface.

"You awake, kid?"

"Yeah," I lied. I sat up and the sun was a thin line to the west, and everything was flat and ugly, and I wondered if I had missed the invisible line as we crossed into another state. "Are we in Nevada?" I asked.

"We have been for a while," Jerry said.

I was disappointed.

"You see that up there?" Jerry pointed out the windshield, and in the distance, I could see lights and the tall shape of buildings. "There she is," he said.

Suddenly there were billboards along the side of the road, and I read them as we passed—*prime rib dinners, no limits, loose slots, craps, poker, shows, 24-hour breakfast, all-you-can-eat buffet, Texas hold 'em, comps.* I didn't understand what half of them meant, but they were bright and big and I couldn't stop trying to figure out the words.

"So what do you want your new name to be?" Jerry asked. "I need to call you something more than 'kid.' I mean, don't get me wrong, it works, but who do you want to be?"

The buildings in the distance were getting closer, and I could see a sudden oasis of neon light in all of the sand.

"I have a name," I said.

"You had a name," Jerry said. "Now you're somebody new. You can't have a girl's name."

I didn't want a new name. I had already lost more than I was ready to give, and I was tired of the change. I wanted food and a bed and I wanted something familiar, and everywhere I looked there was nothing that I recognized.

"I got it," Jerry said. "You're Joey. My nephew."

"*Joey?*" I said. "That's stupid."

"It's perfect," Jerry said. "Close to what you're used to but different. Uncle Jerry and Joey. It works."

"Jerry and Joey," I said. "It sounds dumb."

"It sounds like a team," he said. "Like family." Even though the car was getting darker on the inside, I could see him smile. He reached toward the dash and pulled the knob on the headlights, and the car got brighter again, and I turned my head and looked out the window at the signs and the buildings and the lights in the distance.

"Hey, get a tape out of the glove box, will you," Jerry said.

"It's locked."

"How do you know?"

"Because I already tried it," I said.

"Of course you did." Jerry flicked his cigarette out the window. "Here, take the wheel."

"What?"

"Just steer the car for me for a second."

I reached over and put my hand on the wheel and I pulled it a little bit and the car swerved in the lane.

"Whoa. Gentle. Just keep it steady."

I loosened my grip a little bit and Jerry reached down and started fishing a key off the ring hanging from the ignition. He turned it slowly and slid it off and handed it over to me.

"Here. Open it up."

I used the key to pop the lock, and the glove box door swung down and the light inside came on, and I could see some papers and tapes, and on top of it all was a gun, and I jerked my hand back as though it could lunge out and bite me. I had been around guns enough to know that the bite was more like a great white shark than a snake, and I probably should have been afraid then, but it was just a gun, and men had guns, and I had held one before—gripped the stock—and it was closer to me than it was to Jerry, and if I had to, I could put my finger on the trigger and point the barrel.

"Get the Eagles tape out," Jerry said.

I put two fingers into the glove box and tried to shift things around so that I could find what Jerry wanted. I didn't want to touch the gun because I was afraid I would just break loose and hold onto it but I touched it anyway, to make sure it was real, and it was cold and I was afraid of it, but maybe not as much as I could have been.

"What tape?" I asked.

"*Hotel California*," Jerry said. "It should be on top."

I moved things around a little bit more and I was afraid the gun might shift and fall out onto the floorboards, and I was afraid that maybe it was loaded and if it rolled out, it might go off, and I imagined myself getting shot in the leg and I wondered what Jerry would do if that happened, if he would take me to a hospital or just pull to the side of the highway and roll me out of the car and into the sand.

"Here," I said.

He took the tape from me and opened the case, and he ejected the

34

one that was playing and handed it to me, and I put it in the glove box and closed the door as quickly as I could. I had been paying so much attention to the gun that I hadn't noticed that the outline of the city in the distance had taken on shape and Jerry turned the volume loud and took the Virginia Street exit, and the sun had already slid behind the hills, and as we crawled from the highway to the main street, the buildings grew around us, and everything was lit up bright and there was so much movement that I didn't know where to put my eyes. I stuck my head out the window and could see the buildings rising above us, and there were people on the sidewalks and open store fronts, glass doors rotating into casinos, and even over the sound of the engine I could hear bells ringing and voices, and Jerry slowed the car down to a crawl, and the neon lights jumped from windshield to dashboard to my lap, and I didn't know that I was smiling until I looked out the side window and saw myself looking back in the small mirror.

"This is it, kid, this is our future," Jerry said, and behind us a big truck laid on the horn and a woman yelled out the window, and people on the sidewalk yelled back, and inside an open door I could see a million lights flashing and then the bells rang out again and the air outside the car was warm and electric.

Jerry reached out and squeezed my arm, and his grip was tight and I looked over at him, and he smiled at me and then dropped his hand and turned the volume on the stereo even louder so that the speakers strained around us, and the Eagles were singing about a desert highway and warm smell and air, and he shouted over the top of the music.

"What do you smell out there?" he asked.

I took a deep breath and thought for a second. "Dirt," I said.

"No, close your eyes," Jerry said, "and really breathe."

I hung my head out of the open window and closed my eyes and opened my mouth and pulled all that I could through my nose so that I was breathing the wind.

I came back in through the open window and sat on the seat, and out of habit I ran my hand over my forehead to push the hair out of my eyes, but there was nothing there to move.

"I don't smell anything," I said. "Maybe like car exhaust and stuff." I dug into my senses for a better description. "And pavement. It smells like pavement." I was proud of myself for that description.

Jerry smiled and turned toward me in the seat. "It smells like desperation," he said. "All those people out there are sweating all of their dreams through their fucking cheap shirts."

I closed my eyes and inhaled again, but I couldn't smell anything but old fuel and new air.

"I don't know what desperation smells like," I said.

Jerry turned down the volume on the stereo and stared out the windshield. "Desperation smells like money. You'll notice it eventually. It's what all these casinos cash in on—that smell," and he swung his hand out to pull in the buildings that were crowding our view of the sky.

Ahead, there was an arch that crossed the roadway that said "Reno, The Biggest Little City in the World," and it was lit up in yellow and orange with a torch in the middle, and we passed underneath it with the lights shining overhead, and I felt a sudden sharp pain low on the left side of my stomach, and it was a pain I had experienced at least thirteen times before, and then I felt warmth between my thighs, and I knew that I had started my period, and this was it now and even though the neighbor boys had fucked me by the slough and in the garage and in the orchard by the fields and I was convinced that I was pregnant and I was determined to make a life somewhere with my own thing to love—there was no baby, and there would be no bean bag chairs in my own apartment in Portland that my mom came to visit so that she could see her grandchild, and I wasn't any closer to a bus stop destination for my sister to run away to when I sent her a letter—there was only me, and I wasn't me anymore, and this was now my home, and home didn't mean anything to me, and I knew what desperation smelled like, and all I wanted was some money.

Chapter 5
6 Feet Deep

The LTD cruised down the Reno Strip and the lights flashed across the windshield until they became nothing more than a smear of color, and I could feel the warmth beginning to lift from the air and the blast of open casino doors and laughter and the way that drunken stumbling felt to feet on the sidewalks, and then Jerry made a left turn that took us off the Strip and down another street and then another, and the heat faded and the air smelled metallic and the sidewalks spit trash, and I saw a man leaning against a chain link fence, puking between his feet, and I looked away, and Jerry was still smiling, with a fresh-lit cigarette in his mouth, and then there was more neon, signs stacked with symbols, balls and lightning bolts, pink and green letters, cable television, swimming pool, air conditioning, motel, motel, motel, vacancy, and he slowed the car and we dipped into a driveway and came to a rest in front of the flickering window with a dancing shoe that said "The Slipper."

I had been in a moving car for so long that it took me a minute before I realized that Jerry had cut the engine and we had stopped moving, and it was only the lights that moved around me, and Jerry pulled the keys from the ignition and opened his door, and the air was cooler here and I reached for my door handle, too, but Jerry raised his hand and stopped me.

"Wait here," he said.

My legs hurt from being folded in front of me and my body felt stuck to the seat and all I wanted was to stand and walk and move again.

"I gotta get out of the car," I said. I tightened my grip on the door handle and looked at him as he stood up, but I was able to catch his eye, and I gave him my weakest smile, and said, "Please."

He stretched his back and flicked his cigarette toward the street and paused for a second before he leaned down and looked at me through the open driver's side door. "Okay," he said. "But you stay quiet and you just stand there, okay?"

"Fine," I said. "I just want out of the car. I didn't say I wanted to talk."

"I mean it," he said. "You just stand there. And smile."

I pulled the handle on my door and I shoved it open, and the hinges groaned a little bit, and then I swung my legs out, and it felt good to touch solid ground again instead of vibrating floor boards, and then I pulled myself out of the car and I had the urge to tuck my hair behind my ear, but when I reached up, I didn't touch anything but scruff, and I smoothed it down with the flat of my hand, and then Jerry was walking toward the door that said "OFFICE," and I followed him and he held the door open long enough for me to duck in behind him.

The office was carpeted in blue shag with pink walls, and the counter was long and smooth and sparkly in the overhead light, and a woman stood behind it, staring into a television set that was flickering something I couldn't see, and there was a soda machine in one corner and a slot machine against the wall, and every now and then the slot machine spun a shower of lights and made a sound of bells ringing and then went quiet again, and the soda machine hummed hard in return. Jerry walked up to the counter and tucked in the tails of his shirt, and the woman looked up and smiled, and I could tell it wasn't a smile that she dealt out for any person that walked through the door, and then Jerry said, "Dee, how's tricks?" and the woman's smile clicked over to high beam.

"Jerry, long time, no see," she said, and she put out her hand over a counter that looked like it was chipped with glitter and polished rocks, and I stood beside Jerry and read all of the signs behind her.

"It's been a few months, that's for sure," Jerry said, and he dug into his back pocket and pulled out his wallet and set it on the counter in front of him.

"How long you staying this time?" the woman asked.

"Oh, you know me, give me a week, and I'll probably be here two," he said.

I was listening closely because this was information that I had never heard before, and I had no idea what the plan was or what the job was that I was really brought here to do, and most of all, I didn't know how long we were staying, and it felt strange to think that way, *we*, and I realized there probably wasn't much of a combination to be had of him and I together, and it was really just me and him and we happened to be here together, and if he was only staying a week or two, then that meant I would need an afterward, like something to do later, and someplace else to be.

"Got somebody with you, I see," the woman said, and she smiled at me, and I smiled back, just like Jerry had directed, and she looked me up and down for a second, and I didn't know whether or not she liked what she saw, but she went back to flipping through a book on the counter top and she finally got to the page she was looking for, and then she handed Jerry a pen and he went to work filling out the information that I couldn't see.

"He's my nephew," Jerry said. He didn't look up from what he was writing.

Dee smiled at me again, and I could see that her eyes were very blue, and her hair was bright red and curled in long waves around her face.

"Aren't you a good uncle," she said. "Didn't you have a nephew with you the last time you stayed here?"

Jerry signed his name and then opened his wallet. "Different sister's kid," he said.

There was a sign on the wall that spelled out a thousand rules, all about things that couldn't be done—no visitors, no drugs, no long-distance phone calls, no loud noise, no parties, no gambling in the office if you were under 21, no loitering in the parking lot, no weapons, no refunds.

"So that's one room then, Jerry?" Dee asked.

"Just the one," Jerry said, and my eyes jerked from the signs like they had been yanked on a leash, and I snapped my head toward him.

"Two," I said. "Two rooms." I had never stayed in a room with anyone I didn't know, except when I went to camp in fourth grade, and I hated everyone there and couldn't wait to get back home, even though I hated home, too. But the thought of sleeping in a room with a man I did not know made my stomach sink, and I realized I hadn't thought that this might happen, that we might get to Reno and end up in a motel, and I'd be in a room with him, having to sleep while maybe he looked at me.

"One room," Jerry said. "Two beds."

Dee swung the register book toward her and started writing something down, and then she turned her back toward the counter and walked toward a rack of keys, and I felt Jerry grab my arm, up high where the bicep rubbed the bone, and I felt his fingers dig in, deep into that groove where the tendons are strapped tight, and I almost let out a yelp, but I didn't, and he squeezed one time, hard, and then he dropped his hand and Dee turned back toward us with two sets of keys on plain white tags that had numbers and nothing else.

"You've got two choices," she said. "I've got one that overlooks the pool and one around back that's a little more quiet."

I wanted to tell Jerry that we should take the pool view, but my arm was still burning and I wanted to reach up and rub at it, but instead I shoved my hands into the pockets of the jeans that didn't belong to me. My cramps were starting to gnaw down low, and I knew that if I kept standing for too much longer I'd be bleeding through, so I just dug into the bottoms of my pockets and tried to chew up some lint with the edges of my fingernails.

"We'll take the one around back," Jerry said. "And I'll need to be able to make some calls."

"Local is still free," Dee said.

"Not a problem," Jerry said.

"You want to do by the week?" Dee asked.

"Seven days sounds about right," Jerry said.

Dee looked down at the register book again, turned back a few pages, and then made another mark. "Shouldn't be a problem."

Jerry pulled the rubber-banded money from his pocket and started peeling twenty-dollar bills off the stack, slowly, into two piles on the counter in front of him, and I watched to see how much smaller the wad in his hand would get, but it didn't change at all.

"You plan on hitting the tables?" Dee said to Jerry.

Jerry smiled and I could see small wrinkles under his eyes, and there was stubble on his face under the lights, and I thought maybe he was older than I thought he was, but I couldn't tell. I didn't know anything about how old people were—they were just older or younger than me, and Dee could have been thirty-five or fifty-five, I didn't know, but the skin I could see on her chest, between the open buttons of the Western shirt she wore, was thin and wrinkled and too tan, and she looked old but was probably young and Jerry looked young and was probably old, and all I wanted was to go to bed, but I couldn't imagine ever being able to fall asleep in a room where Jerry was in a bed across the room from me. I once went on a camping trip with my grandpa when I was a kid and for half of it we slept in a trailer in the woods, and even though I had my own bed, he was sleeping in the room with me, and I didn't sleep for three days because all I could hear was the sound of him breathing and snoring and making noise, and it scared me a little bit in a way that made me too nervous to ever relax.

40

Dee took the money off the counter, first one stack and then the other, and then she folded the first stack into her hand—the bigger of the two—and shoved it into her front pocket, then she knocked on the counter with her fist and took the second stack and put it into a little gray, metal lockbox under the edge where I couldn't see, and she glanced over at me, but I dropped my eyes as if I was lost in examining the wear on my shoes, and when I looked up again, she smiled at me, but this time the smile didn't reach all the way to her eyes, and I realized that she was just trying to be nice.

"The pool is closed from sunset to sunrise, okay? That's a real rule around here, and if you break it, I'll have to ask you and your nice uncle here to leave. No swimming after dark. We understand each other?"

I nodded. Jerry jabbed me with his elbow a little bit and Dee gave him a real smile that she hadn't extended to me.

"Yes," I said. "I understand."

"Good, then we won't have any problems. Now, there's cable TV in the room, and if you want clean sheets or towels, you let me know before 9 a.m. each day. Otherwise, enjoy your stay here."

Jerry reached across the counter and took Dee's hand and she squeezed his back, and then he turned and headed for the door, and I trailed after him and kept my eyes down so that I could watch my feet sink into the blue carpeting while the slot machine spun red light.

When the door closed behind me, I followed Jerry to the car and got back in the passenger seat, and the leather was still warm, as though I had never left it, and Jerry got in and shut his door and fished the keys from his pocket and started the engine up and flicked on the headlights, and we crept through the parking lot toward the back of the motel, and we passed by the pool that was dark and fenced-in, and there weren't many cars around back, and Jerry squinted up through the windshield, trying to read the numbers on the rooms, and when we were finally close to 293, he pulled into a spot and I put my hand on the door handle, but then I heard the familiar sound of electric locks dropping into the pockets, and I could hear the engine ticking and Jerry pulled a cigarette from his front shirt pocket and lit it without cracking his window, and he exhaled hard so that the smoke bounced off the windshield and filled the front of the car, and I looked out the passenger window and braced my feet against the floor, waiting for it.

"You have a problem following directions, kid?" he asked. His voice was low, and he said it casually, like how someone might ask if it was going to rain today, but in a library, while other people were reading.

"No," I said.

"I thought I was pretty clear about you being quiet when we got in there."

I started folding small creases into my jeans and rubbing my thumbs against the material. "You were," I said.

I had been in this type of conversation before—first when my stepdad Dale had been alive and then when Chris had started spending more time at the house—and I knew the best thing to do was to just agree and be sorry, and I was, a little bit, but it had just been a reaction, to speak up like I did in there, like putting my hand on a hot stove and jerking it back.

"I just hadn't thought that I was gonna share a room with you," I said.

Outside the passenger window I could see an empty parking lot, and there was someone walking through it, pushing a shopping cart, and there was a dumpster near a tree that lined the asphalt and there were bags and trash caught underneath, and I could see stacks of boxes in the light of a yellow lamp that lined the empty lot beside us, and in the distance there were more neon flashes and signs in motion, and beyond those lights, there were even more, so that it was like a cement mountain range that glowed in reds and greens and blues and golds.

"Why not?" Jerry asked. "Did you think you'd be getting your own suite? You want me to go drop you over at Harrah's? See how far sixty bucks can roll you? I mean, eventually it was gonna get dark outside," Jerry took another long drag on the cigarette and exhaled, and I could hear him but refused to turn my head from the window. "Where did you think you were gonna sleep?"

I was hungry now, for real food, and my stomach growled, and I could hear it, and I wondered if Jerry could, too. "I hadn't really thought about it, I guess," I said.

Jerry tapped his fingers on the steering wheel. "Well, in the future, you let me do the thinking and you do as you're told, and things will just be smooth as butter," Jerry said. "They'll be right as rain. They'll be good as gold. They'll be gangbusters. You understand what I'm saying?"

I nodded. "Yes," I said.

I looked away from the window and Jerry loosened his tie again and leaned his head back on the seat and the car was getting smokey and it was starting to hurt my eyes. He shifted in his seat so that his back was pressed against the driver's side door and he could turn to look at me. His hair had fallen over his forehead and he pushed it back with his hand, and then he picked something off his lip and took another drag from his cigarette and blew the smoke in my direction.

"You're a smart kid, aren't you, Joey? I mean, I saw that in you, right away. That's why I knew you'd be good for this job. That's why I brought you."

I didn't say anything, and Jerry paused for a second and the air was getting thick and I wanted to cough but I didn't.

"But you know," Jerry said. "There's smart. And then there's too smart. There's a difference." He stretched his leg out a little bit and I could feel the seat shift. "So, which one are you? Are you a smart kid? Or are you too smart?"

It was hot in the car with the windows up, and I could feel sweat on my upper lip and I wanted to lick it but I didn't.

"Huh? Are you a smart kid?"

I nodded. "Yeah, I'm a smart kid," I said.

"But?"

I didn't know what he wanted me to answer.

"C'mon," Jerry said, and he reached out a hand toward me, and I didn't want to flinch but I did a little bit, and I knew he saw it, but it didn't stop him from patting me on the arm and I couldn't move away from him because I was pinned as far over as I could get. "But are you too smart?"

He squeezed my arm gently and then dropped his hand. "Huh?" he said. "Tell me."

I shook my head. "No, I'm not too smart."

His grip on my arm tightened and he shook it a little bit, like it was made out of cloth and sewn onto a doll. "See, that's good! That's just right. I knew that about you." He let go of my arm and it fell back into its place beside me and my hand hit the seat with a thud.

He reached past me then, and his hand fumbled with the glovebox, and he pulled the gun out and he set it on the seat between us, and I could see it there, dull and flat and waiting for something to do.

"Don't worry," Jerry said. "I'm not going to hurt you. But you've gotta trust me. You've gotta be smart. But not too smart. Too smart won't be good for anybody."

I shifted my legs and my feet rubbed the floor mat and it made a tight squeak, and Jerry moved away from the door so that he was facing forward again, and he picked the gun up from the seat and he shoved it into the waistband of his pants, and I heard the lock in the door beside me pop up with a metallic click, and then Jerry opened his door and the smoke followed him, and by the time I got my own door open and my legs back underneath me, I realized that I was shaking a little bit, and Jerry was at the trunk of the car, moving things around, and I didn't know whether I should go stand next to him or not, so I just stood there for a minute, beside the open passenger door, listening to the sound of cars in the distance and I thought that I could hear people winning jackpots somewhere across town, but it was just my imagination, and there was a stillness around us, like even the motel had been holding its breath, and the only thing I could really hear was the blood pulsing in my head and the sound of the shopping cart clattering across the empty parking lot beside us, beyond the chain link fence, crushing small rocks beneath its wheels.

When we got to the room door, Jerry set the duffle bags down and took the key from his pocket, and I waited for him to shove it home in the lock, but he hesitated for a second, and then he reached into his pants again and pulled out a wad of cash and held it up to the hallway light so he could look at it, and then he pulled a ten out of the knot and handed it to me.

"There's a burger place three blocks to the right," he said, and he pointed back toward the office and the driveway and the street beyond. "Go get something. And bring me back a double with cheese."

All I wanted was to use the bathroom and clean myself up and figure out how I was going to stop the damp and sticky flow from between my legs that was now drying into my jeans in a narrow stripe, and I didn't really want another burger after I'd had one for breakfast, but I didn't really figure I could ask Jerry for some other options.

"Can I use the bathroom first?" I asked.

Jerry shoved the rest of his money back where it had been and he pulled his cigarettes from his shirt pocket and shook one loose. I waited for him to find his lighter, and he did, and then he sucked the smoke into life and I watched him flick the wheel on the lighter a couple of more times, dry firing it like a gun before he put it back where it had been.

"No," he said.

I'd been sitting in the dirty jeans and squeezing my thighs together for a while, and I couldn't stand the thought of walking around, even if it was dark outside.

"Please."

"It won't take you long. You can have it when you get back. So get going." He stood in front of the door and put the key in the lock and then let the white tag dangle there without turning the knob. "Run along now."

I stood for a second and then I stepped away from him and walked back toward the stairs, past the ice machine that was making a low growl and a soda machine that was dim and flashing on most of the selections, and I looked back over my shoulder while Jerry watched me. He ashed his cigarette and waved me on in one flick of his hand.

There were no people around the motel, no sounds of life except for the occasional muffled blast of a television set behind a window, and everything was shut tight and there was nothing to see, and I took the stairs in twos and hit the sidewalk below, and I could hear my footsteps echoing against the building, and then I was back in the parking lot and I passed the LTD, and I could feel the asphalt under my tennis shoes and my stomach growled and I kept walking, and then I rounded the corner and was heading past the pool when I thought I heard somebody say *hey*, and I waited for a second, thinking that maybe I had just made up the voice in my head, and I strained my ears, but there was nothing, and then it came again, *come here*, and it was coming from the pool, from the shadows in the corner, and I tried to focus my eyes but I couldn't see anything.

"Go to the gate," the voice said, and I walked toward the posted sign that said "NO SWIMMING AFTER DARK," and I pushed on the gate, expecting it to be locked, but it wasn't, and it gave with little resistance, and I could hear the hinges squeak a little bit, and then the voice came again—*over here*.

I walked toward the shadows, to the place in the corner that I could not see, but I could smell the chlorine—like the city pool that I avoided in the summer, with my friends in bikinis and the boys showing off, splashing and flexing and jumping where they weren't supposed to jump—and as my eyes adjusted to the darkness, I could tell there was someone sitting in a lounge chair, stretched out, and I could see something raising and lowering and then the flash of a can in the slim reach of light from the hallways behind me, and I walked toward the wink in the shadows and the voice, but I hung back before I got close enough to reach it.

"I'm not gonna bite you."

I could tell that it was a girl talking, but I couldn't tell how old she might be, and I relaxed a little bit, and I took a couple of steps closer, and the flash of a can raised and lowered again, and then I could hear the rustling of a paper bag. "You want a beer?"

Part of me wanted to say yes, but I also wanted a burger now, because it seemed like something I could fill my stomach with, and I was planning on getting a vanilla shake, too, on Jerry's dime, and maybe some onion rings, if they looked hot enough, but a beer also sounded like a good idea, and two beers sounded better, and I didn't know the voice or the girl behind it, so I cleared my throat and said, "No. No thank you."

"Your loss," the voice said, and I heard the tab snap and then a long swallow, and I shifted my weight on my feet and thought about turning around and leaving.

"You got any cigarettes?" the voice asked me.

I never had my own cigarettes, and the times when I had smoked them, they had always come from someone else's pack.

"No," I said.

"Damn," the voice said. "You're pretty much useless."

I took a couple steps backward and started to turn toward the gate, but the voice reached out and held me before I could head out.

"You come here with Jerry? I saw the car pull in."

I nodded and then realized that she probably couldn't see me, so I said *yeah*, and the voice laughed a little bit, and I wanted to know why but I didn't ask.

"So you must be the new one."

"The new one, what?"

"The new runner," she said. "You know what I'm talking about."

I didn't know what she was talking about at all, and I wanted to tell her that, but I thought that if I admitted how stupid I was, she would find another reason to laugh and I'd be confused again, and I hated that feeling.

"We all know Jerry," she said. "I'm Amber, by the way."

I settled for a quiet *hey*, in return, as though that might be enough for her.

I cleared my throat again. "I thought nobody was supposed to be at the pool after dark," I said.

"Oh yeah? Who told you that?"

"Well, I mean, there's a sign on the gate, and the lady at the office was pretty serious about it."

"Yeah? What lady? Did she have red hair? Kind of curly? Kind of a skinny bitch with mean fucking eyes?"

I smirked a little bit, and even though she couldn't see me, I knew she could hear it in my voice.

"Yeah," I said. "Exactly."

"That's my mom," she said.

I sort of startled a little bit, and I laughed, and I didn't know what to say, so I settled on "Really?" and thought that was safe enough in case she was fucking with me because there was something about her that made it hard to tell.

"Not lying," Amber said. "Ignore her. I do." She raised the can again. "Cheers to Dee, the fucking bitch."

Now that my eyes were adjusted to the dark, I could see that there were several empties scattered around the chair, but I couldn't make out many details about her, and I wished that I could see her in some light. "Damn, I wish you had a cigarette," she said.

"Sorry," I said.

"Can you get some?"

"I, ummmm, I'm supposed to go get food for me and Jerry."

Amber laughed but this time I liked the sound in a way that I could not explain, only that I did like it, and I wanted to step closer.

"Jerry doesn't eat," she said. "But whatever."

"So you know Jerry?" I asked.

"Everybody knows Jerry." She took another swallow from the can. "I mean, not everybody, but you know? There's people that do."

"I don't really know him," I admitted. "I mean, I just met him today."

"Yeah?" Amber said. "That's usually how it goes." She stretched out in the chair, and I heard an empty can hit the pavement and it rolled for a few seconds, clattering, and then it stopped. "Where are you from?"

I hesitated for a second. "California," I said.

"Big place. I've been there," Amber said. "So you're working for Jerry?"

"Yeah," I said. "He hired me."

"What's your name?"

I almost told her the truth—it was what came naturally—but I remembered Jerry standing in that gas station bathroom, cutting my hair, and then turning me toward the mirror by the shoulders so that I could see who I was, and I was somebody else now, and I had to remember that.

"Joey," I said.

"Good name," Amber said. "I like it."

I didn't know what she meant by that and I didn't ask because I didn't really want to know the answer.

"Well, Joey, you'd better go get your burgers. Jerry doesn't like to wait."

"Yeah," I said, and at the mention of food, my stomach growled again and I hoped that she couldn't hear it.

"I'll be here tomorrow, if you get bored and want to come and hang out with me," Amber said. "And I'll be here the next day, and the day after that, and probably after that, because this place is a fucking hell and I am stuck here." She lifted her arm and threw the empty can in the pool, and I could hear the hollow *tink* of aluminum on water. "Come and find me," she said. "And next time bring some cigarettes."

I took a couple steps backward and waited for her to say something else, but she didn't, and I couldn't tell if she was looking at me or not, but her shape didn't move in the chair and there was silence between us, and I could hear cars passing on the street out front and people walking by and laughing, and I wanted to say something else or maybe ask a question, but there were too many in my head and they all sounded dumb to voice out loud, and even though I didn't know many things at all, I knew enough to know when I had been dismissed, and whatever conversation she had started with me was over now, and I needed to step away from the pool and the motel and the room I hadn't been in yet with a bathroom I could not use, and Jerry was waiting for me, and I knew that no matter what all Amber had said about the woman in the office being her mom, and whether she would be here hanging out tomorrow, I knew that in the few things that she had said, there was definitely one truth—that Jerry didn't like to wait.

Chapter 6
Drown

The burger place had tacos, and I was grateful for that. I ordered two and sat outside at a sticky plastic table under the bright lights buzzing from the awnings and a cloud of bugs that hung in the air like moving clouds of smoke, swarming, landing, and lifting again, and I ate fast, barely tasting the first one, and then I ate the second one, slower this time, chewing through the half-soggy tortilla, and I thought about my mom and the tacos she used to make, and I didn't want to think about her, but I couldn't help it, she had been on my mind all day, and I wanted to feel sad and guilty for what I had done, but mostly I was still mad, so I found a way to blame her for what I was doing and make this all her fault.

When I was done with the second taco, I went back to the screened window and ordered another one, and I ordered the cheeseburger for Jerry, and I got my Dr. Pepper refilled, and then I thought about it for a second and ordered some onion rings, too, and then I stood around and people-watched while I was waiting for the white, greasy sack to be handed to me from the other window that said "Pick-Up," and then I walked back to The Slipper while people went by on the opposite sidewalk, headed toward the Strip, and they walked close to each other and held on to waists and shoulders and arms—women with short skirts and high heels that clicked over the cement and flashed light like low sparks, and men with belt buckles and shirts tucked in—and someone called out, *hey baby,* and I looked up, but no one was talking to me.

I walked back to the motel and the lights in the office glowed through the window, but there was nobody at the counter, and I went through the parking lot and slowed down when I got close to the pool, wondering if maybe Amber would call me over again, but everything was quiet and I couldn't see anything in the shadows anymore, and I figured that she was probably gone, so I rounded the building and climbed the stairs to the second floor, and for a second I was worried that I couldn't remember the room number, but I did, and I went to the door and the curtains were drawn but there was light behind them, and I stood there for a minute, unsure about what to do since I didn't have a key, and then I knocked quietly, once, and then twice, and then a few more times but there was no answer and I couldn't hear any sound inside, so I turned the doorknob, already convinced that it was locked, but the door opened and I went in.

The room smelled, but not in a bad way, really, more like a smell of bleach and waxy air fresheners, and there was the hint of pine forest, and the carpet was light blue and the walls were pink, and there were two beds, just like Jerry had promised, and he was already sprawled out across the one closest to the window with the bedspread pulled back and his shoes kicked off on the floor at the foot, and his head was on the pillow and his mouth was open and I could hear him snoring quietly. I put the bag of food on one of the nightstands between the beds, and then I crept into the bathroom and watched for Jerry to wake up as I pushed the door shut, but he didn't, so I twisted the lock and stood there in the bright light and looked at the rolled white towels and the wrapped plastic cups and the little bottles that said "shampoo," and then I ran the water in the sink until it got hot and the mirror started to fog, and I was glad that I did because I couldn't bring myself to look at my reflection and not recognize what I might see. I took a washcloth off the metal rack and soaked it, and then I dropped my jeans and did my best to clean myself off—pulled the paper off the thin bar of soap and rubbed the washcloth until it foamed, and washed and rinsed, and then drained the sink and did it all over again—and when I was done, I took another washcloth from the rack and folded it over on itself until it was a thin pad and I took my jeans off and then my underwear, and the jeans were fine but the underwear wasn't, and I wasn't sure what to do with them—I couldn't see myself washing them in the sink and leaving them to dry on the shower rod, not with Jerry in the room, so I wadded them up and put them in the trash can, and then I took some toilet paper off the roll and wadded it up, too, so that the bottom of the trash was covered, and I took the folded washcloth and put it into the crotch of the jeans and pulled them up, and moved everything into place, and for the first time in many miles, I felt clean.

I unlocked the door and turned out the light and saw that Jerry hadn't moved from the position that he was sleeping in, with his tie loose and his shirtsleeves rolled up, and I sat down on the opposite bed, and my backpack was there, and I unzipped it and thought about changing into something else, but I was too tired and I thought about rustling through the bag from the burger place and eating the other taco, and I wondered if there was a way I could put the TV on without waking Jerry up, and there seemed like too many decisions to make suddenly and all of them sounded exhausting, so I just folded back the bedspread and laid down on the thin, tan blanket underneath, and I pulled my feet from my shoes and stared up at the ceiling and wondered what I was doing there, in that room, with Jerry sleeping on a bed that was just a few feet away from me, and I could hear cars go by on the street, but they were quiet and seemed far away, and I thought that maybe it wasn't too late for me to just pick up my things and go, and maybe it wouldn't be hard to find a way to get someplace else, and I had more money now, and I could pay for something, and I thought about doing that—picking up and getting gone—but my mind finally wore me out and before I knew it, I wasn't staring at the ceiling anymore, I was down by the slough near my house, with Bobby and Wayne and Tony Gutierrez, and we were drinking warm vodka from a pint bottle and trying to find flat rocks to skip, and I could feel the sun on my bare shoulders, and I pulled my hair up and off my neck, and somebody said, *hey, we should go swimming*, and that was the last thing that I remembered before I, too, fell asleep.

My stepdad Dale had a brother named Oren—Uncle Oren to us—and Oren was a mean fuck who didn't give a shit about rules or codes or saying *please* or *thank you*, or taking just one, or waiting his turn, or putting things back where they belonged, and when Dale was with my uncle Oren, they became two of the same, trying to outdrink each other, or yell louder, or hit harder, and Uncle Oren was two years older than my stepdad, so he always had a hand up, and a sharper edge, and a longer reach, and by the time I was four, I knew that going over to Uncle Oren's with my stepdad on a Saturday would be a day when I would want to shrink down and be quiet and not be seen or heard, and it was on a Saturday that they taught me to swim once, in April, when the water was still cold but the sun was getting hot, and I was going on six, and Uncle Oren had a big pond on his property in Cottonwood, where sometimes they would go and fish, and after they were a twelve-pack in on that particular afternoon, sitting on the shore in lawn chairs, throwing rocks at birds, they got the idea that it was good for me to learn how to keep my head above water, and I hadn't been paying attention to them or what they were saying—I had been drawing in the mud with a stick—and then my Uncle Oren yanked me to my feet and then lifted me off the ground, and my stepdad took my legs while Uncle Oren kept me by the arms, and they swung me between them with my body stretched out like a short piece of thick rope, and I could feel my T-shirt catching the wind as they pitched me forward and back, and my skin was cold, and my jeans were slipping down from the force of my stepdad's grip around my ankles, and the sun was so bright above me that I had to squint my eyes a little bit in order to see the hard blue of the sky beyond the light, and they were both laughing, and Dale had a cigar pinched between his teeth, a Swisher Sweet, and they were counting, in loud voices, both of them ticking off numbers, punching them down from *three,* and then *two,* and then *one,* and when they hit the bottom, they swung me high and hard and launched me toward the green and stagnant water—over the thick weeds and black silt where the bullfrogs sucked and went open-throated after dark, and I was airborne for what seemed like a long minute, as if time had stood still and held me between the water and the sky, but it was just a second or two maybe, just a tick of a watch hand skipping past another number, and then I hit the surface and crashed through, past the point where my feet could touch, and my clothes went heavy, and my head went under, and above me there was a dirty brown window of light that I reached toward until it grew so small that it closed, and I kicked my feet like I had seen others do, and my tennis shoes pulled like lead weights on a line, and I sank into the cold water, and everything went quiet around me—and even my heartbeat went out of my head, so that all I could do was feel the wet—and I closed my mouth against the water but felt it come in through my nose anyways so that my entire face burned, and I wanted to suck in a breath and cough, but even then I knew better, so I kicked harder, and I tried to reach for the surface in handfuls that couldn't hold anything more than a trail of bursting bubbles, and every time I opened my hands to grab and pull myself toward the surface, they were just empty and useless, but I kept reaching and kicking—as hard as I could pump my knees—and the water around me got darker until it didn't any more, and that was the day that I learned how to swim.

Chapter 7
The Richter Brothers

The sun was coming through the curtains. I could feel it on my face—hot and close—and for a minute I couldn't remember where I was—not home—and I rolled over in my small bed and saw Jerry across from me, separated by the narrow strip of blue carpet, and he was still in his clothes, still with his head thrown back on the pillow and his mouth open, snoring lightly, and then I remembered where I was and reached a hand up and touched my too-short hair to remind me, and it felt soft and I brushed at it with my fingers and ran my palm over the top and smoothed it forward where it did not touch my forehead.

The room smelled like old food, and I looked over and saw the white bag from the burger place, now greasy at the bottom, and my stomach growled and it felt like a hamster had crawled up on my face in the night and peed in my mouth, and all I wanted was to brush my teeth and take a shower but I was afraid to make too much noise with Jerry sleeping—it was as if as long as he was sleeping, I could stay in this place of limbo, between what I'd done and what might yet happen—so I got up quietly and took my backpack to the bathroom and shut the door, and I dug my toothbrush out of the bottom and found the almost-empty tube of paste I'd taken and brushed my teeth, slowly, and then I ran water in the sink until the water got so hot that steam collected on the mirror, and I got the end of a towel wet and washed my face and dried it off, and I ran the towel over my head and my hair soaked it up as though it was as thirsty as I was, and when I was finished, I pulled my shoes on and walked quietly across the carpet and opened the door as slowly as I could, and then I slipped out into the light.

Everything looked different in the day. There were people in the parking lot, and I could hear voices and cars, and I wished I had something to eat besides a burger gone soggy in the bag, and I walked down the hallway where there was a housekeeping cart just beyond the stairs, and

I went down to the floor below and stepped out onto the asphalt and looked back over my shoulder toward the room, but the curtains were still tight and the door was still closed, so I kept walking and rounded the building and the pool was to my left, and it was empty of people, but the water was bright blue and clean, and I could see spent cans collected under a lounge chair at the deep end, where the sign said "6 feet," and I stood at the fence for a minute and tried to think about what to do in this place I didn't know, with money in my pocket and nothing in my stomach and no real sense of direction or idea of what I might try to find if I did. I knew I was making dumb choices, but I couldn't seem to make myself care, and in a way, I thought that it was because it was summer and I had a hard time thinking when I wasn't in school, and I could still feel my mom's boyfriend's hand on my throat and the sound of his footsteps when he came into my room in the dark.

I heard a whistle and I looked up, but there were only cars parked in front of the rooms and another housekeeping cart going by the lower level, and I wrapped my hands around the pool fence and felt the hot, black metal, and then I swung on it a little bit, and then the whistle came again, this time with a yell, of *hey*, and I turned my head and I could see a guy with no shirt and a pair of jeans, sitting in a lawn chair in front of an open room door, tucked behind a pickup truck, and I looked away but not before I could see someone inside the room, leaning forward on the bed, and she was waving at me, and the guy in the jeans spit into a cup and yelled over, "she's calling you," and I turned toward the room and the guy and the voice from the chair, and I said, "yeah? What?"

"C'mere!" The person on the bed sat up and waved again, and all I could see were bare legs and a pair of cutoffs, and then she came to the doorway, and it was Amber, from the night before. "Joey, right? Come over here."

I nodded and let go of the pool fence and crossed the parking lot, and the guy in the lawn chair was barefoot, and the sun was pinned to his bare chest, and he was squinting toward me, and when I got close enough, he said, "Hey," and then Amber waved to me to come into the room, so I did.

"What are you up to?" she asked, and she flopped back on the bed and kicked her legs up and grabbed a bag of Doritos off the nightstand and tilted them my direction. "Want some?"

"No thanks," I said.

"Sit by me," she said and she patted the bed next to her where the blankets were pushed back to the sheets and the pillows were propped up, so I sat down next to her and kept my shoes on the floor. The room was the reverse of the one Jerry and I had—this one had pink carpeting and blue walls and on the wall above the bed there was a painting of a forest with mist hanging in the trees, and there were clothes everywhere, spilling out of suitcases and drawers, stacked in piles on the little dresser where the television sat.

"You stay here a lot?" I asked.

"For now," Amber said. "My mom just moves me around to different empty rooms every week so that nobody really knows. It ain't terrible, but this whole town sucks, and I can't wait to get out of here. Until then, at least there's cable, right? I'm watching *Alien*." She pointed at the little TV on the dresser that was sitting in a sea of T-shirts. "I mean, I've seen it like a hundred times," she said. "But I fucking love this movie."

I looked at the TV, and there were people in spacesuits walking through some kind of chiseled-stone-looking cave, and it was almost too dark to see anything except their lights washing the blackness around them, and the only sound I could hear was a high-pitched whine of wind coming from the screen.

"I've never seen it," I said.

"What? Are you kidding me?" She yelled toward the open doorway, and the guy in the jeans who was still spitting in a cup and staring toward the lot—"He's never seen this. Can you believe that? Were you like home-schooled or something?"

"No, I wasn't home-schooled."

"You must have been sheltered."

"I wasn't. I just haven't seen it. I mean, I know what it's about and everything. I just haven't watched it."

"Yeah? So what's it about?"

There was something about Amber that told me that she liked to catch people in a lie, so I looked at the screen and everyone was moving back toward the clouded lights of a ship and still there was only high-pitched wind and darkness and it looked sort of boring to me. "It's ummm about an alien."

"No shit," Amber said, and she dug her hand into the Doritos bag and pulled out a handful of orange triangles and started chewing the corners off of them. "See that guy right there?" She pointed at a short man without much hair. "He's about to fuck them all. He's the one who lets the alien into the ship."

I nodded and watched a guy with something on his helmet get put onto a table.

"That's the alien," Amber said.

"Doesn't seem like much," I said. It was just a small thing on the front of the guy's face shield.

"That's the baby from the egg," Amber said. "It grows. And that guy who let them in? That's Ash, and he's really a robot, but nobody knows it."

"He doesn't look like a robot," I said.

"Exactly, but wait until they attack him and they knock his head off and he's like all—what's the word—robotic."

She passed me the bag of chips again, and even though I didn't really like Doritos, I reached in and pulled out a handful and ate a few and they tasted better than I remembered, so I kept reaching in for more.

"See, they don't know he's a robot, and he's the one who makes them get the alien. If it was me, I would have known he's a robot. You can tell."

I watched him talk to the others and he seemed like a regular guy to me and not like a robot at all.

"I could tell he's not really a person like them," Amber said. "If I was them, I'd know there was something wrong with him. I'm good at seeing through people, you know?"

I nodded but she didn't wait for me to answer.

"And that guy with the baby alien on his face is really a host for the egg and the real alien is going to bust out of his stomach in like a few minutes. You're just in time for the best part."

"Oh yeah, I heard about that part," I said.

"Then the alien gets away and the whole movie is about them trying to find it and kill it."

"Jesus, Amber, why don't you just tell him what the whole movie is about," the guy from the doorway shouted from over his shoulder.

"Ignore him," Amber said. "That's my boyfriend, Hurley."

"Oh, so now I'm your boyfriend?" the guy yelled again. "You didn't act like it last night."

"Because you were being an asshole," Amber shouted. "Oh, I love her!" Amber yelled at the screen, and there was a woman with big eyes and curly hair, and she was getting mad at somebody at the table.

"You and fucking Sigourney Williams," the guy shouted from the doorway. "Your fucking hero."

"Weaver," Amber yelled back. "I have such a crush on her," Amber whispered to me. She moved closer so that I could feel her breath on my ear. "Don't tell anyone."

"I thought her name was Ripley," Hurley said from outside the room.

"You're such a fucking idiot sometimes." She moved close to my ear again. "Wait, this is almost the good part," Amber pointed at the screen and clapped her hand on my thigh. I could feel its warmth through my jeans. "It's gonna explode out of his stomach. It's vicious."

I could hear the lawn chair shift and scrape across the narrow cement sidewalk, and then Hurley came into the room and he reached above him and grabbed the top of the doorframe and stretched himself out so that I could see the hair in his armpits and I looked away.

"Everybody gets fucking killed except for Sigourney Williams or Weaver or whatever the fuck her name is and she survives and kills the alien. The end," and Hurley dropped his arms and stretched his back—his chest was hairless, and it reminded me of Tony Gutierrez and Wayne, who had put the cardboard down on the dirt by the slough and had taken turns climbing on top of me while my shorts were hooked around the shoes on my feet.

"You're such an asshole sometimes," Amber said, "You ruin everything," and she reached over and picked up the remote control from the bedside table and pushed a button and the channel switched to Bob Barker, and this was a show that I knew.

"I gotta ice my knee," Hurley said, and he walked past us to the bathroom and I heard something shifting in the sink, and then he came out with a towel dripping heavy with ice, and he pulled up the leg of his pants and put the towel on his knee and leaned back on the bed next to Amber and grabbed the bag of chips out of her hand and tossed them to the floor. "Stop eating that shit, baby. You'll get fat. I don't want you fat." He adjusted the towel and pressed it down with one hand. "Let's go do something," he said.

"I need breakfast, Hurley. You said you were gonna take me to breakfast. You wanna go out with us?" Amber asked.

I could feel the bed sinking where Hurley was sitting, and I was getting sucked toward the depression in the bed where the sheets pulled, and I got to my feet and brushed my hands off on my jeans, and I wished I hadn't eaten any of the Doritos because now I was thirsty and they didn't taste so good after a few minutes in my mouth.

"I probably gotta go," I said. "You know, Jerry, and everything."

"Oh, you're the one, huh?" Hurley said. "Amber told me about you."

"The one what?"

"With Jerry."

"You know Jerry?" I asked.

"Nah, I don't know him. Just what Amber has told me. She just said you're with him—you know, working and shit. Whatever." He leaned back and Amber started running her hands through his hair. He was wearing a belt with a horse head on the front, and green stones all around it.

"I like your buckle," I said.

"Hurley's a bareback rider," Amber said. "He's competing Friday, you should go with us. Him and his brother. They're like champions. The Richter Brothers. You ever heard of them?"

I shook my head. "I don't know much about rodeo."

"Ain't much to know," Hurley said. "You just climb up and ride, right, baby?" And he jumped forward and dropped the towel to the floor so that the ice spilled out and he turned around and grabbed onto Amber and she let out a scream, and he pinned her to the bed, grabbing her by the wrists, and she was squirming around and laughing, but he pressed his weight into her and covered her with his body so that she couldn't sit up.

"I gotta go," I said.

Hurley quit moving around on top of Amber and she went still underneath him. "You should come see us Friday," he said. He held both of Amber's wrists in one hand and reached down to the floor beside the bed, and he picked up a beer can and took a drink.

"Hey," Amber said, "how old are you anyways?"

"What the fuck does that matter?" Hurley said.

"It doesn't. He just doesn't look very old, that's all. I'm just curious."

"I'm seventeen," I said.

"You don't look seventeen," Amber said.

"I mean I'm almost seventeen."

"I don't know," Amber said. "You're pretty small for a guy. I mean, no offense, but last night by the pool, I thought you were a girl."

"Jesus, Amber, don't be a bitch. Not everyone can be as big as me," Hurley said, and he shoved one of her hands down toward the buckle and the crotch of his jeans.

"Whatever," she said, and she squeezed him and then pulled her hand back.

I turned toward the door, and I could hear them behind me, wrestling across the bed again, and then Amber said, "Hey, Joey, next time you were supposed to bring me cigarettes, remember?"

I kept walking out the door and when I got to the stretch of broken cement in front of the room, I stopped for a second. "You want the door open or closed?" I asked.

"Leave it open, man," Hurley said. "This is the best arena in town."

So I kept walking and then I was back in the sunshine and there was asphalt underneath my shoes again, and I could hear Amber laughing from the bed behind me, through the open door, and Hurley was making noises that I didn't like the sound of, but that were something that I was familiar with, and I knew that if I closed my eyes, I could imagine myself under the trees by the slough, with their branches reaching above me, bending and releasing, like the damp square of cardboard I could still feel underneath me, and pressed against my back.

PART II

Chapter 8
Fat

The town where I grew up was covered with trees—so many that they named streets after them—Walnut, Oak, Ash, Pine—but there were no trees here—just asphalt and broken cement and trash clinging to chain link fences, and there was no smell of life—just chemicals like bleach and antiseptic and the smell of vomit and something that was sticky and sweet, like a spilled drink that had been left on a linoleum floor to dry into a thick gel. I stood on the walkway to the room and wasn't sure if I should turn the knob or knock, since I still didn't have a key, so I just stood there, dumb, until I finally pushed my way quietly inside and expected to see Jerry, still in his clothes with his tie loose and his shoes kicked off, asleep on the bed, but the room was empty and the beds were rumpled, and the bathroom door was closed, so I sat down in one of the stained chairs at the beat-up table under the window and waited and wondered about what would come next.

The door to the bathroom opened and Jerry stepped out in a haze of steam, and he was dressed and combed, in what looked like a clean shirt, and his hair was slicked and he ran a finger across his teeth and looked over at me.

"Where you been?" he asked.

"Nowhere. I just got bored."

"'I just got bored' isn't an answer. Where were you?"

I hesitated for a second. "I was hanging out with someone I met," I said. "Amber. Her mom's the lady who was at the front desk."

"Oh look at you, making new friends," he said sarcastically. "This isn't fucking summer camp. You're here to work—not hang out, and especially not hang out with her. Stay away from her."

"You know her?"

Jerry didn't look at me. "Yeah, I know her. She's a hundred pounds of fuck-up in a five-pound bag, so steer clear. And let me tell you something—I don't ever want her in this room, you got it? I don't want to see you talking to her, and I don't want her around."

"She seemed nice," I said. "She invited me to the movies with her boyfriend."

"Oh, that's just beautiful. It could be like a date, right? You want some money for popcorn?"

I dropped my eyes to the stained carpet and followed a dark brown stripe to where it disappeared under Jerry's bed.

"I got bored and was walking around. She invited me into her room."

"Don't go into her room, either. Steer fucking clear."

"Well what am I supposed to do? Just sit here?"

"You'll do what I tell you to do. That's the deal. This isn't a fucking field trip." He stretched his back and walked over to his bed and sat down and pulled his shoes on.

"I brought you back your food last night," I said. "But you were already asleep." I pointed at the grease-stained bag on the nightstand.

"It's smelling up the room. Go throw it away."

"Where?"

"I don't know where. Jesus. Just get it out of here. I can't stand the smell."

I couldn't smell anything, but I went over and picked up the bag and then stood there for a minute. My stomach growled.

"I'm hungry," I said.

"Jesus, kid. Is that all you do? Eat and complain?"

"I'm just hungry. It's past breakfast."

"You want three hots and a cot? Get arrested. They'll take good care of you down at the jail."

"Can I get some food?" I asked.

"You got food last night. You can eat later."

My stomach growled again and this time it was so loud that I figured Jerry could hear it and know that I wasn't just trying to be difficult.

He dug into his front pocket and pulled out a five-dollar bill. "Here. Go get some donuts. Out the driveway and to the left. And don't fuck around. I've got some calls to make." He picked up the phone from the table and held the receiver to his ear, then lit a cigarette and waved at me with his hand. "Go," he said, "before I change my mind and let you eat what's in the bag."

I opened the door and the sun flashed in, too bright, and Jerry winced

64

and shielded his eyes. "Don't fuck around," he said again, "and stay away from that fucking trash," which I guessed to mean Amber, and I shut the door behind me and walked toward the stairs. There was a garbage can beside the soda machines, and I dropped the bag in and it made a heavy *thunk* as it hit the bottom. Part of me was sad to throw away a perfectly good burger, but I wasn't sad enough to pull it from the bag and eat it, and I didn't really want donuts but my stomach didn't care at that point, so I walked down the stairs and through the parking lot and I couldn't help but look toward Amber's room, but the door was closed and the truck that had been parked in front was gone, and I figured Amber and Hurley had gone out like they had talked about, and I wondered if they were somewhere having pancakes and drinking orange juice while I was here, hungry and sweating in layers of clothes, with my hair cut off, and I knew my sister would laugh if she saw me now, and I kept walking through the parking lot, kicking at rocks, and when I went past the office, I could see Dee behind the counter, writing on something, and I waved my hand but she either didn't notice me or didn't care.

I bought three glazed twists and one plain and then added on an orange juice and decided I would keep all the change, and I ate the first twist as I walked, and I was so hungry that I didn't even taste it, so I slowed down for the second one and decided to save the plain one for Jerry, just in case. The sun was hanging higher in the sky and there were people on the sidewalks, and some of them were already loud and staggering, and it was as if the city didn't know the difference between night and day. I went back to the room and opened the door and there was a man I had never seen before lying on my bed with his shoes on the bedspread, and he looked up when I walked in and put the bag on the table under the window and stood uncomfortably by the door, unsure about what I should do.

Jerry was on his bed, with the phone against his ear, and then he said something I didn't catch and he hung up the receiver, and the man on my bed pulled a pack of cigarettes out of his pocket and shook one loose and lit it and stared at me.

"So this is the runner, huh?" he didn't look at Jerry while he said it—just kept his eyes on me as he exhaled a thick wall of smoke and took another drag.

"Yep," Jerry said. "Starting today."

"Doesn't look like much," the man said.

"Neither do you," I said. The words came out before I could stop them but there was something about the man that I didn't like at all, and I didn't care what I said to him.

"Whoa now," Jerry said. "You'd better be nice to Gordo here."

"Turn around," Gordo said. "Let me see you. Give me a spin."

"No," I said.

Gordo laughed and shifted his weight on my bed. He had a lot of weight to shift. He was fat with a stain on his white T-shirt that he was trying to dress up by wearing a black suit jacket over the top, but it only made him look sweaty and wrinkled, and his hair was thin on top and didn't look as if he washed it much.

"Mouth is good," Gordo said. "I'll take a good mouth. Don't take any shit, kid. You'll live longer." He laughed and ashed his cigarette onto the carpet. "What's this one going by?" Gordo asked.

I didn't like all the ways that he was getting in my business, like what I was going by and wanting to check me out. I didn't know what it meant.

"This is Joey," Jerry said.

"Good one. Good name. How old?"

"You can ask me," I said. "I'm standing right here."

Gordo shook his head slowly. "Slow learner, huh?" he said to Jerry.

"Still learning the ropes," Jerry said.

"Let me know if you need someone to break her in," Gordo said, and he laughed and rubbed the tears out of his eyes. I didn't like the way that they were talking—like there was a secret between them that I wasn't in on, and I'd already felt that way when Amber had mentioned Jerry, and I wondered how many others had been picked up for jobs and had stood in one of these rooms wearing somebody else's clothes and waiting for a shoe to drop. I almost asked Jerry right then—asked for the truth and the real story, but I didn't think I would get much out of him with Gordo lying on my bed as part of the inside joke.

"I'm fourteen," I said. "And a half."

"Oh, and a half! Damn. Good for you," Gordo said. He turned toward Jerry. "Went a little younger on this one, huh? Traded down a size?" He started laughing again and his cigarette fell onto the bedspread so that he had to pinch it up quickly and then slap at the smoldering burn it left behind.

"What's in the bag?" Gordo asked me.

"A donut," I said.

Gordo reached into his jacket pocket and pulled out a short bottle, uncapped it and took a long drink. He passed the bottle to Jerry, who did the same.

"Candy is dandy but liquor is quicker," Gordo said. Jerry passed the bottle back to him and he took another drink and then tucked it away. "So what's the deal, Jerry? We got twenty-three minutes until first pitch. Brewers and Rangers. Got a full weekend and night games to get sorted out. Hey, kid," he said to me, "do me a favor and turn on the TV. Toss me the clicker."

I took the remote off the top of the television, turned on the TV and tossed the remote onto the bed. Gordo flipped through channels until he got to some announcers sitting in a booth, and then the camera switched to a baseball diamond and players throwing a ball around to warm up.

"Take the chalk on the Brewers, the Phillies, the Cubbies, the Yankees, the White Sox, and the Dodgers," Jerry said.

Gordo held up his hand. "Slow the fuck down. I can't remember all that shit."

"I'll spell it out to you. Real slow like. Just make the call."

"Give me the phone," Gordo said. Jerry passed it over to him and Gordo punched in some numbers and then started talking while he lit another cigarette. Jerry repeated the names all over again and Gordo echoed them. "Wait," he said to Jerry as he held up his hand. "Are you fucking listening to me? No, I said Phillies. Yeah. Put Ray on the phone. I don't give a shit. Put Ray on." Gordo shifted the receiver to his other ear. "Ray? Is he fucking retarded? I'm just asking. Jesus, I know it's your son, but I'm asking if he's fucking retarded." He paused for a second and listened. "Hold on." He put the receiver against his shoulder. "Hey, Ray says Koosman's got a rotator cuff problem. The line on the Phillies has been moving all day."

"Stay with the Phillies," Jerry said. "I don't give a shit about Ray's information he gets from some niece's boyfriend's cousin in the fucking front office."

"What's the action, Jerry?"

"A dime," Jerry said. "All on the lines. Spread another nickel around."

Gordo lifted the phone back to his ear. "A dime," he said. He paused for a second. "Spread a nickel," Gordo said, and then he hung up the phone. On the TV, the players were gathered around the mound, and the pitcher spit a long, brown stream into the dirt.

"You got any beer, Jerry?" Gordo said.

"Haven't had time to lay in supplies," Jerry said.

Gordo flipped the channels on the TV and then went back to the game. "We've only got half a show here," he said. "We could run them all day if we head over to the Cal Neva."

Jerry was sitting on his bed, smoking a cigarette. He opened the bottom drawer of the nightstand and pulled out a paper bag but didn't open it. "I've gotta get some work running today," he said, and then he looked over at me.

"I thought you weren't supposed to go to the Cal Neva," I said to Jerry. I remembered what Lalo had said before we left Susanville and the way Jerry had reacted.

"Jesus, Jerry, you didn't tell me you brought your mom on this trip," Gordo said. He pulled the bottle from his jacket again and took another drink.

"Mind your business, kid," Jerry said.

There was a knock at the door and everyone went quiet and looked at me. Jerry moved forward on the bed and pulled the curtain back a little bit so he could see out onto the walkway.

"Fuck," he said.

"Too early for the Po-po," Gordo said, and then he laughed.

"It's for you," he said to me. "Go ahead and answer it."

I looked up, surprised. "Me?"

"Yeah, you and your fucking boredom."

I didn't move from the chair.

"Go ahead," Jerry said. "Crack it and tell her to go away."

At first I couldn't imagine who was at the door—my mother had found me, maybe, had tracked me down, and I tried to picture her standing on the walkway, in her jeans and tank top, angry and small, but I didn't think she would be angry, and she wasn't very small, and I could remember the way she had watched Chris hold me by my neck with the backs of my shoes tapping against the wall, and then she had looked away and went back to eating, and it had been the same when my stepdad Dale had been alive, with his long reach, always yanking me, always grabbing me by the hair and threatening to "rub my nose in it," which was something that he liked to say.

I stood up and pulled the door open a little bit, and the light hit my eyes, and at first I couldn't see who was standing there, and then I realized it was Amber, and she said, "Hey," and I smiled and opened the door a little bit more. She looked over my shoulder and into the room. "Hi, Jerry," she said. "I didn't know you were coming back."

"I guess my postcard got lost in the mail," he said.

I could feel Gordo watching both of us, and I used my body to block the room from Amber's view, but she looked past me and I could tell she was looking at Gordo.

"Who are you?" she asked over my shoulder and smiled.

"You know who I am, baby. I'm fucking Santa Claus," Gordo said. "You wanna come over here and sit on my lap?"

Amber made a face. "No thanks," she said. She put her eyes back onto me. "Me and Hurley are taking off to the movies," she said. "You wanna go?"

I leaned my weight into the crack between the door and the jam. "I can't," I said.

"You sure?"

"He's busy," Jerry half-shouted from his bed. "Bye-bye."

"Jesus, Jerry, you don't have to be rude. I just thought I'd ask him, that's all." Amber was wearing a pair of short cutoffs that had the pockets rabbit-eared out of the bottom and a tube top that left a gap beneath her breasts where the fabric didn't meet her chest. Her skin was brown, and I could smell coconut on her. "Maybe next time, huh?" she said to me, and I smiled and nodded my head.

"Have fun," I said.

"I always do," and she turned away from the door and I watched her walk back toward the stairs, with her flip flops slapping the backs of her heels. I shut the door and sat down in the chair again. I hadn't realized how much the room smelled until I had cracked the door open and sucked in the air, and I looked over at Gordo sweating on my bed, and I knew I'd have to smell him on my pillow and my sheets even after he finally went away, and the thought made me want to gag a little bit.

"Gonna start calling you The Warden, Jerry," Gordo said. "You get enough jailbait up in here to turn this place into a bona fide institution." He slapped the bedspread and I could see dust motes rise into the air.

"You should have never fucking talked to her," Jerry said to me. "Now she's gonna be sniffing around here every chance she gets."

Gordo raised his head and sniffed hard at the air. "I'd like to smell her out myself," he said. "Bitch in heat. Pick those pockets right off her thighs."

69

"She'd break your hand off," Jerry said.

"I only need one finger," Gordo said. He raised his right index finger and curled it back and forth like he was pulling a trigger.

Jerry laughed and then clapped his hands together. "Okay, enough of this bullshit," he said. "I've got work for you."

My heart dropped a little bit and my stomach did a slow roll that churned the donuts into a wet mash that mixed with the orange juice I had drank too fast while I was walking.

"Hey, Joey, I got a joke for you," Gordo said. "You'll like this one. You know why women have two holes down there?"

I winced a little bit and shook my head and waited.

"So when they get drunk, you can pick 'em up and carry 'em like a six-pack." Gordo laughed so hard that he banged his head against the wall behind the bed. "I bet she likes to drink," he said between hard sucks of breath. "Here, have some," he said, and pulled the bottle out of his jacket and tipped it toward me.

"I don't want your backwash."

"Honey, you only wish. It's a good thing you don't have tits. You look like a boy. I don't do boys. Even girly ones." He hit his cigarette and lowered his eyes at me. "Hey. Let me ask you something? You get your period yet?"

I felt like he was looking at the wad of washcloth stuffed into my jeans.

"Yeah," I said. "You get yours?"

Gordo wiggled his fingers at me like he was exorcising the boogeyman. "Ohhh, honey, you got me there."

"Go put these on," Jerry said. He dug into the paper bag he'd pulled out of the nightstand and came up with what looked like a pair of tighty-whities—the kind that my stepdad Dale used to wear. My mom's boyfriend Chris wore boxer shorts. I'd seen them on her bedroom floor many times.

"I'm not wearing those," I said.

"You will. And you are," Jerry said. "Lalo's wife makes these special." He held them up and put his hands around the waistband so that they hung in front of him, and then he pulled at the front and I could see that the opening flap had been sewn closed with a pocket inside that had been stitched across, behind the waistband.

"That's pretty fucking smart," Gordo said. "Let me see them."

"I'm not wearing them if everyone keeps touching them," I said. I grabbed them out of Jerry's hand and inspected them myself. The pocket was shallow but wide.

"What's the pocket for?"

"Go get dressed," Jerry said. He checked his watch. "You'll find out soon enough."

"We gonna ride the rails, Jerry, or what? I'm being patient over here, but the pipes, they are a calling." He ran the back of his hand under his nose and made a loud sniffing noise. Jerry shot him a look.

"I'm showering first," I said. I picked up my backpack from the floor and carried it with me into the bathroom. I shut the door behind me and put the underwear on the counter. I felt like everything was a piece of a puzzle that I was supposed to be putting together—what Amber knew, what Lalo had said, why Gordo was there, but all I had were corner pieces and there was no substance to the inside picture I was supposed to be seeing, and it was like there were still a thousand pieces spread out on the table in front of me and they were all the same color of white, like the underwear on the counter. I wanted to stab that fat fuck Gordo. I wanted to jab him in the stomach and watch his guts spill out. But all there was in the bathroom was a small, thin bar of soap and I didn't think my toothbrush could do much damage, and I doubted I could really stab him. *Unless he touched me*, I reasoned. If he touched me, I could sink in a knife. Behind the door, I could hear the volume on the television go up, and I could hear the sound of announcers talking about pitching and speeds and percentages and things that didn't matter to me, and then I heard the tick of a batter connecting, and the announcer came through clearly—"a long fly ball, and it's going, Chavez is running back, and it's still going, Chavez is underneath it, he's at the wall, but this one, ladies and gentlemen, is gone."

Chapter 9
How It Works

I took a long shower and washed my hair, and when I was done, I stood in the steam of the bathroom and rubbed a towel against the mirror so that it cleared in a few wet streaks, and I took my clothes off the counter and slipped into them, pulling on the underwear carefully like they might bite me, and I looked at myself in the mirror, naked except for the underwear and it felt strange to see myself like that, in men's underwear, sagging at my crotch, with my flat stomach and small breasts, like two different pictures that had been torn apart at the navel and put together with each other in a way that almost, but didn't quite, fit, and I ran my hand over my hair and smoothed it forward, and I wondered if this is what boys felt when they stood in the mirror, looking at themselves in their underwear and feeling powerful in a way they couldn't describe. I stepped into my jeans and let the waistband of the underwear sit above the jeans as I buttoned them so that they held the underwear up, but I could still feel them hanging on both of my thighs and they felt like I was wearing a pair of shorts under jeans, and I wondered if anyone would notice the ways the leg holes seamed at my thighs, and then I put on a T-shirt, a tight one that Jerry had given me, and my breasts pressed against my chest, and then the looser one over that, and then the long-sleeve and I buttoned it halfway, and then I rolled the sleeves up, and with the steam and the heat from the shower closed into the tiny room, I was already sweating, so I took another white towel from the tiny rack above the toilet and wiped down my face, and then I stood in front of the door and counted to three and turned the lock and pulled the knob and stepped out into the room.

Jerry was sitting on the edge of his bed drinking beer from a can, and Gordo was on my bed, jangling his legs back and forth on the pulled-back bedspread, and he was sweating and rubbing at his nose, and Jerry was tapping his fingers against the mattress in a slow wave, moving index to pinkie and then back again, and the baseball game was still on and Jerry ran a hand through his dark hair, and there was a blue shadow on his cheeks from the stubble he hadn't cut back, and from the way they were both tight-lipped and staring at the small TV screen, I could tell that whoever was supposed to be winning wasn't.

"Okay," I said.

Jerry looked up from the TV and I could feel his eyes make the scan from my head to my feet, and he told me to turn around, and I did, in a small tight circle, and Gordo gave a short whistle, and said, "Not bad, not bad at all."

There was an envelope on the nightstand, and Jerry leaned back and picked it up and handed it to me.

"Now put this in the underwear pocket," he said.

I looked at both of them as they stared back at me, and I didn't like being in the center of the room, so I turned to go back into the bathroom where I could stuff it in private, but Jerry said, "no, do it right here," so I unbuttoned the top of my jeans where I could see the white triangle of underwear underneath, and I pulled out the elastic waistband so that it went tight against my hips, and I took the envelope and fumbled it into the pocket, and it was hard to do with one hand, and I had to dig around and realign and then it was in, and it felt awkward to have a flat shape in the curved part of my body, and I pulled up the top of my jeans and fastened them again, and Jerry told me to stand back again so he could get a better look, so I did, and then he told me to walk with it, so I crossed the few feet of dirty carpeting to the room door, turned and walked back, and Jerry caught me by the arm as I walked in front of him and he reached forward and pushed at the front of my jeans, and I tried to pull away from him so that he couldn't reach me, but he just gripped my arm tighter, and then he patted me, just above my crotch, and said, "how does it feel?"

"Weird," I said. "It's uncomfortable."

"You'll get used to it."

"I don't like you touching me," I said.

"It's business, kid. It's not personal."

Jerry dropped my arm and I went and sat in the chair and waited for the next thing to do, and Jerry lit a cigarette and Gordo shifted on the bed so he could pull another beer from the box on the floor, and then Jerry took an ink pen from the drawer by the bed and told me to hold out my hand, and I wanted to say why, but there was a look in his eyes that told me it wasn't a good time to put up resistance, so I did as I was told and Jerry leaned forward and took my hand, flipped it palm up, and then he wrote three numbers on my skin—712—and then he dropped my hand and put the pen back in the drawer, and he got up and turned the sound down on the TV and Gordo opened his mouth to say something, but Jerry turned on him, as if to say, *shut your mouth*, and Gordo dropped his eyes and started pulling at the creases in his pants.

"So listen up, kid. This is how it works, and you'd better listen real close to what I'm about to tell you because if you forget an important detail, you're gonna wish you'd never met me in Redding." He took a drag on the cigarette and blew a jet across the room. "You go in the casino, through the doors on the side of the building, down the block, not the ones facing the Strip, you get it?"

I nodded, and he waited for me to voice it, so I said, "Yeah, I get it."

"You walk past the machines, and you don't stop and you don't touch anything, and you don't talk to anybody. If somebody talks to you, you say you've gotta get back to the room and meet your mom."

"Who's gonna talk to me?"

Jerry looked exasperated. "Like anyone, but especially anyone in a suit—you'll see them. Dark suits, older guys. They're the floormen and their job is to keep anyone underage out of the casino, but you can go through it to get to the rooms, so that's all you're doing—getting to your room. That's why you don't stop and you don't watch, and you sure as fuck never put anything in a machine and pull a handle, no matter how curious you get." He ran his hand through his hair, and turned to Gordo. "I swear I get fucking sick of giving this speech," he said.

"You should just write a training manual," Gordo said. "Like they do for McDonald's."

Jerry laughed and then looked over at me. "This is serious shit, so I really hope you're smart enough to listen."

I nodded. "I'm listening," I said. "Jesus."

"You're gonna pray for fucking Jesus if one of those floormen decide to take you to one of the back rooms and have a little talk with you. Now, you follow the signs to the hotel desk—got it? You can't miss the signs. But you don't go to the desk—you go to the elevators. At the Eldorado they're to the left of the desk. You don't look at the people at the desk. You just walk like you know what you're doing and where you're going and you've done it a million times, and if one of them tries to stop you, what do you say?"

I paused for a second. "That I have an envelope in my underwear?"

Gordo laughed and slapped at his thigh and finished his beer and crushed the can a little bit in his meaty hand. He was sweating and I hoped he wasn't getting it on my pillow, and I didn't know how I was ever going to sleep on that bed again if it smelled like him.

"Don't be a smartass," Jerry said. "You say you're going to your room. You've gotta meet your mom."

"Yeah, I have to meet my mom," I said.

"If they ask you what room you're going to, you just smile and keep walking. They won't stop you. They're too busy and they don't really care, but they have to look like they do, so if you don't give them a reason to care, they won't. You understand that?"

I nodded again, and he waited and I said, "Yes, I understand."

"Good. Good. So you take an elevator, and you see that number I wrote in your hand?"

I looked down at my palm and held it up. "Yeah. 712."

"Okay. That's not the real room. You go up to the seventh floor, but each number I wrote down is one higher than the real room, you're going to, get it?"

I looked down at the numbers again. "So 601?"

"Exactly," Jerry said. "But you never get off on the floor of the room. You go one higher, and then you come out of the elevator, and you take the stairs down one floor. You get it?"

"Where are the stairs?"

"You look for the fucking sign. They're always at the end of the hall. You just push through the door and walk down the stairs, and you come out on the floor you're supposed to be on. So you take the elevator to seven, but you walk down to six."

"Okay," I said. It seemed like an awful lot of secret bullshit to go through but I wasn't going to say that to Jerry.

"Then you go to the room and you knock. Three times."

"Three times," I repeated back.

"When the door opens, you say you're with Jerry. That's it. You just say, 'I'm with Jerry,' and whoever answers will know what you're talking about, and they're gonna let you into the room. You stay close to the door. You get that? You don't go into the room—you stay by the door." Jerry took a drink from his can and then he dropped the rest of his cigarette into it so that I could hear it hiss for a second before it went out. "Then they're gonna hand you some money—and I want you to count it. You always count it. Take your time. Don't rush it. It has to be $300. You understand that? It's always $300."

"What if it's not?" I had never held $300 in my hand before and I couldn't imagine counting it up that high while somebody watched me.

Jerry lit another cigarette. "If it's not, then you pull that door open and you walk. Get it? Repeat it to me."

"I walk."

"Exactly."

"And if it is $300?"

"Then you reach into those fancy underwear and you pull out the envelope and you hand it over."

"What if it's not and they come after me or something? Or they won't let me leave."

"They will. That's why you stay by the door. Nobody wants a scene."

"Then what do I do after I give them the envelope?"

"Jesus, kid. If you'd let me fucking finish, everything would be clear. You shove the money where the envelope was."

"In front of them?"

"No, you ask to use the fucking bathroom and you take your time, and maybe you order some room service and watch a fucking movie. Yes, in front of them if that's what it takes. But you do it before you go back out that door. When you step out into that hallway, you don't have anything in your hands, you don't have anything in your pockets. You keep it tucked where it goes."

I was still stuck on having to do this whole exchange with some stranger watching me digging around in a pair of underwear that didn't belong to me.

"Then you go back the way you came—back to the stairs, and you go back up to the floor where you came out of the elevator, and you go back down to the lobby, and you walk back out the way you came in. And you make yourself fucking invisible. You got all that?"

"So I have to carry all this in my underwear?"

Jerry looked like he might hit me, but he smiled instead. "Yeah. That's the way it works. And when you get back out onto the sidewalk, you beat feet back over here, but you don't run. You don't look like you're in a hurry. You be casual, but you don't fucking windowshop, get it? You don't stop for a milkshake. You don't take your time. You get that money back to the room."

I could feel myself starting to sweat a little bit. I had the envelope and I knew that after Jerry finished with all these "Do's" and "Don'ts" I was going to have to leave the room and do it for real, and it was so much easier just listening to the story of how it needed to be done rather than actually being the one doing it.

"Now," Jerry said, and he sat back on the bed with his cigarette. "You tell me what you're supposed to do. And start at the beginning. And don't leave anything out."

I told the story back to him, from the door to the casino to the front desk to the elevator to the stairs to the knock to the counting to the return. When I was finished, he seemed satisfied and he looked over at Gordo who nodded his head, and they both turned their attention to the TV in time for somebody getting a double and driving in a run, and Gordo clapped his hands and said, "The luck is turning, Jerry—the luck is turning."

I heard a high-pitched beeping sound and I looked around at what it might be—it was like the alarm on a watch but louder, and I remembered that Bobby had a watch with an alarm like that and he used to set it for when he had to start getting home so he wouldn't miss curfew when we were out.

"What was that?" I asked. Jerry wasn't wearing a watch and it didn't sound like it came from Gordo and his hands looked too fat to wear a watch anyways.

"Gonna be a busy day," Jerry said, rubbing his hands, and he lifted up his loose shirttail so that he could pull something off the waist of his pants, and it was a little black box with a clip in the back, and he looked at it and sat it down on the nightstand and took the pen out of the drawer again, and a small pad of paper that said *The Slipper* with stars around the name and a legless high heel floating over it, and Jerry wrote down some numbers and then he tore the paper off the pad and handed it to me.

"What's this?" It looked like a phone number.

"Jesus, kid. Can you just shut up for a minute?"

Gordo snorted from the bed. I wanted to tell him he sounded like a pig, but I bit down on my tongue and ignored him.

"This," Jerry said, holding up the little black box with the clip that he'd set down on the nightstand, "is a pager. You ever see one?"

I shook my head. I'd heard of them, but I'd never actually known anybody who could afford to use one. Jerry tipped it toward me and I could see there was a little screen at the top, and Jerry pushed a button on the side and the little screen lit up with green numbers. "People call this and then you go call them back."

"*I* call them back?"

"Yeah, you. You remember that payphone down there—the one by the office?"

It was on the sidewalk down the block, I had passed it a few times on my way to get burgers and tacos and shakes and fries. "Yeah," I said.

"Well *you* are going to go down there and call the number I give you and you're gonna get the information I need."

I looked at the phone on the table. "We have a phone right here. Why don't you use this one?"

Jerry smiled. "Because we aren't really here, remember? We're invisible. We never use this phone."

"Gordo's been using the phone all day," I said. I shot Gordo a look and he narrowed his eyes at me.

"Gordo is doing business. This phone in the room is for business."

"Then what's the payphone for? I don't get it," I said.

"That is for pleasure. Other people's pleasure. We never mix up the two."

I didn't understand what he meant, but he held up his hand to stop me from asking, and then the pager went off again in three shrill beeps, and he pressed the button and looked at the top of it and he motioned with his hand to get the piece of paper he'd handed over to me, and I gave it back and he took the pen out and wrote down another number beneath the first one.

"Now," Jerry said, "you'd better go deliver what you have so you can come back and make some calls. Gonna be a long day for you."

I felt myself shrink down a little bit, and I realized how much I hated anything that had to do with work, and this was going to be work, and I was scared and nervous, and my stomach felt slick, and I wished that maybe I had just taken the Greyhound to Portland and right now I was in the mist and the fog and the rain and I was figuring something else out, and then I thought that maybe I shouldn't have left at all, but it was just a tiny voice in my head and it was easy to shut it out because if I closed my eyes a little bit, I could see Chris at the dinner table, watching me eat, and waiting for me to make a mistake that I didn't know that I was making so that he could come into my room at night and correct me.

"Hey, and kid, I forgot to tell you one thing," Jerry had stepped forward and turned up the volume on the TV, and the Padres were up at the bottom of the eighth, and Gordo was cracking another beer, and I could hear something grinding and I realized it was his teeth. "If you get caught," Jerry said, "I won't know you anymore? You understand what I'm saying?"

I shook my head.

"What he's saying," Gordo said from the bed, and he leveled his black eyes at me, "is that you'll be dead to him. And then you'll be dead. Do you get that?"

"Oh, and kid, one more last thing," Jerry said. "Don't ever open the envelope. Don't open it for nobody at no time. I mean that."

"What's in the envelope?" I asked.

Jerry looked me in my eyes. "Sandwiches," he said. "With everything."

Gordo shifted his weight on the bed and I heard the springs groan and then he pushed himself to the edge, and stood up and stretched his arms above his head so that I could see that he'd sweated through the yellowed armpits of his T-shirt and the rest of it looked damp and stuck to his skin, and he walked toward the bathroom. "I gotta take a piss. Good luck, Joey." He smiled at me. "I hope you make it back," and then he shut the bathroom door behind him and I could hear a hard stream hitting flat water.

Chapter 10
Eldorado

I was sweating when I walked out of the motel room and that made the envelope all the more obvious as it rubbed against the elastic waistband of the underwear, and I blinked for a minute until my eyes adjusted to the bright light of the sun glaring off both the pink and blue building and asphalt below me, and then I walked slowly down the corridor to the stairs and I stepped out into the open again, and I knew that anyone who looked at me would know just what I was carrying in the crotch of my jeans. I looked at the number Jerry had written into my palm, and I kept reminding myself not to rub my hand on my jeans or else the numbers might blur, so I walked awkwardly, with my arm stiff at my side so the ink would dry while my hand dripped sweat from my wrist to my fingertips.

The parking lot was quiet and I willed myself not to look at the pool or for Hurley's red truck parked in front of a room, and instead I focused my eyes on the driveway and the exit, and I walked out to the street without looking into the office to see if Dee was behind the counter because looking at her was a way for me to think about Amber, and I was thinking about her but I told myself not to, and I crossed the narrow street and then I was on the opposite side, where a chain link fence separated the buildings from the cement, and there was trash in the fence, and I saw a tennis shoe lying by itself in the gutter, and I wondered where the other shoe had gone and how someone could only lose one shoe, and when I got to the corner, I turned right and walked toward Virginia Street, and then I made another right and kept walking, and I was pulled into the crowds of people who were moving from one casino to another with their drinks and their Big Gulp-looking cups of coins and everyone flushed and talking and laughing, and I wondered how they could all seem so normal when all I could think about was how I was walking—trying to only move my legs from the knees down—and a woman bumped into me and sloshed some red drink onto me and said, "Sorry, man," and I didn't even slow down or smile or nod my head, just wiped the drink off my shirt with my hand and kept walking past the doors that were open with the bells ringing into the street, and the lights were everywhere so that the Strip looked lit up even though it was still afternoon and the sun was high above us, and there were signs for slots and craps and blackjack and prime rib and buffets and girls and shows and everything was "LIVE!" and "IN PERSON!" and "BACK BY POPULAR DEMAND," and machines were loose, and tables were two-deck shoots, and by the time I got to the Eldorado I thought that my head would explode.

The Eldorado held down the corner of North Virginia and West 3rd Street, and Jerry had told me to walk around the block until I got to the North Sierra Street entrance since it would put me closer to the hotel desk and the bank of elevators I needed to get up to the seventh floor. I had to keep reminding myself that I went to the seventh floor and then down one and everything was one up and the number on my hand wasn't real, and I looked at my palm to remind myself of the room I was supposed to go to, and when I held up my hand, the numbers were gone.

I had wiped the drink off my shirt and then rubbed my hand dry on my jeans, and it had been such an automatic reaction that I had forgotten about keeping my palm dry to save the ink and I had rubbed it clean, and I stood there outside the Eldorado, with the entrance in the shade of the buildings around it, tucked into the side street, and I stared at my hand and tried to will the numbers to rise again, and I walked back down the sidewalk to the sun so that I could get a better look in the light, but there was nothing to see, just a faint smear of blue that had blurred into nothing more than a mark that looked like an old bruise, and for a second I felt my heart reach up and grab ahold of my throat and I tried to think of all the choices I had—to go back to the room and tell Jerry that I had lost the number, and I could already see him run a hand through his hair and set his jaw in that way that told me I'd crossed into the dark territory again, and I would have to explain that I was an idiot, and he'd probably kick me out then, and maybe beat me up a little bit, and I'd be pushed out to the street with nothing but the money I had in my sock in my backpack, and I'd be on my own in Reno with no idea of how to catch a bus, or where to sleep, or what my next plan would be, and I realized that I had never made another plan because I thought this would be easy, doing deliveries and making money, and I had only been on the job for twenty minutes and I'd already fucked everything up because I was too stupid to keep a number on my hand, and then I saw fat Gordo sitting on my bed with his beer can and his cigarette burning my bedspread and his sweat rubbing off onto my pillows, and how he would light up at the opportunity to join in with Jerry to tell me what a waste of time I'd been, and I could already see him laughing at me and see the spit collecting in the corners of his mouth and his thick tongue flicking out to lick at it while he told me some sex joke about stupid women—and then I thought that maybe I could just take off right then and disappear and not go back to the room, and that seemed like the worst idea of all because then all I'd have was what was in the envelope, and I already knew what was inside, and I didn't think I was ready to use it to barter for a way out of town. I took a deep breath and counted to ten and let it out and remembered the cartoon from when I was a kid stuck in front of PBS at somebody's house while my mom went out drinking with some guy, and there was the girl going to the store for her mother, and all she had to get was a loaf of bread, a container of milk, and a stick of butter, and she has it all memorized like a little song she skips to as she makes the trip and then she goes up to the counter and the man asks her what she wants, and she goes blank—just like that—but those of us in front of the TV could still remember the song, and I remembered chanting it to her while she stood there stuttering—*a loaf of bread, a container of milk, and a stick of butter*—and even *I* was frustrated with her because it had all seemed so easy, and I looked down at my hand at the number that wasn't there, and I said "it's 7-1-2. The rest is up to you," and I laughed at myself for falling apart, and I pulled myself back together and walked back to the Eldorado side entrance and pushed my way inside.

If outside was afternoon, inside was night, and the light from the door only stretched in like a short finger before everything became one color of flashing lights, and the room hung with cigarette smoke, and the carpet was a bright red blanket flung through with gold diamonds, and there were machines all around me with people sitting on stools, pulling handles and jamming buttons and pumping loose change, their eyes as dull as nickels, and sometimes a bell would go off, and there would be the sound of coins hitting the metal plate, piling up, and somebody would cheer a little bit, and inside it smelled like an empty ice cube tray that had been left in the freezer—flat and cold and stale—and I could see women in heels with trays of drinks and everything looked like it was underwater, like I was standing at the edge of an ocean of metal and flash with the sound and bodies treading through the light, and even though I narrowed my eyes and tried to focus, I couldn't see a sign anywhere that pointed in the direction of the hotel desk.

I started weaving my way through the machines, and then I realized that the carpet made a pathway in its design, and I followed it and wished I had breadcrumbs I could drop so that I could find my way back, and then I realized that I was walking in a wide circle, and I slowed down and started reading everything with words, and there were so many directions—to the buffet, the restrooms, the players' club, the cashier, the Showroom Bar—and I stood staring at a sign with arrows moving in opposite directions to direct me through the maze toward places I didn't want to go: "YOU ARE HERE," and I kept repeating my new song in my head, "7-1-2. The rest is up to you," and I turned around and made a left on the next pathway through the machines, and I was about to go back and try a different direction when I looked up and saw a sign labeled "Check-In" and a long desk with signs for the hotel, and Jerry had said the bank of elevators was to the left, so I kept walking in that direction, and a woman behind the desk smiled at me and I thought she was going to say something, so I just smiled at her and didn't slow up and then I hit the button for the elevators—Going Up!—and I stood and waited before a pair of doors slid open behind me and the car was empty and I hit the button for 7 and I prayed that no one would step into the elevator with me, and nobody did, and then the doors closed and the sea of machines disappeared and I was tucked into the tiny room of advertisements for nightlife and discounts and 24 hours a day of service and Friday night seafood and Sunday morning mimosas, and then I was on the seventh floor and I could feel my knees start shaking.

The hallway ran in two directions when the door slid open, and I stepped out and tried to figure where the stairs might be, but everything looked the same—the dark, red-and-gold patterned carpet of diamonds and spades and walls stark white with gold diamonds edged in red painted at chest height—and the only thing that broke up the sameness were the doors set at intervals with their gold numbers on narrow plaques affixed to their centers, and I tried to see to either end, but the hallway went so far in both directions that it seemed like it stretched into the adjacent states on either side, so I turned right and started walking, and I could feel my feet sinking into the deep pad of the carpeting and I could hear the sound of televisions behind the doors of the rooms, and there was a room service cart parked against a wall, and now and then I could hear laughter leaking out from somewhere, and then I saw a green sign with a red symbol of stairs lit up against the ceiling, and I pushed on the door and then I was in the stairwell, and the air was cool and there was no sound except the echo of footsteps coming from above, and I went down the two short flights to the sixth floor, and then I recited the number to myself—712 was 601—and I counted the doors and looked for the room, and then I was in front of it, and like the little girl in the cartoon who stood at the counter to give her mom's order to the clerk, I forgot what I was supposed to do again.

"You knock. You knock on the door," I whispered to myself, and my voice felt strange in my throat, like I hadn't spoken aloud in a very long time and had gone rusty from disuse. "Three times. Knock three times." So I put my hand to the wood and tapped one, two, three, and then I waited, and I felt like I used to when we had to sell stuff from school for fundraisers—money for choir, money for teams, money for field trips—Christmas ornaments, tins of popcorn, magazine subscriptions, and all I ever wanted was the prizes for selling the most—the tiered bait they threw at us to reel us in and cut us loose to knock on doors and fumble our way through the spiel to somebody who wanted just about anything but a ten-year-old on their doorstep trying to hustle them for some money, and I would feel the air go out of my lungs, standing there with my catalog of crap and explaining to some adult about why we needed the support and could they and would they, and every year I would want one of the good prizes—the turntable stereo, the Casio watch with the built-in calculator, the mini Donkey Kong arcade console—and every year I would last about three houses before I gave up because I couldn't stand waiting for the door to be opened by somebody who didn't want me there any more than I wanted to be there and asking them for money while they flipped through the catalog I pushed at them, looking bored and being polite, and saying no over and over again to the crap that nobody was willing to buy.

I was hoping that no one would be inside and then I'd just go back to the motel room and tell Jerry that it wasn't my fault—I did exactly what he'd told me to do *but nobody answered and I guess they weren't there, so it just didn't work out and I'm sorry but it's not my fault and I guess this just isn't happening today*, but then someone said "yeah," and it was a man's voice, and I said, "Jerry sent me over," and then I heard the knob on the door turn and he opened it up with the chain still attached to the lock so he could look out in the hall, and then I saw him look in both directions, like they did in the movies when they were convinced that somebody had been followed, but there was nobody around, and then he shut the door so he could unfasten the chain, and then he pulled it wide and motioned for me to come in.

He was a younger guy, with long hair pulled back in a ponytail, and he had a thin moustache and green eyes with long lashes, and he was wearing a pair of jogging shorts and a T-shirt, and his feet were bare, and farther into the room I could hear the television airing a sitcom, and there were towels on the floor, and the bed was pulled apart so that the sheets and thin brown velveteen blanket hung off the mattress, and we both stood there, in the entryway, shifting on our feet, and then he finally said, "Well?" and I figured that was my cue to get to the part that I was worried about the most: counting the money.

I cleared my throat and held out my hand. He looked down at it, and at first he didn't understand what my gesture meant, but then he realized what I was asking for and he walked back into the room and pulled a stack of cash off the dresser, and he came back and handed it to me. "Three hundred, right?" he said.

"Exactly," I said, and I was proud of myself for sounding normal and strong and like I wasn't about to piss myself out of fear. It felt strange to stand in someone's room and to see their things and smell their smells, and I could smell cologne and fresh shower and dirty socks and the remnants of food drying on a plate that was sitting on top of the TV, and with the door closed behind me, I realized he could do anything to me right now and nobody would know I was trapped inside of here, and then I realized that if I never came back to the motel, Jerry wouldn't bother to come looking for me here.

I started smoothing out the bills and counted them, and there were twenties and fives and tens, and they were all bundled together, and I kept losing track, and then I dropped three tens on the floor and had to reach over and pick them up, and then I got through the rest of the stack and the total came out to $280 and I looked at the guy and he blinked at me slowly, with those long eyelashes dusting the tops of his cheeks.

"There's only $280 here," I said. I had to clear my throat again in order to be heard.

"No, there's $300," the guy said.

My hands were shaking, and I went through the money again, slower this time, and with every minute that ticked by, I became more convinced that something bad was about to happen, and it felt like those scenes in scary movies where somebody is trying to get their key into the ignition and the killer is right there at the window and the key is skipping all around the slot, and the person is screaming and the killer is tapping on the glass with the knife or the axe or the chainsaw spinning fresh gristle and the key just won't go in, and I stood there shaking and sweating, but I counted it all again, and I realized that two twenties had been stuck together, and there was $300 and he was right and probably knew that this was my first time.

"Sorry," I said.

"No problem."

"So, ummm. Okay," I said. Now he held out his hand and looked at me, and I almost handed the money back to him but then I remembered the whole reason that I had come to his door, and I turned my back to him a little bit and I reached underneath my shirts and under the waistband of my jeans, and I pulled the elastic in the underwear and the envelope was still tucked dry in its pocket, and I caught it by the corner and pulled it free, and the guy took it from me and opened the flap and he looked inside and said, "All good," and then we both looked at each other and he reached toward me and I flinched and almost brought my hands up to block my head because I was pretty sure that this was where he started beating me unconscious before he raped me, but he just slipped his hand past me and opened the door, and I stepped backwards a couple of times and then I was out of the room and he pushed the door shut with a soft click, and I was standing in the hallway with the money in my hand, and I knew that Jerry would be pissed if he saw me like this, so I lifted my shirts again, and slid the money under my waistband, and I kept pushing until all of it was sealed in the pocket, and I heard a door down the hall open and I shoved my shirt down and smoothed my jeans, and then I walked back toward the stairs and climbed the flights to the seventh floor and found the elevators again, and then I rode back to the lobby and walked past the front desk and this time I was smiling at the lady before she could even look at me, and when I stepped back into the maze of machines and tables and signs and lights, I didn't hesitate and cut down pathways and ignored the signs, and I went from the land of no time back into the heat of the afternoon, and behind me I could hear someone hit a jackpot so that the tray began to fill with coins and the bell started ringing, and I didn't even jump when I heard the sound, and then I was on the sidewalk and I had $300 in my underwear and nobody had looked at me, and I had done my first delivery—just the way that Jerry had told me to—and I could hear cars picking up speed as they headed toward the freeway where big trucks droned under the overpass, and there was music spilling out of open windows, and I let myself take long strides as I walked back to the motel room, stepping through the crowds and making way for the people who staggered and held onto each other and the ones who were dazed and adjusting to the sun again and the ones who had walked through doors with wallets spilling money and were walking out now with nothing but air left in the folds, and it took me a few blocks to realize that I was smiling and probably had been for a long time because my cheeks felt stretched and my lips were starting to hurt, but I had gone into the casino with my stomach in my throat and I had come out with the money, and no matter what happened the next time I made a run, I wasn't a virgin anymore.

Chapter 11
Pretty Things

When I got back to the room I expected a celebration—a party, some cake, a lot of back slapping and congratulations—but Jerry was sitting on the edge of the bed with his eyes stuck to the baseball game on TV and fat Gordo was on the phone, yelling at someone on the other end, and when I stepped in from the walkway, Jerry looked up, and said, "So, you got it?" And I shut the door behind me and pulled the money—wrinkled and wadded—out of my underwear without caring about turning my back, and Jerry took the cash from me as I handed it over in fistfuls, and he licked a finger and started counting the bills—fast and just peeling back the corners—and when he hit the magic number, he smiled and said, "Good job, kid," and then he took a twenty off and handed it to me and shoved the rest in his front pocket and went back to watching the game, and he and fat Gordo were both jaw-tight and chewing on their tongues, and I sat in a chair and picked at the rubber on my shoes.

"That's it?" I said. "Twenty bucks?"

Jerry looked over at me without blinking. "That's payment."

I cleared my throat but I didn't shift my eyes away from him. "No way," I said.

"No way? No way fucking what?"

"It's not enough money."

"You're kidding me, right? You go take a walk, knock on a door, in and out, and you come back. I'm over-paying you."

"Forget it," I said. "You get three-hundred bucks and I get twenty."

"Take it or leave it."

"Then I'm leaving it. Get somebody else."

Jerry licked his lips, slowly, and even from a distance I could tell that his tongue was dry and I thought that maybe I had pushed him too far but I wasn't backing down, and I wasn't afraid to stand up and run out the door if he came after me, and I wasn't worried about Gordo at all because he was too fat to get off the bed without a lot of effort, and as I was sitting there and wondering if I should get up and grab my stuff and run, Jerry reached into his pocket and pulled out another twenty and tossed it my direction and then he went back to watching the game without looking at me. I shoved the money into my jeans and thought about running out anyway, but I didn't even know where I would go, so I just sat very still and watched the game on the TV without seeing it, and when the inning was over, Jerry reached behind him and took a piece of notebook paper off the nightstand and there were four numbers on it and he told me to go to the payphone down from the motel and call them back, and he handed me a pen, and all I was to say was, "did you page Jerry?" If the answer was yes, then I was to ask, "Which hotel and which room number?" And then I was supposed to say "Three-hundred," and I was to wait for them to say "okay," and I was supposed to write it all down, and if they answered and hadn't paged Jerry, I was to hang up immediately, and Jerry handed me a bunch of dimes and told me to hurry up and not make people wait, and I turned myself into Joey, the person who wasn't really me, and Joey could make phone calls and Joey could carry the envelope and come back with the money, and Joey was invincible and smart and strong.

It was Saturday and the casinos were packed with people and I was able to get swallowed into crowds while I weaved my way down carpets that were brighter than the sky outside, and it was easy to find the casinos now, all crowded together and just a matter of buildings and doors and machines and bells and so many lights that I couldn't hold all of them with my eyes, and I found the hotel desks—always tucked in the back, in some corner—and the elevators and went up and then I went down and I knocked on the right doors and made the exchanges in the entryways of rooms that didn't belong to me, and it was like nothing had happened in the hours I was gone and walking and sweating and trying to look like I belonged, and I was disappointed that after all that I was doing and worrying about, the whole thing was pretty boring, and then I was being sent out to make phone calls like a secretary, and I could see my mom sitting at her desk at Tri-County Tractor, punching lighted buttons on a phone, putting people on hold, transferring them to the shop or the sales floor, and her boss leaning over with his grass-green tie held in place with a little gold deer, so that he could look down her cowl-knit sweater, and I could hear her in the same voice that she used when my sister and I used to call her at work to tell on the other one when we were fighting, and how she would answer the phone, all business, and I used to wonder why she always said she was "so tired" from her job and now I knew why. Every time I got back to the room there was another slip of paper with phone numbers and a pile of dimes.

"You want me to go right now?" I asked. "Like go make these calls right now?"

Jerry looked up at me and I could hear Gordo yelling at somebody about yeah, yeah, he knew, he knew, and just run the line, and Jerry said, "Now. What the fuck you think we're doing here?" So I pocketed the dimes and shoved the piece of paper into my back pocket, and as quickly as I had gotten into the room, over and over again, I was walking back out, and there was less swing in my step, and I realized that for all I had brought back to Jerry, I'd only gotten a little bit, and it didn't seem fair but I figured that it wasn't a good time to go back inside and bring it up to him again.

I went to the payphone in the blast of heat, and everyone around the motel was moving slow as a blood clot, and I didn't see Hurley's big red truck, and I knew that meant Amber was out somewhere, and part of me wondered what they were doing, and I knew that it didn't really matter because whatever it was, it had to be better than what I was about to do, and I hated talking on the phone, and I hated making calls, and I was glad that there were only a few things that I had to say because I knew my voice would give out if I had to take it any further, and my shirts were hot and I wanted to put on a pair of shorts and a T-shirt and be like I used to, but I wasn't sure who that was at the moment, so I just stood at the payphone that smelled like piss, with the phone book, all gutted and torn up, swaying from a wire against my thighs.

I put my dime in and punched the first set of numbers, and the phone on the other end rang and rang, and then I heard someone pick up and I went through Jerry's script, and it sounded like an older guy, but who can tell age on the phone, and he at first he asked me "Who's this?" and then I just plunged forward with what Jerry wanted me to say so that I didn't start making up shit, and the guy was all "Yes, and yes," and he was in Fitzgerald's and I knew where that was already, and then I hung up and dialed the next number, and it went about the same, and then the next and the next, and everybody answered like they had been waiting by the phone, and the last guy I talked to had been all anxious, like "When will it be here? When can I expect it?" And I just hung up on him and it gave me the little bit of power that I needed to walk back to the room with everything written down on another wrinkled piece of paper.

There was one at Fitzgerald's, two at the Harold's Club, and one at the Eldorado, and I had their rooms and I knew that meant I was shoving envelopes back into the sweaty space below my belly button, and I wasn't too happy about any of it, and I was hungry now, with my nerves all worn off, and I wanted something besides a burger or a taco or a bag of chips out of a machine, but I didn't figure Jerry was going to offer to take me out to dinner, and I thought that maybe it wouldn't be so bad to hit one of those buffets, but I didn't know how they worked and I couldn't imagine doing it all by myself and sitting at some table alone with trays of food stacked around me, so I tried to pretend that I wasn't hungry, and I told myself that—"you're not even hungry"—and I was hoping that my mind would talk my stomach out of the truth.

When I got back to the room, Jerry had already packed envelopes again and Gordo was still on the phone, and the TV screen was coated in a fresh wash of beer that was still dripping off the console, and there was a can on its side, underneath, and I guessed that the right team hadn't won, and Jerry was pacing around the room and staring over at Gordo, and fat Gordo was waving his hand at Jerry in the universal sign to calm down, and I could tell that Jerry was getting more worked-up by the minute, and maybe it was a good thing that I was about to leave and get out of the room again.

"You got the info, kid?" Jerry asked. He had a cigarette pinched against his lips and I could tell that he was ready to chew on the filter, so I tried to smile and make everything seem as if it was easy and right and good, and I said, "absolutely," and I handed Jerry the paper and he looked down at what I had written, and then he squinted at the page and walked over to me.

"What the fuck does that say? I can't read that."

I looked down at the numbers I had written and they seemed clear to me. "Eldorado 349 and 714," I said.

He yanked the paper out of my hand and stared down at it again. "You have to learn to be clear for fuck's sake. This shit all looks like chicken scratch."

I shrugged since there wasn't much I could say in my defense, but I had always been proud of my handwriting, and I almost said it looked all

91

fucked up because I was starving to death and this was probably how people in concentration camps took down numbers, but I thought he might get pissed at that, and fat Gordo was nodding without talking into the receiver, and Jerry turned to him and said, "So?" And Gordo just shook his head and held up his hand again, and Jerry sat back down on the edge of the bed and watched the end of the baseball game where the announcers were talking about this pitcher and that hitter and a bunch of bullshit that sounded boring to me but seemed like some kind of gospel to Jerry.

Jerry handed me the envelopes and wrote the numbers on my palm, all one up from the real rooms, and next to each number he put an "HC" or an "F" or an "E" so I'd know if it meant Harold's Club or Fitzgerald's or the Eldorado, and I knew by this time that I'd better not rub the ink off onto my jeans because this was too much to remember and I wasn't just picking up a few things from the corner store for my mom anymore.

"You good?" Jerry asked me, and I nodded, and that seemed to satisfy him, and I waited for him to tell me more instructions, but he didn't have anything more to say, so I walked out of the room and went back the way that I had come in, and my feet were starting to hurt in my shoes, and I felt like I was doing a lot of walking for one day and it was definitely worth more than $40 a trip, but if I did all four, I figured that would be $160 and that was more money than I had ever had at one time, and if I added it to the money that was still rolled in my sock in the bottom of my backpack, and the money that was stuffed in my front pockets from everything I'd been doing all day, I would pretty much be rich, so I forgot about my feet and the little bit I was getting peeled off the stack, and I started back toward the Strip, and then I saw Hurley's pickup swing into the motel parking lot and he nosed it into a spot in front of one of the downstairs rooms, and I knew that I shouldn't have noticed them or stopped or waved or even lifted my head from memorizing the way that the asphalt went soft in the sun, but I did, and then I heard Amber's voice yell, "Joey!" and I knew that everything I had done right was over and mostly everything that was going to come next would probably be wrong.

Amber stepped down from the passenger side, and there was another guy with them—someone I hadn't seen before—and Amber was dressed in her cutoffs and a spaghetti strap shirt that was yellow with an orange flower in the center of the front, and her hair was pulled back in a ponytail and she was wearing a pair of Converse low tops with no socks, and when I let my eyes slide the length of her, I saw that she had on a gold anklet that winked in the sun, and even though I could have kept walking and done that thing that people do where they smile and wave and acknowledge and say, "Good to see you, I'm on my way out," and I could have been at Fitzgerald's in ten minutes, walking fast and chewing up sidewalk with my rubber soles, I had never been very good with the whole idea of "keep walking" and as soon as she waved to me, I stopped and turned and walked over to where she was standing next to the truck.

"What are you doing?" she asked.

I wasn't sure how to answer the question, so I just shrugged and said, "Just some stuff for Jerry," and I hoped that would be enough, but then I realized that I had opened a door and now she wanted to step in and look behind it.

She lowered her voice. "You ummmm, carrying stuff?"

I looked up at her and her eyes were liquid and big and there was a pink stain of sunburn on her nose and I could smell her next to me—lavender and all kinds of things I should have known but didn't—and I knew it was as if I had a shovel in my hands and I was standing on soft dirt and being offered the opportunity to walk away, but I looked up at her and said, "yeah," and I could hear the invisible shovel break into the ground so that I could dig myself in deeper.

"Yeah?" she said. "So like right now? You've got some?"

I wasn't sure about what she meant by "some," but if she meant I had envelopes, then yes, I did, and if she meant that I had room numbers and hotels and phone numbers and leftover dimes in my pockets, then yes, I had that, too, so I nodded my head and said, "Yeah."

"Oh my god, that's crazy," she said, and she grabbed me by the shoulders and turned me toward the truck, and across the hood I could see Hurley and the other guy I didn't know, and Amber said, "Joey is holding," and I sort of knew what she meant by that but it was a lie that I had gotten good at telling myself—that there weren't any drugs in the envelopes, and I had almost gotten good at convincing myself that they were sandwiches in a way—just bread and meat and cheese and not drugs, not speed, not "motorcycle meth," as Bobby used to call it when he saw bikers go by on the road, and Hurley and the other guy seemed to know exactly what Amber meant by *holding*, and Hurley smiled and the other guy dropped the cigarette he was smoking and they both looked at me with shiny eyes, and I knew that I was the only one who had been late in figuring out the truth about what I was hired to carry.

"Come inside with us," Amber said, and she walked toward the rooms and dug a key out of her pocket, and she was in 133 now, and I waited for her to open the door and the entire time that she fumbled with the key and waited for Hurley and the other guy to walk up behind us, all I could think was that I needed to go, I needed to go, I needed to go, but instead I just stood there as if I had nothing but time and it wasn't running down my ribcage like sweat.

I went in and it was cleaner than the one she'd been staying in before, but I could tell the room was just holding its breath and waiting for her to get serious about moving in, and Hurley came in and the other guy followed, and I didn't know whether I should sit down or stay close to the door, so I did both and pulled out a chair from the small table underneath the window, and Hurley turned on the TV and found music videos on a channel and then he pulled off his shirt and flopped down on a bed, and Amber pulled a six pack of beer from the bathroom sink and pulled one from the ring, and she tossed it over to me, and I knew that I shouldn't be doing what I was about to do, but I did it anyways, and I popped the top of the can and took a long drink, and then Amber walked over to me and said, "Let me see it," and I didn't know what she meant at first, but it didn't take me long to figure it out, and I looked up at her, standing over me with her hand out, and I said, "No, no way."

"Oh c'mon, Joey. It's not like it's a big secret," she said. "I mean, did Jerry tell you I've delivered for him? Did he tell you that?"

I was surprised by what Amber said, and at first I couldn't believe it, but then I figured why wouldn't I, so I shook my head and said, "No, he didn't say anything about that."

"Yeah, a few times. Like a year ago or something. Or maybe like six months. I don't know. But I had to go take some speed to some guy over at Harold's." She pulled the rubber band from her hair and shook her ponytail loose, and I could feel some of her hair brush against the top of my shoulders and fold into my neck, and I didn't realize she had been standing so close to me until she did.

"It was no big deal," she said. "Jerry gave me like a hundred bucks for it. How much are you getting? I mean, if that was a hundred bucks like a long time ago, he must be giving you a hell of a lot more now."

I felt my face get hot, and I didn't look up at her. I could feel sweat start to bead on my upper lip and I didn't want to lick at it, so I shifted in the chair and tried to look toward the TV.

"Yeah," I said. "It's a lot."

"But like how much?" Amber said. "My mom made me quit because she got all pissed off at Jerry, but I would have kept going. So how much are you making?"

"Jesus, Amber, you don't ask people how much they're making. It's like none of your business." The guy I didn't know was sitting on the edge of the bed and he was watching us, and he had stood up for me and I didn't even know his name, and I could see that he was wearing a big belt buckle, with lots of silver and gold and green, and I wondered if it was heavy on his jeans.

"That's Hurley's brother, Reece," Amber said. "He thinks he's a know-it-all but he's too young and doesn't know shit." She shot him a look and then he smiled, and I already knew that I liked him better than Hurley. He was thicker and blonde and where Hurley was dark, Reece was light, and he had an easy smile that seemed to get him a long ways, and I looked over at him and he dropped his eyes and skipped them across the carpet so that he could focus on the TV and the woman who was writhing around on the hood of a car while a guy with long hair stroked a guitar between his legs and swung it at her, and when Reece turned his head, I could see something on his neck, and I realized that his skin was all twisted and red and there was a shine to it, and I stared at it for a minute and tried to figure out what was wrong with him, and then Amber leaned down close to me and I could feel her breath in my ear—"show it to us," she said, and I shook my head again, but I knew that the only way I was getting out of this was to either get up and walk out or dig into my underwear and pull out an envelope, so I did the only thing I could think of and leaned back in the chair and flattened my stomach by holding in my breath, and then I slid my hand down, and moved my shirt out of the way and reached beneath my waistband and I pulled out part of Jerry's stash.

"Oh, fuck yes," Amber said, and she held up the envelope to the room and the sliver of light coming through the crack in the curtains, and she turned it over and over so that she could see the silhouette of what was inside, and then she set it down on the table and started to open the flap.

"Don't," I said, and I grabbed her hand and held it in mine.

"Hurley is up in his divisions today," she said. "We're celebrating."

Hurley groaned and pulled off his boots and knocked them to the end of the bed and then across the carpet, and then he pulled his T-shirt up and over his head, and I could see that his ribs were all bruised, and he rubbed at the marks with his hand and then winced a little bit.

"Where are you in your division, Reece?" Amber asked. "Like third, right?"

Reece looked over at us and nodded, and I could see the scar on his neck light up and I wanted to ask him about it.

"They're gonna bring back big stacks of cash money," Amber said. "Look at that belt buckle Reece got last month," and she pointed over at him and he lifted his shirt and rolled his hips up, and I had already been staring at it, and I said, "That's pretty cool," and he settled back down on the bed and balanced his beer can on his chest.

"I know you're looking at my scar," Reece said. "You like it?" He turned his face away from me so that the skin on his neck pulled tight, and I could see that it looked like a burn with a letter in the middle.

"I didn't notice," I said.

"Liar," Reece said. He took a drink and raised himself up so he could pull a can of chew out of his jeans pocket, and I could see that there was a bleached ring where the can had worn into the fabric, and he dug two fingers in and took a dip and packed it into his lower lip. "It's a brand," Reece said.

I didn't know what he meant at first. "A band?" I said.

Hurley laughed. "Yeah, he's a real big fan," and then Reece punched him on the arm, hard, and Hurley balled his hand into a fist and slammed it down on Reece's left thigh. "Faggot."

"It's a brand," Reece said. "Like the ones you put on cattle, you know?"

"Oh, a *brand*, yeah, I get it."

"Nah, I'm the one who got it. See, that's what happens at my house if you fuck off your chores and don't go fix the fence your dad told you about and the cows get out onto the road."

"It's for remembering," Hurley said. "Always know where you come from."

Reece pulled his neck tight again and turned his head toward the wall. He pointed to the center of it. "See that. That letter? That's the Lazy 'R.'" The name of our ranch. Never leave home without it." He drained the beer from his can and then spit into it.

"Did it hurt?" I asked. I had never seen anyone with a brand before or that had been given one as a form of punishment, and I wondered what my stepdad Dale would have done if he'd had access to that kind of hot iron. Once when I had woken up in the middle of the night and gone to the bathroom for a drink of water, he had come in and turned on the light, and he had a big cup with him—what he called his "ice water cup"—tall and plastic, and he filled it at the sink and told me to drink it, and I stood there, in my pajamas with my feet getting cold, and it took me a long time to finish it, and I started to walk toward my room but he grabbed me by the arm and pulled me back inside and shut the door and filled the cup again, and told me to drink it, and I couldn't, and he made me do it, pulled me by the hair and tilted my head back, and when I choked down that one, he poured the cup full again and I was crying by then, and he told me to drink it, and I threw up halfway through, water coming back up fast, and then he hit me, hard, and said maybe I'd remember to get a drink before I went to bed, and the whole time I just kept thinking that my mom would hear us—that she would get up and make it stop—but she never came in and never said anything to me about it afterward.

"It still hurts sometimes," Reece said, and then he got up and took another beer out of the bathroom sink and I could hear ice shift around, and then he settled back down onto the bed and locked his eyes on the TV.

"You know we could make a hell of a lot more money with a pinch from that bag," Hurley said, and he pointed at the envelope on the table. "Take a few dimes and sell them for double. I know about five people who'd fight each other to take it off my hands."

At first I thought he was talking about the dimes in my pocket, but then I knew what he meant, and I reached for the envelope again so that I could put it back with the others, but Amber stopped me, and I wanted to roll through the stop sign her hands tried to make against mine, but she squeezed me then, in a way that made the hair on my arms stand up and all the muscles go weak, and her hand was warm and small, and she picked up the envelope and opened the flap and she held the baggie up and looked at it. It was just crystallized powder and didn't look like it would be worth anything at all, but I knew that Jerry was getting three-hundred bucks a pop for something that looked like nothing more than a sandwich bag with some tablespoons of sugar inside.

"Methedrine," Hurley said. "Biker booze."

"You don't know shit," Amber said. "This is like the best stuff in town."

She unknotted the baggie and smelled it, and then she licked her finger and stuck it into the powder and licked it again, and made a face and shook her head, and Hurley laughed from the bed. I wanted to take the bag back from her but I didn't.

"You don't fucking taste it," Hurley said.

"I know, stupid. I just wanted to see what it was like."

"It's not coke."

"No shit," Amber said. "Let us just take a little to sell at the arena," she said to me. "It's Saturday. The place is crazy with riders." She smiled at me. "Besides. We'll give you a cut of the profit."

I shook my head no, but it was like my voice was caught in my chest and all I could do was swivel my head back and forth on my neck as if it was a ball on a stick.

"Just a few pinches," she said. "Nobody will know."

"I can't," I said. "I just can't. Jerry will know."

"Nobody will know. Just a little."

She settled herself onto my thigh and put her arms around my neck and leaned into me and I could feel her breath on my neck, and then she was whispering into my ear and I felt warm and as if my head was buzzing, and she smoothed my hair back from my forehead and she rolled her hips on my thigh so that I could feel my jeans grind against my skin and I knew that if I was wearing shorts I would feel more of her than I was ready for. "Just a little bit," she whispered.

She took the bag and slid a magazine across the table toward us, and I recognized the same cover as the one we had in our room, "Welcome to Reno!" and there was The Biggest Little City arch across the gloss and she flipped to the center of it where there were advertisements and ripped the page down the center so that she separated coupons from the restaurants they belonged to and strippers from their clubs, and she didn't lift herself from my thigh, and I could feel her moving around against me, and I couldn't move, and maybe it would just be a little bit, and then she opened the bag and dumped a small pile into the ripped page she pulled from the magazine and knotted the bag up and tapped it with her fingers so that what had clung to the sides settled back to the bottom, and she put it back into the envelope and handed it over to me.

"See?" She said, but it looked like a lot to me. "Just a little bit," and then she carefully folded the ripped magazine page around the pile and formed the paper into a pocket, like she was just making a note to pass to somebody in class when the teacher turned his back, and I wondered how many times she had made this tiny envelope before, and then she picked it up from the table, stood up so that everything that had been warm against me went cool again, and put the folded magazine page into the front pocket of her cutoffs and kissed me on the cheek. "Thank you," she said. "You'll see. It'll be just fine."

Amber walked toward the bathroom and turned on the light, and I watched her in the doorway, and she stood with her back to me and slipped each strap of her shirt down her shoulders and to the top of her arms and then she pulled her arms from the thin strings, and Hurley and Reece were staring at the TV, and I tried to find a way to join them with my eyes, but I kept watching Amber, and she pushed the shirt down so that it curled into a thick roll around her stomach, and she kept pushing it until it rolled over her waist and hips and thighs and knees and calves so that she could step out of it, and I saw the thin gold chain on her ankle, gripping her skin above her tanned feet, and then she picked up a T-shirt from the counter and pulled it over her head, but before she did, I could see that she was watching me in the side reflection of the mirror that was mounted over her left shoulder, and there was just enough angle to it that she could see me behind her in the chair, and she stood there with the shirt in her hands, and her skin was brown with sun and there were freckles on her shoulders, and I could see them, and I could see that her spine was a narrow ridge down the center of her back and her cutoffs hung on her hips and I could hear the music on the TV but I couldn't look at it, and she slipped her T-shirt over her head and walked back out into the warm room, and Hurley told her to turn on the air conditioner that was mounted under the window, and she took his beer out of his hand and took a long swallow, and she kept watching me, and she had told me that nobody would notice that she had taken some from the envelope and everything would be okay, but even if no one knew, it was me who still knew that she had, and I should have felt worse about it, and maybe I did, but part of me had gone numb and electric, as though I had grown a forcefield while sitting in that chair, and I knew I had to leave so I stood up and the chair rocked back and knocked over some beer cans on the table, and I said sorry, I have to get going, and Reece looked up from the TV but Hurley didn't, and Amber lifted her hand toward me in a short wave while she stretched herself out on the bed next to the brothers.

"Thank you, Joey," she said, and as I shut the door to her room behind me, I could still feel her breath in my ear.

Chapter 12
The Strap

I made my runs to the Eldorado, to Fitzgerald's, and I was finishing the last one at Harold's Club, and it was my favorite place because it was all cowboy themed and I loved the mural on the wall and I always took a long time to stare at it and get myself together before walking in, and then I was in and walking the maze of carpet, and I could smell the cigarettes and the sweat and the people and the oxygen struggling for room in the crowd, and I took the elevator up to the tenth floor and walked down and found Room 947 and I knocked and went through the shuffle at the door, and it was just a regular guy with a crew cut and a black tank top, and he was wearing glasses, and we did the exchange in the entryway with the door closed but not latched behind me, and it was the end of my run and I was happy to get the last scratchy envelope out from poking me in the stomach and he handed over the money and I shoved it in the pocket where the envelope had been, and my elastic was stretched and I knew that was a good thing, and then he shut the door behind me and I stepped out into the hall and started walking back toward the stairwell and I was glad that I was finished, that nobody had noticed one of the bags had been dumped into a magazine so that what was supposed to be wasn't there anymore, and I was thinking about how thirsty I was and that I needed a nap, and I was tired of baseball on TV and the smell of fat Gordo on my bed, and I was walking down the corridor, with my feet leading the way, when I heard somebody whistle, and I knew by then to ignore every sound—the bells and the rings and the spins and the coughs and the flip of cards and the craps table buffering dice, and I heard somebody whistle behind me again and I was three doors away from the stairwell, and I kept moving my feet, but then there was a loud voice that said "hey!" and I wanted to keep walking but that word was the hardest one to ignore, so I turned and looked over my shoulder and the guy from 947 was standing in the hallway and waving his arm at me,

100

"come back here for a minute," and I knew that in fifteen more feet I'd be free, but I turned anyways and stopped walking.

"Hey, kid, come back here for a second," he yelled, and I was so used to quiet and carpet and closed doors that I walked back to him as though I had been hypnotized by his voice, and when I got to the door, he smiled at me, and I thought maybe he just wanted to place another order—it wouldn't be the first time that somebody said "come back this time tomorrow"—but then I felt his fingers on my arm—up high where the muscle is still trying to make peace with the bone—and his grip was tight and he jerked me back into the room, and then I heard the door click behind me and I knew that everything that had gone right had just been a preparation for what was about to go wrong.

"You think you can screw us?" I noticed there were more people in the room than I had seen when I had been standing there in the habit of handing over and taking back, and they had materialized out of the shadows of the room, and the curtains were pulled shut and there was no sun peeking through the gaps, and I just stood there without saying anything as he shook my arm like it didn't belong to me.

"You hear what I'm fucking saying? Look," and he guided me into the bathroom where there was a scale on the counter, and I could see the envelope torn open and gutted on the white Formica and the bag that was inside was sitting on one beam and there was a number on the scale below it that I could not read.

"I don't know what you mean," I said, and I didn't.

"Look at this," and he took me by the back of the head and yanked my face toward the number and my eyes started to water.

"You're light, you little fuck," he said. "You didn't think we'd notice? You thought you could fuck us over?"

He hit me then, up against the side of my head, but it didn't really hurt, and I knew it was best to just agree to everything even if I didn't, because that hit had been the warning shot and I knew from experience what would come next.

"What's the number, Terry? How light is this fuck?" A guy I hadn't seen before, with dense curly hair and a T-shirt, leaned down toward the numbers and I could smell his breath in my face and it was bad, like he hadn't been acquainted with his toothbrush in a long time, and I turned my head, but then the guy that was holding my arm loosened up long enough to shove me over to the guy with the bad breath and the guy with glasses stepped away.

"About three grams," the guy with bad breath said. "Fucking you out of three grams."

The guy with glasses laughed. "You think I pay full price for a short? You trying to scam me you little fucker?"

"No," I said. "I'm sorry. It's just a mistake."

"Yeah? A fucking mistake?"

The guy with curly hair who was holding me twisted my arm behind me and it hurt and I cried out a little bit and then bit my lip. "It was a mistake," I said.

"I bet it was a mistake," the guy with glasses said, and he unbuckled his belt and pulled it free from his jeans, and then he doubled it over and held the two ends in his hand. "Hold him," he said, and the guy with the curly hair and bad breath gripped me and I tried to fold in on myself, but he yanked me to my feet, and then the belt hit me, hard, in the stomach, and then he hit me again in the chest, and then in the legs, and then again in the stomach, and the guy with bad breath just held onto me so that I couldn't fall even though my legs went like Jell-O and I stood there, held to my feet, and the guy with glasses hit me with the belt again, and I had been hit with a belt many times in my life, but I was grateful that this time I wasn't bent over a knee with my pants down.

I was crying and I didn't want to be, but I held my breath until I could steady my voice and I said, "I'll give you some money back," and it was all I could think of, and the guy with the glasses started laughing and he punched me hard then, in the stomach so that I did finally bend double no matter what was holding me, and I fell to the floor and I could see the carpet up-close, and I was amazed at how bright it was, and I knew that I was crawling even though I didn't mean to be, and the guy with bad breath caught me with the toe of his shoe and slung me into the bed so that I hit it at an angle, and I tried to grab the bedspread so that I could pull myself up, but then the guy with glasses reached back into what felt like yesterday and hit me in the face, and I went down then, flat on the carpet, and I could feel him roll me over and dig around in my jeans until he got his hand on the money, and I felt him pull it free from my waistband, and he said something to the guy with bad breath, and they were both laughing, and I tried to stand up but he hit me again—this time in the ear—and everything went quiet for a minute except for a ringing in my head, and I watched them pull some money off the stack and then they shoved the rest of it back into my pocket and the guy with bad breath kicked me one more time in the ribs, and this time I gagged and coughed up a white foam onto the carpet, and they both grabbed me around the arms and dragged me toward the door and then it was open, and I could see the hallway lights, and there was no one in either direction, and they dragged me past the room next door and dumped me to the floor and the guy with glasses kicked me one more time and I rolled over onto my side and it felt like my guts were going to come out through one of my fingers, but I didn't make any sound, and I could hear them walking away, and the guy with bad breath said, "Don't ever fuck us over again, asshole," and then they shut the door and I was on the carpet in the hall and I could taste my own blood and spit and acid from my stomach, but I was still alive and I laid there for a while, until I could count to one hundred, and when I hit one hundred, I counted again, and then I crawled toward the wall and I got my feet underneath me, and I thought I was going to fall down again, but I told myself not to and I kept upright, and I inched down the wall, and a couple came out of one of the rooms and they looked at me, and then they moved over to the opposite wall, as far as they could get, and kept walking, and there was blood coming out of my nose and my lip was split and I could feel my face getting tight from swelling, but I could have been worse, and I knew that, so I got my legs steady and kept walking, and the more that I moved, the easier it was to stay moving, and I held myself steady with the weight of the wall and my feet shuffled as if they already knew the rhythm of movement that I was hoping for, and I hit the door to the stairs and then I kept going and made it back to the tenth floor, and it took me a long time to lift my legs and step and do it again, but I did, and then I was able to push the button on the elevator, and I was able to leave the casino, and I kept my chin tucked to my chest and I wiped the blood with the tail of my shirt, and some people looked at me but most didn't, and I passed the mural of the cowboys on the wall, and they were branding a steer and their jaws were set, and there were horses in the background, and I was the steer and I was the cowboy and I was the horse, and I folded myself into the desert of the background and I limped my way back to The Slipper.

When I got inside Jerry was gone, and I knew he'd be back before I was ready, so I dumped the money onto my bed and I counted it and they had taken a hundred bucks from the wad, and I was happy that they hadn't taken more, and I pulled my backpack from under my bed and dug into the bottom and pulled out my money sock and counted out the hundred to replace what I had lost so Jerry wouldn't know the difference, and I put all of it together and opened the nightstand drawer between the beds and took out the bible and opened it up to wherever the pages folded, and I shoved the money in, but not before I read what it said, and I didn't know anything about the bible, but I liked the name Matthew, and even though my face was swollen, I couldn't help but read what was at the top of the page:

> When Judas, who had betrayed him, saw that Jesus was condemned, he was seized with remorse and returned the thirty pieces of silver to the chief of priests and the elders. "I have sinned," he said, "for I have betrayed innocent blood." "What is that to us?" they replied. "That's your responsibility." So Judas threw the money into the temple and left. Then he went away and hanged himself.

And I laughed because I knew enough to recognize money and sin, and I was glad I could replace what had been beaten out of me, but it hurt to breathe and I turned off all of the lights in the room so that the only thing I could see was the yellow streak of lamp from the hallway through the crack in the curtains, and my nose had stopped bleeding and it was closing up, and maybe that was a good thing so that I couldn't smell fat Gordo on my sheets, and I wanted to rinse my mouth out in the sink but it felt like a million miles to walk to the bathroom so I curled up on my mattress, wearing my clothes and my shoes, and I pulled myself into a tight ball so that my knees touched my chest and I could feel the bruises on my body already beating with blood, and I knew that they could have killed me if they had wanted to, but I was still alive, and I should have been grateful, but I wasn't.

Chapter 13
Saturday Night Special

I woke up to the sun knocking on the curtains and a bruise high on my cheek that was throbbing with the same insistence as the light in the room, and my face felt puffy and there was a split in my lip that still tasted like blood when I ran my tongue over the groove, and Jerry was sitting upright in his bed, in his clothes, smoking cigarettes, and when I rolled over and opened one eye to test it, to see if it would still work, he looked over at me and said, good morning, kid.

I was sore, and it hurt to move my arms, and my back felt like somebody had held a birthday party and used me for a pinata, and I groaned a little bit through my teeth, and then I straightened my legs and flexed my arms a little bit, and everything still worked, and I tried to sit upright, but my head felt like it would burst from the pressure if I didn't comply with gravity and stay flat and even with the floor below the bed.

"You're still alive," Jerry said, and I wanted to agree with him, but I felt like I'd have to get better to die, and I remembered the day before, when the guy in room 947 had beat the shit out of me, and I remembered the look on his face when he had swung the belt and it had made contact with my skin—that sound of something thin and flat cutting through the air and then the solid *thwap* of it biting into me—and me ducking the blows and raising my arms, but they kept coming at me from all sides, and I could remember how the room smelled like shrimp shells that have sat too long on a plate, and I remembered that there was a movie on the television, and that two women had been fighting over a letter that the other one did not send, and I remembered that the carpet was soft when I hit it, finally, down on my knees, and that the bedspread, when I grabbed it, was slick in my hands, and I remembered that I had opened my mouth to make a sound but the only thing that would come out was air, in one long burst from my lungs, and then when I had the chance to make another sound, it grabbed for my throat and then got scared and disappeared into my stomach, and I remember that there was a pair of jeans slung over a chair in the corner, and I remember that the curtains were only open in a thin crack where they gapped in the center, and there was thin light outside—the first rise of neon sunset in the Strip—and I remember that there was a small bathroom counter that I tried to stumble toward, and there was a hairbrush on it, and the brush was full of blonde hair. But what I kept forgetting was how I made it out of the room, how I made it up the stairs, how I stayed low and moved fast, how I walked the casino floor with my head down and one arm gripped around my waist as I tried to hold myself together, and I forgot how I stumbled out the side doors, like so many other stumblers, and I forgot how I made the walk back to the motel, across the parking lot, up the stairs, and to the room, and I forgot how I got inside and I forgot how I dug into my backpack for the sock at the bottom and replaced the money one of the guys had pulled out of my pants and how I had stuffed it all into the bible in the nightstand and fallen into my bed and curled into myself as if I could shrink smaller and maybe disappear.

I used the flat of my hands to push myself upright in bed, and I shook my head a little bit to clear the cobwebs, and my face felt as if it rose and sank again with the movement, but it was good to move around a little bit, and I could see out of both of my eyes, and I looked at Jerry and said, "I feel like I got hit by a car," and he just laughed and said maybe that would have been better for me.

"So what the fuck happened out there?" Jerry asked.

I didn't want to tell him anything at first, but I couldn't make up a story—like I had fallen on some stairs, so I just told him that a guy in a room had beat me up and he looked concerned at first, like a vice principal that hears how the school bully jumped you after sixth period when you weren't doing anything but waiting for the bus, and Jerry got a washcloth wet in the sink and put it to my face, and then went down the hall for ice and balled up the loose cubes in a towel and held it to my head and then my ribs and then my back, and then he lit a cigarette while he iced me down, and said, "you sure can take a punch, kid."

"You think you can make it into the shower? It'll help loosen you up," he said.

I stretched out my legs and kicked one toward the edge of the bed and then the other, and then I put my feet on the floor, and my head was throbbing, and my hips hurt, but the more I moved around, the better I felt, and I got up and limped my way toward the bathroom, and when I got inside, I turned on the light and looked into the mirror. I was expecting it to be bad, that what I saw would match the way that I felt, but I didn't really look bad at all—there was the bruise that I could feel and a little bit of swelling on the left side of my face and a small split in my lip, but otherwise I didn't look like I had just had the shit beat out of me the night before. I stood there for a minute, and then I put some toothpaste on my brush and scrubbed my teeth and that made me feel better, and I thought that the fucked up thing about getting hurt is that the injuries never quite match on the outside the way you feel on the inside. I once broke my arm while riding my dirt bike—I was eleven and shouldn't have been riding at night, but I did, and I hadn't seen a pile of wood in a field, and I had hit it, head-on, and one second I was on the bike and riding toward home, thinking about a TV dinner and whether or not there was still one left with the chocolate pudding that I liked to eat when it was still hot from the oven, and then I saw the pile of wood before I could even turn the handlebars, and then I was on the ground, and there was no *middle* to it—just before, when I was riding, and then after, when I was on the ground with the dirt bike's throttle stuck in the soft dirt and the back wheel spinning like crazy and the motor wound tight, and I had to get up and pick the bike up off the ground, and then I realized that my right wrist wouldn't work, and it hurt to move my hand at all, and when I finally pushed the bike back home and made it up the driveway and went in the house and showed my mom, there was a long, numb thread that ran from my fingers to my shoulder blades, and my teeth were chattering, and by the time we got to the emergency room, the pain had turned from cold to hot, so that it felt like there were spikes being hammered in, and then the doctor came and told us that I had broken both bones in my wrist and he had to snap them back together and that was the worst part—the five minutes it took him to grind my bones back into place—but on the outside you couldn't even tell that I had broken anything—there was only a small scrape in the skin where the ground had rubbed against it, but inside my bones had come apart, were rubbing against each other, and just by looking at my arm, nobody would ever know the pain.

I ran the shower as hot as I could stand the water, and I let it blow across me, and I bent my head to the force, and I took a long time to soap and lather and scrub and wash, and I held my face to the steam and the heat, and everything loosened up, and by the time I stepped out and put a towel around myself, I felt okay again. I took my time putting clothes on, and I brushed my teeth again, and when I came out of the bathroom, Jerry had three Tylenol and a little box of orange juice sitting on the nightstand for me.

"Better?" he asked.

"Yeah," I said. "I'm okay."

"Good. We've got an errand to run," and he pointed at the pills and the juice and told me to take them, and I did, and then Jerry walked toward the door and waited for me to follow.

"Where're we going?"

"Like I said, we've got an errand," and he headed down the hallway into that hard blast of sunlight, and I pulled the door shut behind me and followed him, and the parking lot was empty except for Jerry's car parked below us, and we took the stairs and I thought that we might be walking somewhere, and I wasn't sure how much I was ready to stretch my legs on the Strip again, but Jerry walked to the driver's side door of his car and I went to the passenger's side and wasn't sure if I should get in or not, and then Jerry waved his hand at me, impatiently, like I was too dumb to figure it out on my own.

The car was warm and smelled like old cigarettes, but it wasn't a bad smell, and I was grateful to be off my feet again, and Jerry lit a Merit and hit the buttons on the windows and then I could smell the air outside and hear the sound of traffic moving on the other streets, and he backed out slowly and nosed the car toward the entrance, and for the first time since we had driven in and parked by the back rooms, we were leaving together in his car, and I missed the way it had felt when we had driven from Susanville, with the wind and warmth and the unknown all stirring around me, and I was happy to be in the car again, and Jerry turned on the stereo and he flipped through the stations until he found some old rock and roll, and then he drove for a minute, and even though I could hear other cars, there were very few to see, and I wondered what time it was because it didn't feel early and it didn't feel late, but there weren't many people on the sidewalks and everything felt sleepy and slow, and before we even got up to a speed where there was enough air to blow the staleness out of the backseat, Jerry pulled into a parking lot and shut the engine off and we were there.

I looked up at the wood and cement building and read what had been painted on the side that faced the small gravel parking lot, and in black letters it said "Gold & Silver Pawn," "Open 24 HRS," "We Loan More & Sell For Less," and Jerry pulled the keys out of the ignition and swung his door open and said, wait here, and I settled into the seat and was glad Jerry had put the windows down before he stopped the car and took the keys.

I could feel the warm breeze picking up and it was enough to move the hair around on my forehead, and I could smell food in the air and I was hungry, and there were small bursts of bacon and syrup smells and I rubbed at my stomach, and then I remembered how sore my ribs were and winced and dropped my hand, and the sidewalks were still mostly empty so there wasn't much to look at, but then I saw movement over next to a dumpster in the corner of the lot, and I watched it and turned my head so that I could get a better look, and there was a man leaning up against the side, cupping his hands to light a cigarette, and there was a woman beside him and she was smoothing down the front of a very short and tight skirt, and she was looking around, but she couldn't see me below the doorframe if I hunched back in the seat, and I watched her pull her own cigarette from a shiny purse she had on her arm, and I wondered if she was a hooker and then I saw her shoes and guessed that she probably was, and I thought of Hooker Stacy that we'd all known around town when I was young, and I was homesick and winced again in the same way I had when I'd touched my ribs. She even dressed like Hooker Stacy had—in the thin, tight skirt, all shiny and high gloss, and the heels that clicked like flint, and I hadn't seen Hooker Stacy in a long time, even though she had a way of popping up when you least expected her to—rounding a corner onto Main Street, leaning against the wall by Tips Bar, walking down the side of the road toward Dog Island Park—and my sister and I used to point her out when we were in the car together, going somewhere—hey, there's Hooker Stacy—and it was as if we had spotted a rare bird in town and we were recording our encounters, and my mom would tell us not to point—it was rude—but Hooker Stacy was hard not to look at, and she was part of our landscape, like a war memorial, and here I was, far away, and she was still a memory of home.

The man adjusted his belt buckle and flicked his smoke into the dirt, and the woman walked away from him, and he yelled something at her, something that made her turn her head and smile, and I watched her high heels cut through the gravel as she walked without missing a step, and then she hit the sidewalk and turned left and I followed her for as long as I could, through the back window and then the mirrors, and then she was gone, and the man walked across the parking lot and went the opposite direction, and then he was gone, too, and I was alone again, in the car, waiting for Jerry. I had already looked at everything there was to see and the glove box was locked, even though I tried the handle again, and I thought about pulling the book off the backseat, but it was easier to just sit where I was and close my eyes a little bit and feel the breeze on my face and the sun through the glass as it warmed me, and I let myself slip a little into a dream that kept me close to the surface so that I could swim back to shore if I heard the sound of Jerry returning.

I don't know how long I waited since there was no time in that place, and being half-asleep helped make it bearable to be bored, but then I heard the driver's door swing open and Jerry slid in, and he didn't have anything in his hands and I wondered what had taken him so long just to come back with nothing.

"Let's take a little ride," he said, and I didn't have any complaints and was happy to be in motion again and away from the room and the payphone and the envelopes and the walks down the Strip, and I wondered what Amber was doing—if the door to her room was open so that she could smoke in the sun—but I didn't want us to head back just so I would know, and I was glad that Jerry made a left out of the parking lot and drove us in the opposite direction from everything that I had come to know, and I looked for the hooker as we eased down the street and thought maybe that I would be able to see her, standing somewhere, seeing everything and nothing in the same way that Hooker Stacy used to do, but she had faded into the buildings by then, and as we kept driving, the buildings thinned like a stream of blood in a bathtub so that they trickled into nothing, and then there were just metal buildings with fences around them and junk in the yards, and places advertising auto repair and the grass grew up high and dead and there were bare spots of earth where the sand pooled at the surface, and then the buildings disappeared from the mirror and I watched the slow rise of small hills and more scrub and yellow, as though the landscape was lumpy and the roots of what was living had to fight for each patch of ground they took, and there were flecks of green from the stronger plants that dug in but were still ugly, and everything looked gray and washed as if they were in a picture that hadn't quite developed, and Jerry kept driving with the music moving from one guitar solo to the next.

When we had been out of town for ten minutes, or ten hours or ten days—it was so hard to tell—Jerry took a right at a stop sign and drove between the low, squat rise-from-the-dead yellow hills, and he looked behind him to see how much road there was left, and he kept going until the asphalt crumbled away, and then he followed the dirt and the big Ford bounced and swung and dipped and Jerry slowed down so that the gravel pinged off the undercarriage and then we came to a flat spot with nothing in any direction and Jerry seemed satisfied and he hit the brakes and the engine cut out with the music and everything went quiet except for the wind slicing through the windows, stronger now, without trees or buildings to block it, and I knew that if I stood out there and closed my eyes and spun myself in a circle for a minute or two, I wouldn't know which way to go to get back to town.

I looked over at Jerry and the muscles in his jaw were jumpy, and I knew that he was mad at me, and I knew why without having to dig too deeply in my head for the answers, and I knew that he was mad because I had gotten beat up, because he had figured out I had been the cause of the violence and I was the one to blame, because somehow he knew that I had done what he had told me not to do, and he thought I had forgotten that he had warned me about doing what was smart, but not being too smart, and how he had told me not to let Amber into the room, and I hadn't, but he probably knew that I had found a loophole and had been going to hers, and I knew he had figured out that we had dipped into the envelope and Amber had pinched, and it wasn't the guy in Room 947 that had caused all of the mess because really it was me.

"I don't usually do this," Jerry mumbled, and I could feel the muscles in my stomach tighten and it hurt to hold my breath, and I figured that if he hit me, I'd be ready for it, because I already knew how it would feel, and then I wondered if he might make me get out of the car and tell me to walk away from him, and to keep walking, and I would, and he would tell me to pick a point on the horizon line and head that direction, and I would fix my eyes on it and try not to think because that's the best way to prepare for a bullet that was coming for the back of your head.

Jerry dug into his belt and I knew it was going to happen and I figured he wouldn't shoot me if I was still in the car because he wouldn't want to be stuck with wiping up the blood, so I reached for the door handle and yanked up hard, but the door wouldn't move because at some point when we were driving, Jerry had hit the locks and I had never even noticed.

"Where you going, kid?"

My throat was too dry to speak so I licked my lips and my tongue felt like I had borrowed it from a cat. "Nowhere," I said.

"Don't be so antsy," he said, and he opened his hand and there was a small gun on his palm, a gun not much bigger than his hand, and it was dark-handled and silver and shiny, and then he reached into his front pocket and pulled out a box of bullets, and he started loading the gun—pressing rounds into the clip and snapping that into the recess of the handle—and then he handed it over to me and it was heavier than it looked and I didn't know what to do with my hand so I just held it out, with the gun hanging over the sides, and Jerry hit the locks on the door and said, "let's go try it out."

Jerry walked to the hood of the car and leaned against the grill, and he pulled a cigarette out, and I leaned beside him with the gun in my hand, and I kept holding it away from myself like it was a snake that might bite me, and I heard the words in my head, *a snake that might bite me*, and I remembered that was the way my stepdad Dale talked about his guns, and I realized that I hadn't been around a pistol since Dale had died, because going out to the hills and shooting at things had been one of his favorite pastimes, and he and his drinking buddies used to take me and my sister out with them, on a sunny Saturday, and they would drink and put the cans on the hills off Jelly's Ferry Road, and they would take turns popping their guns off at the targets, and Dale had big pistols, a .44 magnum that he was especially proud of because he said it was the same as Dirty Harry's and when he pulled the trigger on it, it made a noise like a cannon so that the echo bounced off the hills in rolls like thunder and the sound didn't die down for a long time, and I could remember what it was like to stand out there or sit on a tailgate and I would hold my hands to my ears and jump every time somebody pulled a trigger and one of the cans in the dirt leapt up and rolled over, and I hated the noise and the smell and the anxiety I would feel, waiting for the noise, and sometimes I would cry a little bit, and Dale would get pissed off at me, and I would wipe my eyes with my dirty hands and leave smears on my face, and Dale would stagger over, with his pistol pointed at the ground and he would hold it out to me and tell me to take it, to hold it, to put my small hand around it, and I wouldn't want to, but not doing it was worse than just going ahead and touching it, and he would tell me to think of it like a snake that might try to bite me, and to hold it like that, and I would, and he'd swing my hand into his and point it toward the hillside, and then he'd put his finger over mine and force it to the trigger and together we would pull—his finger mashing mine down against the metal—and I would jump and flinch and I could not cover my ears.

"It's just a little J-22," Jerry said, and this didn't mean anything to me, so I nodded as if I understood. "Not really any stopping power, but it'll back someone up if they come at you. Takes a .22 long rifle—" he pulled the box from his pocket and shook a bullet out and handed it over to me, and it was easier to hold than the gun, and I rolled it around in my palm and it seemed funny to me that something that felt like that could rip into someone and shred them up on the inside. "Nothing much to that either," Jerry said, jerking his head toward the bullet in my hand. "Probably best you don't even load it, but I want you to know how to use it, just in case, even though you never will."

Jerry opened his hand and reached for the gun, and I handed it over to him, and he pulled on something on the gun and then he pointed toward a weed in front of us that was about twenty yards away, and he pulled the trigger, and I saw the weed flutter a little bit in a wind, and then Jerry sighted down the short barrel and held his arm out straight and pulled the trigger over and over again, five more times, and the little plant danced and the dirt jumped up, and even though I wanted to flinch and cover my ears, I didn't.

Jerry took the box of bullets off the hood and stacked six again, and then he handed the gun over to me and told me to point and pull the trigger—that's all there was to it—and I did as he told me, and I closed one eye and looked down the barrel at the weed out in the sand, and I squeezed the trigger and the gun barely twitched in my hand and I heard it pop without even feeling it much, and I saw the dirt blow up into the wind, just to the left of the plant, and Jerry told me to try it again, and I did, and then again and again and again and again, and then Jerry reloaded it a third time and showed me how to do it—how to put the bullets into the clip and then load the clip into the gun—and he smoked another cigarette, and let me shoot it until I stopped jumping when the noise went off, and there was a haze surrounding us that smelled sharp and warm, like the green sap from a broken branch, and the sun beat down on us in the openness of nothing, and the longer I stood and felt the small heft of the gun, the more relaxed my arm became until I understood what Jerry kept telling me as he stood behind me and held my arm and taught me to sight down the short barrel—*it's just an extension of your hand, pretend you're pointing at what you want to hit*—and we stood there, in front of the car, while the light glanced off the short, silver barrel, and Jerry stepped out from behind me and let me shoot on my own, and he sometimes reached over and steadied my arm and showed me how to take a stance that looked more like I meant what I was doing, and neither of us heard the pickup truck come down the dirt road and pass behind us until the dirt clouded up, and I looked over to see the driver—an older guy with a dirty baseball hat on, driving a beat-up four-wheel-drive with a dog in the back—and I wondered what Jerry and I looked like out here, and I tried to imagine it from the driver's point of view, at what he had come up on out in the middle of nowhere with the sand and the dirt and the dead weeds and the wind blowing across us in small gasps, and I thought that we probably looked like a father and son out for the afternoon, and the father was just a man teaching his boy how to shoot.

Chapter 14
Packing

Jerry drove fast coming off the dirt and then gravel road so that the car rocked and bounced, and when we finally hit asphalt again, he swung the car left and onto the road, and we fishtailed as the Ford's tires broke loose, but Jerry kept us in the lane and then we flew back to the city rising up in the distance. The sky was cloudless and flat and sharp blue, but a wind had come up suddenly and it pelted the windshield with dirt and sand and I could hear it hitting the car in sprayed handfuls until we were tucked between the high rise of buildings that blotted out the land, and then it quit suddenly, like a frustrated mother on a beach who grabs her child's arm from throwing another fistful and says, stop that—stop that right now.

I watched the buildings and the people on the sidewalks, and they were crowding quickly, with the rodeo in town for the long holiday weekend, and I realized that if I was still home, I would be out trying to hold onto the daylight for as long as I could as I felt the summer slip through my hands like so much desert sand and dirt being blown by the wind. Jerry was sweating and he was gripping the steering wheel hard, but he sat back in his seat, twisting the dial on the radio, skipping through stations until he landed on one for a minute and then another, finding the songs he liked, and he pointed out casinos as we passed—the Peppermill, at the far end, in the center of its own parking lot, and then the Harold's Club, Fitzgerald's, the Eldorado, slicing into the corner of North Virginia Street like the edge of a fence stake that hadn't been driven into the dirt—and he told me about how he had played at the tables or been in a fight or fucked some woman or been too drunk to tell the difference between the floor and the walls, but his stories kept jumping around like the songs he couldn't tune into for more than a few seconds of guitar or drums or a blast of chorus, and I cracked my window a little bit and breathed in the warm air and I could hear the bells ringing and the people making noise and I knew that by the time we got back to the motel, I'd be sent off to hustle another delivery and I'd be back to work, and I wondered if Amber was at the arena with Hurley and Reece, and I was still mad at them for the trouble they had made for me—especially Hurley for having the idea in the first place, but it was harder to be mad at Amber and the way she said *just a little bit, nobody will notice*—and I thought maybe if I could get a chance, I could go join them and watch and hang out for a little bit even if I *was* mad because they were my friends now, and I liked having friends, but it was Sunday, and Reece and Hurley had to compete in the afternoon, and I knew that there wouldn't be any break for me between the room, the payphone, and the runs for me, but there was also the money to think about, and I had a lot of it now, stuffed into a pair of socks that were rolled into a T-shirt buried in the bottom of my backpack that was shoved under my bed, and in the short time that I had been pulling envelopes out of my underwear and replacing them with cash, I had become hungry for more, a hunger pang that I couldn't quite feed, and I thought about what I might do with the money, and how far it might get me, but I had never dreamed in dollars and I didn't know how far it could reach.

I thought about Bobby and what he would be doing this weekend, and I knew that he and Tony Guiterrez and Wayne would be wandering around and looking for things to distract them, and I wished that I was with them even if I hated them and I missed the easy days of watching TV and eating Pringles and dodging chores and pretending. I thought about my sister sometimes and what she was doing in my absence, and I figured she was getting the best of everything now, and I hoped that she was learning how to watch where Chris put his eyes, and sometimes I thought about my mom, and I tried to picture her in my head, but the image of her was always fuzzy, like a channel I couldn't quite tune into, and when I could finally get a grip on her and what she looked like, all I could see was her picking up her purse to go out somewhere, and I tried to see her doing something else, but in the end she was always walking out the door and I could only see her back and the easy shift of what she was wearing, with the sun in her hair lit up golden, and the easy stride of her legs in a pair of jeans with the white stitching on the pockets that gripped her hips as if they were afraid they might slide off and get left behind too, and her purse slung over her shoulder and her car keys in her hand, and in my mind I had to settle for either watching her leave or worse still, not doing anything at all.

When Jerry made the right turn into the motel driveway, I was surprised to see Hurley's red truck parked in front of the lower row of rooms, and Jerry slowed the LTD and eased us around to the back, behind the low row of buildings, and I tried to see if there was anyone at the pool—if Amber was there, stretched out on a chair with her hair pulled back off her face and a beer in her hand—but the light was too bright and bounced off the water, and then we were around the corner, and Jerry pulled into a spot and the world went quiet again, except for the sound of the street and voices in the distance, and I wanted to stay in the car, and I wanted to just be left there to sleep and watch and be alone, but Jerry swung his door open, and he shoved the pistol he had bought for me into his front pocket, and for a while I had forgotten about it, had forgotten about the heft and the pull and the sound it made as I squeezed the trigger over and over again, and I didn't quite feel as if it was mine yet, but it was, and if I had been home, the first thing I would have done is gone out to show it off to my friends.

"Time to get some work done, kid," Jerry said, and I felt the ache in my ribs and the way my back stung if I leaned into it, and there was still the place on my cheek that hurt when I put my hand up to touch it, and I wasn't too excited to go out and make the walk and stand in front of another hotel door, but there was the pistol that I kept forgetting about, and somehow it made me feel braver even though I knew I would never touch it or use it again no matter what happened when I made the quiet knock on a bright numbered door from one of the hallways.

"I've gotta make some calls," Jerry said, and I knew this was my cue to take my time getting back to the room, so I got out of the car and leaned against the fender and Jerry lit a cigarette and headed toward the stairs. "C'mon, first," he said, and he waved toward me, so I followed him across the cement and up the stairs and over the landing to our room, and we went inside and the air was stale, and Jerry kept the door open for a minute so that the air came in and stirred things around, and there was bright light in the window and I liked that I could feel the heat through the glass, and then Jerry drew the curtains closed so that the room went dark and he switched on a lamp and shut us in.

"Go suit up," he said, and that meant I had to get the underwear on, and I went into the bathroom and pulled a washed pair off the shower rod, and I closed the door and I pulled my jeans off and put the whites on, and they were still a little damp from being washed in the sink, but they felt cool against my body and I liked the way they shrank against me, and then Jerry knocked on the door, and I said, "Just a minute," and I could hear him pacing on the other side, so I hurried up to pull myself together, and I ran some water in the sink and smoothed down my hair, and it was already growing out from the gas station haircut, and didn't feel so sharp at the ends anymore, and I had finally reached a point where I could look into the mirror and almost see me.

When I came out, Jerry was sitting on his bed and he had the gun he'd bought me in his hand, and he told me to come over to him, so I did, and he told me to put the pistol in my pocket, and at first I thought that he meant my jeans pocket so I did, but then he said, *No, the inside pocket, knucklehead*, and I realized what he meant, and nobody had called me knucklehead since my stepdad Dale, had died, and I felt my face get hot, and then I turned my back toward Jerry and pulled the waistband of my jeans out so I could squeeze the gun in, but I ended up having to unsnap them and pull the zipper down, and I was embarrassed a little bit, but I could hear him behind me, tapping his fingers on the bedspread, and I knew that this was all business for both of us now.

The pistol made the pocket sag and it felt strange and heavy against my lower stomach, and when I pulled the jeans over it, there was a slight bulge in the fabric and I had to shift it around to get it to sit right, and then I zipped up and snapped the button, and I turned around and faced Jerry and held my arms out from my sides so that he could get a better look.

"Perfect," he said. "Can't even tell."

I felt like there was no way that someone *couldn't* tell, but I palmed at the front of the jeans and moved my thighs a little bit, and shifted its weight, and then it was nestled against me, and I knew that if push came to shove—and I was the one getting pushed and shoved—there was no way I could get the pistol out fast enough to be of any threat unless I practically undressed myself from the waist down, and I wondered why Jerry had really bought the gun for me when it wasn't really going to be of any use.

"Try to sit down with it," Jerry said, so I stepped backward and eased down to the edge of my bed, and the pistol didn't really fold with me, and I had to shift it more and cup it until it was practically between my legs, and I could feel the underwear sagging so that only the seam in the crotch was holding them up, but I could sit.

"Now stand up again. And quit pushing at your fucking crotch. You look like a major league pitcher on the mound with all that fucking ball movement. I mean Jesus Christ, kid—if it can't get up, it can't get out."

I stood up and this time I let the pistol slide itself into position, and if I didn't mess with it, it sort of molded itself to my body, and then I sat down again without Jerry telling me to, and then I stood again, and I repeated this a few times and by the fourth time I went through the routine, and even walked to the door and back, the pistol didn't feel like it was there at all.

There was a knock at the door, and I recognized the rhythm of the tap, and it was fat Gordo, and Jerry pulled the door open and Gordo came through in all his sweat and dirty suit jacket and the yellowing T-shirt underneath, and the room felt too small again, and fat Gordo went over to my bed and made himself comfortable and I wanted to test how quickly I could pull the pistol and get it straightened out and sighted in and pop it loose on fat Gordo, but I just stood in the middle of the room and Gordo reached over and picked up the phone, and he lit a cigarette while he was punching in numbers and I realized that this was the silent signal that I was excused.

Jerry waved me out the door, and I walked down the corridor to the soda machine and pumped in a few dimes and made my selection, and the can that shot out was cold and I snapped it open and stood in the shade of the hallway and drank, and I realized that I hadn't had breakfast, and I was sort of impressed with how long I could go without food now, and then my stomach growled and I wished I hadn't thought about it and jinxed myself. I walked forward to the railing and looked down, but I couldn't see anything from where I stood, except for the vacant parking lot, and there were the usual bunches of trash and split bags, and a dirty mattress that had gone swollen and coughed out handfuls of stuffing, and I walked to the stairs and went down to the parking lot, and there was no one around and the wind that had been blowing around us while we were coming back from the desert had now gone from exhales to quick puffs, and the air was warm, and the sky was still flat and full overhead, and I walked over to the pool and leaned against the fence for a little while, but it was empty and the water was still the milky blue it had always been, and there weren't any traces of Amber left in the winking aluminum of spent cans rolling around on the cement, and I was about to pull the gate open and go get comfortable in a chair when I heard my name called and I looked over my shoulder, and Amber was standing in the doorway of 155 and she waved me over.

"Where were you guys today?" she asked. "I went looking for you."

I felt a pull in my stomach at the thought of Amber looking for me, and that I had been on her mind at all, and then I realized the pull was really just the pistol shifting around as I walked, and I pressed my legs together, and Amber moved from the doorway and I stepped past her, but she grabbed me as I walked in, and she held me by the shoulders and looked at my face, and the pain from the bruise had already sunk below the surface, like bruises do, and I could feel it deeper now, closer to the bone.

"Jesus, who did this to you? Did Jerry do this to you? That fucking bastard." And she moved me by the shoulders and turned me into the light that was filtered through the doorway so that she could take a closer look at my face.

"Jerry didn't do it," I said. "It was a guy I was delivering to. A guy we shorted."

"Oh, shit," Hurley said. "He figured out we pinched? What an asshole." Hurley was on the bed and his brother, Reece, was sitting beside him, and they were both smoking cigarettes and there was a haze in the room, and I could smell something sweet, like drinks that had been sitting too long in plastic cups, and Amber came back in the room and closed the door behind her and then all I could smell was her, and her strawberry shampoo, and I wanted to press myself into her skin and inhale until the light faded from the sky and the sun went the color of her name as it sank into the low slung hills on the horizon.

"I'm so sorry," Amber said. "Jesus. I didn't know this would happen. Are you okay?"

"Some serious shit," Hurley said. "What'd he do? Scale it up right there?"

Amber rubbed a thumb over my cheekbone. "Does it hurt?"

"Not anymore," I said.

"Stingy dope fiend," Hurley said. "Pinching is a matter of economics. Everybody knows that."

"I thought you'd be at the arena," I said. "It's the rodeo, right?"

"Hurley and Reece don't ride until tonight and we're just killing time," she said. "It smells at the arena. I hate being there for too long." Amber let go of me and walked toward the bathroom.

"You're just sensitive," Hurley said, and he laughed and ashed his cigarette into a beer bottle, and Reece had his shirt off and his chest was tan but there was a clear line that separated his chest and stomach and upper arms from the rest of him, and it was as if he was wearing a white shirt and his tan arms were sticking out below the short sleeves. He was cute, in a way that I thought that Bobby was cute, and I wondered that if things were different, Reece and I would be like Bobby and me had been, and I wondered what it would have been like when I was on the cardboard down by the slough and Reece had been watching us instead of Bobby, and I thought that Reece would have done something, and I could see him balling his hands into fists and beating the shit out of Tony Guiterrez, or rocking one of his cowboy boots back and kicking Tony Guiterrez right in the ribs so that he lifted off me and I rolled free, and then I remembered that I had a pistol in my underwear now, and if I'd had it then, I would have just pulled it loose and put it against Tony Guiterrez's stomach and pulled the trigger over and over again when he decided to pin me down and fuck me by the slough—*you don't have the stopping power*, Jerry's voice whispered in my head, and I figured that no matter what Jerry said, me popping Tony Guiterrez over and over again in six yanks of trigger pull would have been enough to make him stop anything, and then Reece would have walked over, with his shirt off and his bone white skin shining in the half-light, and he would have put his arm around my shoulders and walked me home.

"I want to get fucked up but these pussies keep talking about riding tonight, and they're boring," Amber said. "Let's get fucked up. We've been sitting in this room all night. I'm bored. I'm sick of sitting around. I mean, we wasted a good high and Joey got beat up for it."

They had said they were going to sell what they took, and I guessed it hadn't made it through the door after I left, and I imagined them dumping it from the torn piece of magazine and taking turns with a straw they pulled from one of the McDonald's cups that were stacked around the room and I looked at Amber and tried to figure out if I could tell if she was high but I couldn't.

"Baby, we got money on the line," Hurley said, and he stretched out and tucked one arm behind his head and adjusted the pillow. "But you can help me relax a little bit." He smiled. "Come over here and give me a blow job." With the door closed, I could smell the sweat in the room, and the sheets and comforter were all pulled apart and there were flies circling the trashcan under the table.

"Oh, you look so strong like that on the bed. Gets me all kinds of horny," Amber said. She was putting on mascara while she messed with her hair, and I watched her hands move around her face.

"I ain't strong, baby. I'm just big," Hurley said, and he tugged at the crotch of his jeans.

I wanted to tell them about what I was hiding—about what I was holding now instead of the envelope that had been so interesting just the day before—but I knew that I couldn't and there was nothing worse than having a great secret that I couldn't share, and it was like my head would explode if I didn't get the truth out, so I just adjusted my own crotch and sat down in one of the chairs under the window and took one of the bottles out of the six-pack on the table and looked around for the opener, and then Reece signaled toward me and reached out for the bottle, and he put it to his belt buckle and popped the top, and I smiled at him in a way that I hoped he would understand, and maybe he did because he smiled back at me, and Amber had moved into the bathroom and she had a curling iron that she was twisting through her hair, and the TV was too loud and they were watching an old western where men in black and white were shooting at each other in a bloodless black and white way, and I wanted to spend the rest of the day with them and go to the arena and watch Reece ride and sit next to Amber in the stands and feel the press of her leg against mine, and even as she curled her hair in the bathroom and brushed some powder on her face, I couldn't stop looking at her, and my stomach always quit being hungry when she was around me no matter how long it had been since the last time I'd had something to eat, and I swapped the soda I'd carried in with me for the bottle of beer, and I swallowed as much as I could until I thought that maybe I could replace one kind of buzzing in my head with the sound of another.

"I saw that fat fuck Gordo drive in," Amber said. "Why is he always hanging out in your room?"

"He's a homo," Hurley said. "He's queer for Jerry."

I'd never thought about Gordo as a homo, but I could see the way the description might fit, but no matter what they thought about Gordo, there was no way that Jerry was queer.

"He calls in bets for Jerry," I said. "He's like a what-do-you-call-it? Bookie?"

"He ain't no bookie," Hurley said. "He's worse than that. He's a fat fucking gambling homo. He probably sucks dick no matter if he wins or loses." Hurley laughed and dropped the rest of his cigarette into the bottle that he had balanced on his stomach.

"So does Jerry win or does he lose?" Amber called from the bathroom.

"I don't know," I said. All I really did know was that Jerry's mood sometimes changed when the games were beginning or ending, and it was an up and down ride that felt like a roller coaster with the phone ringing and numbers being punched in the background.

"My mom says he's a big loser," Amber said. "I mean that he loses a lot of money, you know?"

"How does your mom know so much about Jerry?" I asked.

"They used to fuck. A long time ago." Amber said this matter-of-fact, and then she put the curling iron on the counter and picked up a can of hairspray and started coating her hair in a cloud that hissed around her. "She says Jerry was always about big promises, you know? The next big thing. Gonna cash in, gonna do this, gonna do that. But it was a long time ago." She moved the can around her head and I watched it mist in a cloud.

"Fuck, lay off that shit," Hurley called over. "That shit burns my eyes and I gotta ride tonight, baby."

Amber kept spraying and I could smell it drifting into the rest of the room. Hurley got up and opened the door and started waving the outside air in. I looked over at Reece and he hadn't moved from the bed, and he was watching me and I could feel his eyes on me like they had as much weight as the pistol in my underwear and I wanted to walk over and tell him that I had it—*I have a gun in my underwear*—and I tried the phrase out in my head, and I realized how it sounded and I knew that if I said that to him he'd think I was a homo just like Gordo.

"What time are we leaving?" Amber asked, and she looked shiny, and her eyes were bright and green and full of her pupils that stretched like black dinner plates, and her skin was even tanner than it had been when she'd opened the door, and I thought maybe it was just the light and the fact that it had shifted in the sky and I could see her better, and she winked at me and came up to where I was sitting, and she sat down in my lap suddenly, before I even knew what was happening, and she put her arm around me and I was against her so closely that every breath I took tasted like the way that she smelled, and I tried to shift in the seat so that I could move the pistol out from under her, but she shifted with me and she smiled at me, and she ran her fingers through my hair, back and forth, and she rubbed the bruise over my swollen cheek with her thumb, gently, so that I could only feel the pressure of her touch, and all of my senses went electric like somebody had flipped a switch and I wanted to reach up and make her closer to me, to push her shirt up and over her shoulders so that I could have all of her, naked against me, and the thought of me doing that made my breath pull tight and I didn't know where to put my hands without them resting somewhere on her body, so I reached out for the beer bottle on the table, and I held it and let my other hand fall to my side so that it hung over the chair like a lead weight that had been dropped over the side of a boat as it trolled out to sea.

"You have to come with us tonight," Amber said as she kept running her hands through my hair and rubbing my cheek in a gentle rhythm that I don't think she knew she was making. "Please. I'll be so bored if I have to sit there and watch by myself."

"I thought you were bringing Debbie with you," Hurley said from the doorway. "This is getting to be too much of a fucking dick fest as it is. We need some more chicks up in here."

"Debbie has to work," Amber said. "Besides. I'd rather have Joey come with us."

Hurley looked at me, and I dropped my eyes, and when I could finally raise them again, I moved them onto Reece, but he was staring at the TV screen.

"Please," Amber begged, and then Hurley came in and took Amber by the hand and pulled her off of my lap and she stumbled into him and he pulled her against his chest and kissed the top of her head.

"You won't be bored, baby," he said. "You'll be too busy watching me win."

Reece looked up from the TV and I thought that he might say something about how he would be winning, too, but he didn't, and I didn't know if they competed in the same categories or if they had different events, and I wondered what it would be like to always have to take second place to my sister, to watch her take the money and the trophies and the plaques and the applause, and I guess I would probably feel like Reece did as he sat on the bed with the scar on his neck standing out like a piece of red licorice so that I could see the "R" lit up bright as if it were still burning through his skin, and his shoulders were rolled forward so that he was hunched down and looked smaller and insignificant, as if he was just part of the furniture that was wearing away, another battered piece of mismatch that was nicked and scratched and something that Amber would never sit on, even if he was the only chair left in the room.

Chapter 15
The Bell Ringer

Jerry and fat Gordo decided that I needed to make one more run and then I could sit the rest of Monday out, like I was on some kind of sports team and we were in a tournament and I was going to start the game and play my position and then I was getting pulled and could sit the bench for the rest of the innings, so Jerry handed me the paper and I went to the phone and made the call, and the guy was restless on the other end, like he had blown through all his allowance and still wanted Now and Laters, and I walked back to the room and the sun was already high even though it was still pretty early and the housekeepers were still hosing the puke off the sidewalks.

I walked past the office and Amber's mom, Dee, was out front, with a long-handled push broom in her hands, sweeping the entryway and the sidewalk and the driveway in front, and she stopped when I passed her and she put both of her hands around the broom handle and leaned on it, and I looked over at her and gave her a short wave as I headed back to pick up and get gone and finish up and be done, and then I was hoping that maybe I could hang out with Amber and we could get some food at some place that I hadn't been able to walk to since Jerry and fat Gordo were heading to the Cal Neva and I didn't give a shit if they did, and maybe they would be gone all day, and maybe they'd never come back, and I could move in with Amber and go on the rodeo circuit with Reece and ride up to Carson City with them next week, and maybe that's the way my life would bend as summer started its slow descent into fall.

"Seen you walking by quite a bit lately," Dee called over as I walked past her and I didn't know what to say to that so I just nodded and said, *yeah*, and kept walking, and I could have made it all the way past her where talking would have been awkward if she would have let me slide by with a "yeah," but she lit a cigarette faster than I could walk, and then she said, "Uncle got you working a lot lately, huh?"

I stopped and looked at her, and I could see the wrinkles around her eyes and she was wearing a pink tank top that dipped low on her chest and her skin was too tan and too thin, and she pinned me to the asphalt with her stare as I sorted through my uncles until I realized that she meant Jerry.

"Yeah, just running errands for him," I said.

"Is that right?" She took a drag from the cigarette and held it in and then her nostrils flared, and I hated it when people did that because it made them look like a horse.

"Just doing stuff," I said, and I kicked at some loose rocks with my feet, and I had the motel paper folded in my back pocket with room numbers and hotel names, and all I could think about was maybe it was time I got some waffles while I was in Reno.

"You know, you can get away with things all the time, but you only have to be caught once." She stared at me and didn't move the broom, and I kept waiting for her to go back to clearing the driveway again.

"I don't know what you mean," I said.

"Just something my daddy used to say to me," she said. "You only have to be caught once."

I shoved my hands into the pockets of my jeans so that I could grip the bottom of the fabric and dry my hands, and my pistol was in the room still, under my mattress where Jerry told me to leave it unless I was going out on runs, and I thought about what Dee's face would look like if I just pulled it out and gripped it at my side while she was talking to me, and I wondered if it would have any change on her expression. "Well, that sounds like good advice," I said.

"Mmmm hmmm," she said. "He wasn't much for paying bills or being around, but he had all kinds of words of wisdom."

I kicked at another rock. "Yeah? My stepdad Dale used to say 'put your brain in gear before disengaging your mouth,'" and I looked at her then, and I didn't drop my eyes and I willed myself to keep from breathing and I held my breath just to see how long that I could. Dale had actually never said that but once I had been Christmas shopping for him at the mall in Redding, wandering stores with my mom, and I had found a plaque that said those words and I thought they were funny even though I didn't really know what they meant and I had used my allowance to buy it for him and had wrapped it up, in my room, and put it under the tree, and when he opened it, he didn't laugh at all, and

127

I thought that maybe I should have bought him the T-shirt that had the cartoon of two buzzards sitting in a tree and said: "Patience my ass, I'm gonna kill something," but he had put the plaque up in the living room, next to the television, and I used to look at it every time I sat down to watch Looney Tunes.

Dee laughed and she loosened her hands from the broom handle and blew a lungful of smoke toward the open sky, and then she dropped her cigarette and toed it out and picked up the butt from the ground and turned and walked toward the small trash can she had moved onto the sidewalk in front of the office to catch her dirt and the scraps of trash she pulled from the low line of shrubs below the window.

"You take care of yourself," she said to me, and she tossed the cigarette butt into the can and then she went back to sweeping and picking wrappers and wadded tissues out of the bushes, and I kept walking across the parking lot and passed the pool and rounded the corner of the building and climbed the stairs and thought about pumping some change into the soda machine so I could get a drink, but I decided to wait because I wanted everything to taste that much better when I was done with running for the day.

When I got back to the room, Jerry and fat Gordo were getting ready to leave, and I gave Jerry the piece of paper and he opened the drawer in the nightstand and pulled out an envelope, and he handed me the pen and I wrote the room number on my hand, in the code that he had taught me, and fat Gordo took his pint bottle from his inside jacket pocket and took a drink and sat in one of the chairs under the window, and it was the first time in days that the TV was off, and I missed the sound of the other voices.

"So you put the money in the bible," Jerry said. "You know the drill. I'm gonna expect $300 when I get back here later," he said, and he lit a cigarette and walked into the bathroom and took a comb out of his back pocket and slicked back his hair. He was wearing his white shirt and tie and the shirt was wrinkled in the back, and Jerry took a jacket off a hanger he had anchored over the bathroom door, and he put the jacket on, and he adjusted his collar and gave himself another going over in his reflection.

"When are you coming back," I asked.

"When we're done," fat Gordo said, and he took another long swallow and capped the bottle and put it back in his pocket.

"Done with what?"

"Hey, kid, c'mon," Jerry said. "You stay in and watch a movie or something, okay? Get a pizza." He dug into his pocket and pulled out his money clip and flicked a ten off the top and tossed it on my bed.

"It's boring," I said.

"Yeah, well, that's not your call. Don't go anywhere."

I took a deep breath and tried to make my face look as defeated as it could, but he didn't seem to notice.

"You hear me? Don't leave the room and don't let anyone in. Period. We'll be back later," Jerry said.

"Yeah, I get it," I said.

"Hey Jerry, why don't we say fuck it and go over to Sparks—hit the Bunny Ranch tonight."

Jerry turned toward him and made a face. "I ain't driving over there for watered down drinks that cost too much. I wanna watch the games."

"They got a girl over there that'll suck your dick through your jeans."

"I don't wear jeans. And I ain't paying somebody to fuck me."

"It's not like I have to pay. I just thought it'd be something to do. I mean, I fucked last night for free."

"Is that why your ass still hurts?" I said, and Jerry laughed so loud that I jumped a little bit.

Fat Gordo swung his leg out toward me, but I stepped back from his reach.

"You better run out of here little girl," Jerry said to me. "Before Gordo loses his cool. So pack it up and get gone." He waved his hand at me and I walked over to my bed and shoved the ten in my front pocket, and I pulled the pistol out from under the mattress, up near where my pillow was wadded and tight, and I shoved the gun down into the front of my pants, careful to keep out of Gordo's reach, and then I took the envelope he'd laid out for me, and I sucked in my stomach and pulled the front of my jeans out and shoved it into the pocket and I was glad my period had dried up and gone away and there was more room for everything to fit.

I turned toward the door and Jerry stopped me before I could get my hand over the doorknob. "Get this done," he said, and I nodded.

I left the room and went back into the sun, and it was hot out and my shirts were sweaty and I thought maybe it wouldn't be a bad idea to just do this delivery and then come back and order a pizza and pull the curtains and find a movie and let everything go away for a little while. I was tired and my feet hurt, and I was bored, and there was never anything to do, and I knew if Jerry came back and I was out somewhere, eating waffles, drinking with Amber and the Richter brothers, I'd be in trouble and I was tired of being in trouble, and I didn't want the hassle today if I could avoid it. I could get a pizza with olives. With mushrooms. With three kinds of meat. I could get half with ham and pineapple. I could pull cans of soda out of the machine. I could just live a little bit without the smell of men in the room.

I walked through the parking lot and Dee wasn't in front of the office anymore, and I was grateful for that because I didn't want any more time with her and her broom and the way that she looked at me, and I was thinking about pizza and maybe watching *Alien* on HBO, and I saw that Hurley's truck was parked in front of the first floor rooms again, but I just kept walking, but then a door swung open and I didn't have to look up to know that I was gonna hear my name called, and it was, and it was Amber, standing in her cutoffs with her arm on the jamb, and she waved at me and I waved back, and she said, "c'mere," and maybe I should have kept walking, but I felt like all I ever wanted to do was keep walking so I stopped and went over to where she was standing in the doorway to her room.

"Where you going?" she asked. "Running?"

I felt my face heat up a little bit and I tried to ignore her because I hated being caught for being so obvious, but I said, one delivery to go, and she smiled at me, and her hair was damp from the shower and I could smell her strawberry shampoo, and she stepped away from the doorway and said, "come in for a minute," and I should have probably said, "I don't have a minute," but my life had become just like the inside of a casino where there was always the possibility for drinks and I didn't know what day it was anymore.

"I gotta get this done," I said, but I didn't say it with much conviction, and Amber knew it, and she grabbed me by the arm and pulled me inside and shut the door behind me.

"So, you have some?" she asked.

Hurley and Reece were stretched out on the bed, in their normal positions, and Reece was spitting into an empty bottle and Hurley had one hand on his belt buckle and he was balancing a beer on his bare chest, and they were both staring at a music video for some country star that I didn't recognize.

I stood in the entryway and lifted my hand, and Reece said, "Hey," and Hurley took a drink from his beer and put it back on his chest. "So," he said. "You holding?"

I nodded and Amber was rubbing my arm and she was all kinds of smiles, and the room was stacked with clothes spilling out of drawers and there was a Burger King bag on the table with a half-eaten Whopper still stuck to a carton, and a scattering of fries, and it smelled like sweat and shower and steam, and there were drink cups and beer bottles and a lazy swarm of flies landing and lifting around the room.

"So, we want to make a deal with you," Amber said.

I looked at her and didn't say anything.

"You know, like maybe get some and pay for it this time. Right, Hurley?" Hurley looked up from the TV and nodded his head slowly against the pillow that was propping up his head.

"What do you mean?" I said.

"I mean like we want one of the envelopes."

"I can't," I said. "I mean, I'd like to, but I can't, you know? They're already going out to people."

"Yeah, but it's not like they already paid."

I thought about it for a second. "No, but they called. They confirmed."

"So what?" Hurley said. "I once called for a taxi and then they showed up and I'd already gotten a ride with one of my buddies. Life goes on."

"Yeah," Amber said. "Life goes on. It's not like they're gonna call Jerry."

"Yeah but they could page him and he'd know they didn't get their delivery."

"How's Jerry gonna know? You're the one who makes all the calls, right?"

"Yeah," I said. "I'm the one who knows the rooms."

"So you just sell one to us instead," Amber said. "No big deal."

"But it's like three hundred bucks," I said.

"Hurley," Amber shouted toward the bed.

Hurley raised up on one shoulder and dug into his front pocket and pulled out a wad of cash, and he counted off three hundred-dollar bills and tossed them forward on the knotted sheets.

"He won big this weekend," Amber said. She stepped forward and took the money and handed it to me. "See. It's all good."

I wasn't sure what to do. All I had to do was deliver the money, but there was no rule about where it came from, and I had replaced the money that had been taken from me when I shorted before, and Jerry had never known the difference, and it's not like we got a receipt that I had to provide a copy of after every sale. Amber shoved the money at me.

"It's paid for," she said.

The thought of being able to make a delivery without going into another casino sounded good to me, and I was tired, and I didn't want to duck and weave down the carpet and take an elevator and go up and walk down and knock on a door where anything could happen when all I had to do was pull it out right here and take the money and be done for the day, and it wasn't like Jerry would know and even if the room called back, I figured Jerry would ignore it and think it was just somebody else, and as long as the money was in the room, what did it matter if I sold it in the motel or walked it over to the Strip?

"Yeah, sure, I guess it'll be okay," I said and took the three bills out of Amber's hand and turned my back and pulled the envelope out of my underwear and replaced it with the money, and I shoved the pistol over so that it could tuck against the cash, and I turned back and gave the envelope over to Amber and she took it and her face lit up like a slot machine.

"Are you gonna sell it?" I asked.

She looked confused for a second and then she smiled. "Maybe," she said, "but first we're all gonna get wired," and she opened the envelope and tossed it on the table and she took the bag out that was inside and unknotted the top, and Hurley stood up from the bed and took it from her and held it up to the light, and he smiled, too, and Reece looked over at me and I thought that he shrugged with his eyes but I wasn't sure.

"Let's do a line," Amber said, and she started clearing off the table and Hurley dumped some of the powder out onto the dark wood laminate, and then he pulled out his wallet and grabbed his driver's license, and he started running it back and forth over the pile until he had divided it into four small mounds, and then he slid the card back and forth against the mounds so that they formed into lines and the lines got longer and then longer still, and then he took another hundred dollar bill from his front pocket and rolled it tight and Amber walked over to the dresser by the television and pulled out two beers and she handed one to me.

"Oh my god, my stomach starts hurting so bad before I do a line," she said, and I was never good at math, but there were four of us in the room and there were four lines on the table, and I knew that I needed to get gone and put the money in the bible and look up pizza delivery and get settled into the room.

"I gotta go," I said, but it was like my feet wouldn't move, and I just stood there, still in the doorway, and Hurley bent down and put the rolled hundred to his nose and took a long inhale, and I watched the line disappear like I'd seen in movies and then he pinched his nostrils together and sucked in his spit and he shook his head fast and he picked up his beer and took a long swallow and then drank again and coughed, and then he clapped his hands together.

"Fuck, I hate the drip," he said.

"That's the best part, baby," Amber said, and she took the rolled bill from him and put her nose to it and did the next line, and then she closed her eyes and it was like I could see her counting without moving her lips, and then she snorted hard in a sharp inhale and shuddered and Hurley handed her his beer but she pushed it away, and then she flashed her eyes at me, and they were wide, and she laughed and said, "Do it, Joey," and she handed me the bill that was still rolled tight.

"Yeah, I don't know," I said. I had never done more than smoke weed and drink, and that was no big deal, and one time me and Wayne and Tony Guiterrez had huffed some paint in Wayne's garage and all that happened was that I got a headache and a silver ring around my mouth from sucking into the bag, but Amber was rubbing at her arms and smiling so big that I thought her mouth might split through her head, and Hurley had the TV remote in his hand and he was flipping through channels and turning up the volume and Reece was staring at me, and I hadn't even realized that he'd gotten up off the bed until he was standing right beside me and rubbing his hands together and looking down at the two lines that remained.

"You're gonna love it," he said, and he reached out and touched my arm, and Amber opened her beer and put it on the table in front of me.

"You're gonna need that," she said.

"What do I do?" I asked.

"Just bend over, put the straw to your nose and suck really hard," Reece said. "It might help if you pinch the other nostril. Makes it easier."

I bent over and put the tightly-rolled bill down against the table and put my nose to the top and I forgot what I was doing and I breathed out a little bit and the line blew apart, and Reece grabbed me and jerked me back from the table.

"Inhale, don't exhale," he said, and he took Hurley's driver's license that was still on the table and herded the line back together again, and then he stepped aside so that I could lean over, and I closed my eyes and pinched my right nostril closed and before I could think about it, I just inhaled as hard as I could and kept going until the whole line was gone, and then my face caught on fire.

"Fuck, it burns," I yelled, and I rubbed at my nose and my eyes were watering, and there was a bitter taste in the back of my throat and I snorted it back and that made it worse and I thought I was going to gag, but I grabbed the beer off the table and started drinking as much as I could swallow until my face died down like cooling embers, and I could feel my heart beating in my head, and Reece loosened my hand from the rolled bill and he bent down and knocked his line back and then that was it—I'd done it, we'd done it, it was done.

All I wanted to do was talk. It was like I had just discovered language and I had to try out all the words at once, and Reece handed me a piece of gum, and it was the best thing that I had ever chewed on, and my teeth couldn't stop moving, and after we had spun through the channels on the TV for what seemed like hours, we smoked a joint from some weed that Amber had bought from the motel housekeeper named Lucinda, and I felt invincible—like I could bite through wire and put my fist through glass—and then we went driving until we got tired of roads and my thoughts stuck together until they were braided like a rope, and my past didn't matter and I wasn't afraid of the future, and finally we went back to the room and Hurley lined us up again and I wadded another piece of gum into my mouth even though my jaw felt like it had gone loose and broken from the bone, and Reece put on music videos and I thought about telling them the truth about me—because we were best friends and I could tell them anything and I was tired of my lie, but then we drank more beer and it tasted like fresh water, and Hurley turned the volume down on the television and he said to us, "we should get our own brick and sell this on our own. We could make thousands," and I spit my gum out and popped in a new piece, and we got quiet for the first time in hours.

"But like how?" Amber said.

"I've got a bunch of people who would pay for this all of the time," Hurley said.

"They would," Reece said.

"We could get it from Jerry," Amber said.

"We could just rob Jerry," Hurley said. "That fucker ain't nothing," and he laughed.

"We couldn't get away with it," Amber said. "Right?" and she looked at me. "I mean, he's a little bit crazy, isn't he?"

I had forgotten about the gun in my underwear and the gun in his car that he'd put in the room and the way that he got serious and the way he had cut my hair in the gas station bathroom and the way that he had talked to Lalo up at the house in Susanville.

"Maybe a little bit," I said. "Maybe a lot."

"So what do we do?" Amber said.

"Too bad we couldn't just rob him. We could get everything and disappear," Hurley said. "Just the four of us. Take the cash. Get the rest of the dope. Sell it off. We'd be set."

"We could rob him," Reece said. "Don't pussy out, Hurley."

"We could get puppies," Amber said.

"I could get a new truck," Hurley said. "Put the puppies in the back. Head to the ocean or something. Go to Oregon. Colorado. Get the fuck gone."

"Yeah," I said, suddenly excited. "We should go to Oregon. Portland is like the best place," and I knew that that's where I would end up, and I could already see the four of us sharing an apartment, and there were beanbag chairs and our puppies, and Reece would go out and buy groceries and we would have things like pots and pans and plates that we'd picked out together from a store.

Amber smiled at me. "We could do it, couldn't we? I mean, there's like four of us and one of him."

"And fat Gordo," I said.

"He's a fat faggot," Hurley said. "We could waste him."

Reece looked up from where he was drawing patterns into the carpet with his finger.

"Tell us everything, Joey. Tell us everything you know. Start from the beginning," Amber said.

Hurley turned off everything so that we were lit only from the flicker of the TV screen and the ghost of lamps blurring through the curtains, and the light was slippery and hard to pin down in the room.

Reece stretched his body out next to me, and I could feel heat coming from his bare skin and my heart was a hammer on the iron of my ribs, but all I wanted was for Amber to touch me, and I thought about when I used to go to slumber parties and I would find someone that made my heart beat and I would stay up all night, whispering to her and telling her all my stories so that she would feel sorry for me.

"Yeah. Tell us everything, Joey." Amber whispered. "Tell us."

So I did.

PART III

Chapter 16
Tricks Are for Kids

Amber and Hurley and Reece had been shut inside Amber's room for an entire day, and I hadn't knocked on the door even when I wanted to, and I hadn't slept well since, but I had made five trips in and out of the Eldorado, and I had become immune to the reels spinning and the sound of people gathering and betting and losing and winning, one of the slot machines by the door, bells ringing like emergency, when somebody had hit it big. The carpet was woven with gold thread that surged and waned and cut a swath through the smoke that hovered and hung in low clouds like rain in a swamp, and I was bored with the people who were blank-faced with their buckets of coins or stacks of red, white, and blue chips, as if dumping money was a national pastime, like baseball in the Cal Neva and apple pie in the buffet, or maybe they kept their underwear stuffed with a pistol and envelopes holding knotted bags of no-tomorrow—and when one of the machines hit and the siren spun red, I would stand for a minute and watch the crowd gather, as if just by getting close some of the luck would rub off on them—and by then I could recognize the floormen by the way that they dressed and the stoop of their shoulders, and I would steer clear of them and drift into the crowd as the suits would make their way to whatever machine was coughing up nickels or quarters into the metal tray with a sound like hail beating a tin roof, or the best of all—dollars—falling like lumps of silver light catching in the churn of the wheel that rotated on top of the machine while it screamed loud enough to draw everyone's attention so that the jackpot pumped like capillaries heading back to the heart of the casino, and even the passersby on the sidewalk would stop and stare through the open glass door at the win, and I liked to watch for a minute at everyone lost in the *what ifs* of some fantasy of money they hadn't won, but maybe they'd be next, and I could almost smell the dreams coming off the watchers in waves of *want*—of things they would buy if only they, too, could hit it big—and usually some of the lookers on the sidewalk would come inside and sit down at a free machine and start feeding it the rent money, or the car payment, or the grocery bill, because I had learned that in the casino there was no past of what had been scraped and saved and no future of what would never be got again—there was only the *now*—an eternal pause in the clock that didn't reveal day or night or the passing of time, and everything hung on a second hand that never ticked past the next number—only the pull of a handle, or the roll of the dice, or the flip of a card, like the river and the turn, all that hitting and folding, and the free drinks that probably ended up costing more than the bottle they were poured from—I was used to all of it now, and I didn't even look up as I crossed the casino and headed toward the doors with the pocket in my underwear, stuffed with an envelope of cash and the weight of the pistol pulling the cotton into the crotch of my jeans.

I was hoping it was my last run of the day, but the day had trickled as I stepped out onto the sidewalk of another twenty-four hours that had about as much definition as smoke, and I could smell the burn of paychecks as people clotted like blood on the sidewalk and clung to each other and laughed at the freedom that only the spending of money seemed to provide, and I was hungry and my stomach growled and I thought that maybe I would drop the payment in the room, and then I would head back out and get a burger or a taco, and I was bored with the menus of the places that I had already been, but as my mom was fond of saying, *beggars can't be choosers*, and I knew that I had to be back in the room before Jerry got back since he was always coming and going, and I had to be ready to walk to the payphone if that was what came next, and it wasn't like I was going to put my name on a waitlist at a restaurant in a casino and stand in line for a table and have a steak, though sometimes I did wish that I could go to one of the buffets and be overwhelmed by all the things they advertised, all available in one room, tray-to-table, all-you-can-eat, and I had seen the pictures enough times in the elevators—the shrimp bowls and the crab legs and the slabs of prime rib as thick as my thigh, and the fried chicken and the mashed potatoes and the pasta and the ham and the desserts stacked in rows, three and four deep, and the soft-serve machine and the thirty-two toppings and the pies and the cakes and the whipped cream fluffed into bowls as big as a shark's mouth—and as I stood on the sidewalk outside of the Eldorado and let my eyes adjust to the dimming light, I thought of it all, how many plates I could fill and how I would wait for a few minutes and eat some more, and I imagined what it would be like—to have so many choices and nothing but opportunity—and I figured it must be the way the people felt who shuffled past me, on their way to the next casino where the machines might be looser, the minimum bets smaller, the chances better, the odds in their favor, and then I heard a voice say *Joey, come here*, and I was yanked from the buffet and fat Gordo was standing against the building, leaning his weight into the wall and smoking a cigarette and staring at me.

"What are you doing here?" I said. I pushed at the crotch of my jeans and tried to shift the contents into a more comfortable position, and Gordo didn't move from his position of keeping the wall upright.

"Jerry sent me," fat Gordo said, and his eyes were red and running and there was sweat on his forehead and the T-shirt he had been wearing for what I counted as days now was hanging limp from his neck as if to try and escape the smell that seemed to come off of him in squiggly lines like in the cartoons.

"Where's Jerry?" I asked, and I figured he must be close by because lately he didn't travel far without his dirty companion that was crumpled like a dirty suitcase he carried from building to room.

"He's around. Don't worry about it. Hey, you see that guy over there?" He pointed toward a man leaning up against a low car, smoking a cigarette and looking the opposite way down the sidewalk.

"Who?" I said.

"*Who?* What are you, a fucking owl now? That guy. By the Datsun."

He swung his cigarette toward the curb and I turned and saw the guy over by the car, watching the sidewalks, and I nodded and shifted my weight from heel to toe and back again, and waited for Jerry to walk up and give me a look for lagging when I should have been halfway up the block toward the motel by now.

"Go over and talk to him," Gordo said. He tossed the burnt end of his cigarette onto the sidewalk and pulled out his pack and lit another, and his hand was shaking as he flicked the wheel of his lighter, and when he finally sparked it into flame, he coughed on the inhale and I could hear his lungs rattling like empty bottles inside his immense chest.

"I don't think so," I said.

"No, do it. Jerry wants you to."

"Jerry didn't tell me that."

"Yeah, well, he told me to tell you."

"Why?" It wasn't like Jerry to give me a delay in getting back with the money, and if he wasn't here, I didn't trust fat Gordo to be telling me anything that I should put some faith into.

"Just do it. Do what the guy says," Gordo said, and I watched a loaded runner of sweat slide from his forehead to his jawline and he wiped it away, and I wasn't sweating at all. Above us the clouds were banking together in disconnected ways so that the sky looked like skin cells under a microscope.

"I have to go back," I said. "Get back to the room."

"Do this first," fat Gordo said. "Just go spend a little time with that guy."

"No." And I thought about just moving down the sidewalk then and crossing at the corner and walking back to the motel, but it was as if through his own odor, fat Gordo could smell my plan, and he reached out and grabbed my shoulder in one of his ham hands, the one without the cigarette smoldering, and I stepped back and away from his greasy grip so that he had to lurch forward to take ahold of me, and I knew that I ought to beat feet to the pavement and run, but I didn't want to draw attention to myself, and I wasn't afraid of fat Gordo, and part of me wanted to know why it was so important that I went and talked to a shaggy haired guy with a skinny mustache in too-tight jeans who was leaning against a brown and gold metallic 280Z.

"Just take a ride with him okay? That's it. Just take a ride. Go around the block."

"No," I said again, and I could feel the envelope with the money in my underwear, pulling everything down toward the cement, and I wanted it out and I could feel the pistol, sagging into my thigh, and I thought about Amber and whether or not she would still be locked-up in the motel when I got there, and maybe I could dump the money and go to her room, and I could sit with her on the bed, and watch the way that her legs rubbed together as we watched TV, and listen to how she moved like a cricket against the sheets, and I could smell her, clean and chlorined, and my arm ached to brush against her skin, and there was also a part of me that wanted to do more speed and forget about everything and talk about nothing for as long as the burn ran down the back of my throat.

"Look, I'll give you a kick for your time. Here." Fat Gordo dug into his pants pocket and pulled out a twenty and pushed it toward me, but I didn't reach for it.

"That's it?" I said.

"It's a ride around the block. For twenty bucks. Don't be a greedy little fucker. This is free money."

I still didn't reach toward the bill, and he held his hand between us, his fist closed around the green, but I could still see the number sticking out from between his fingers.

"Give me fifty," I said. I could tell that something about him wanted me to do this so badly that it would be a waste for me to just give in and take what he was offering, and it was something that Jerry had taught me—that if someone wants what you got, then you have all of the power—so I just stood there and shoved my hands into my pockets, and I could feel the edges of the money I'd stashed in the envelope poking through each side, and I didn't look down at my feet as I usually did, and I just stared at fat Gordo and waited, and then he ran his hand through his hair and it was damp and limp and matted to his skull in places where it shouldn't have been, and I knew I was just wasting time and messing with him, and I had no intention of taking a ride with a man when I was supposed to be dropping off an envelope of cash in a bible in a room built on pink and blue, like cotton candy pulled from a cart on a carnival midway, and then get some tacos afterward.

"Forty," Gordo said, and he reached into his pocket and pulled out a twenty and he slicked it with the other twenty and he kept his fist closed around the money but I could still see it, and I liked that it was adding up, and I wondered how long I could hold out until he quit, and where the line in the sand was drawn, and I could tell that I was pushing at the grains already, and forty was a lot more than zero, and I wouldn't mind taking a ride, even if it was with a guy I didn't know, and he was skinny and looked harmless, and his car looked fast, and as I shifted my weight back onto my toes, I felt the pistol poke into my lower stomach and I remembered that I was safe as kittens.

"Okay," I said. "Fifty."

"Fuck you," Gordo said, but he dug back into his pocket and peeled off a ten, and I held out my hand but fat Gordo darted his eyes up and down the sidewalk and flared his nostrils like he was about to bolt from a stall, and he said, "Don't be so obvious. Give me a hug and I'll put the money in your back pocket," and that was almost the breaking point for me because there was no way that I wanted any part of my body pressed against his, but I relented and said okay, and then I leaned forward a little bit and held my arms out and he stepped toward me, and I thought he might do something creepy, like touch my ass or try to grope me, but he was quick about it, all business, and he was in and out of my pocket before I'd even put my hands against his back, and for a second I was engulfed by him, but only for a second, but long enough to smell all the ways that he looked—greasy and wet and panicked and unwashed—and then he stepped away from me and took another drag off what was left of his cigarette, and then he shooed me away and I walked toward the guy and the car that was parked at the curb.

The guy watched me walk toward him, and he stood up from where he had been leaning against the fender, and he smiled, and his teeth were even and white, and his thin mustache pulled back from his lip and I couldn't tell how old he was, but when he said, "Hi, I'm Brad," his voice wasn't what I expected, and he was wearing a gold bracelet on his left wrist and a ring on his right pinkie that flashed in the dimming sunlight as he reached out to shake my hand, and I took his hand and it was soft and warm, and I could feel the bones in it when I shook it, the way they shifted and moved and rubbed together like sticks, and I thought of a bird's foot and I wasn't afraid of him at all.

"What's your name?" he asked.

"I'm Joey," I said. I looked at him for a second. "Is Brad your real name?"

He smiled and ran a hand through his hair while looking at his reflection on the roof of the car. "I'm Kentucky Mike," he said.

"That sounds like a fake name. Brad sounds real."

"That's the problem with the world, I guess. Everything is backwards. Is Joey your real name?"

"Maybe," I said.

He laughed. "Well I'm gonna call you Vig."

"What the fuck does that mean? Big?"

"Vig."

"Why Vig?"

"You'll have to ask that degenerate bastard over there," and he nodded his head toward fat Gordo who was still holding up the wall. "So you wanna take a ride around the block, Vig?" he asked, and I nodded and said I guess, and he walked with me to the passenger side of the car, and I thought he was going to unlock the door, but instead he opened it for me, and waited while I sat down, and the car was spotless, clean and new and fresh, and it smelled of soap and pine, and then he walked around the hood and got in his seat, and the engine gunned to life, and I could feel it vibrating behind the glovebox, and the dials on the dash lit up and he had a cassette deck, and it hummed a dark blue, and I could feel the music when it started, as though the passenger seat was sitting on a speaker, and the car was warm and the seat was leather, and it wrapped around me in a way that felt like I was being hugged by someone I liked very much and missed after a long absence that I couldn't remember taking.

"You like music?" Kentucky Mike said, and I nodded and he turned the knob on the stereo, and the Cars came on, and I knew all about how much the singer wanted his best friend's girl, and then Brad pulled into the thin traffic on the Strip and drove with one hand, with the gold bracelet hanging loose from his wrist and bouncing against the wheel, and we were so low to the ground that it felt as if I was sliding across the pavement, and then he mashed the gas pedal and shifted into second gear, and then third, and the back wheels spit street, and he gunned us through a yellow light and then he signaled and moved over a lane, and when the entrance to the freeway came up, he took the onramp, and I saw the blocks we were supposed to be circling fade out in the side mirror where objects were supposed to be bigger than they appeared.

"You don't mind if we go someplace quieter?" Kentucky Mike asked, and I didn't know what he meant by that, but I was listening to the Cars and glad that I wasn't walking, and I looked out the window at the buildings that thinned and then faded, and we crossed into empty desert and there were lights on in the distance, and the sun was sinking behind the slope of hills, and there was scrub grass, and a few houses with swaths of bright green lawns that stood out like a rash in the sand, and then Kentucky Mike turned on the headlights, and I wondered if this was how I would leave Reno, in a brown metallic 280Z, with an extra fifty bucks in my pocket, and then I remembered the envelope in my underwear and the pistol beside it, and I wondered if I would have to shoot Kentucky Mike, and if it came down to it, I figured I could if I had to, but I knew that was easy to think when there was wind in my hair and music thumping underneath me, and I looked out of the corner of my eye at his silhouette as he drove, and he wasn't bad looking, and he had a half-smile on his face, as though he was about to reveal a great surprise that he had spent a long time planning, and then he moved over into the slow lane and signaled right off of the freeway, and at the top

145

of the incline he took a right at the stop sign, and there was more sand and scrub plants and weeds choking from the lack of soft dirt, and then there was nothing, and he drove and made another right and then a left, and there was emptiness around us, and I thought about movies and how you know everything is going to go bad once there is nothing to buffer the people in the scene—no houses or cars or buildings or people—and I stared out the window at the waning light that had turned the horizon pink and then purple, and then Kentucky Mike pulled the car over onto the shoulder and he cut the engine so that the only sound was the stereo playing, and the Cars had given up on the girlfriend and were telling me that they didn't want to hold her down, didn't want to break her crown.

Kentucky Mike shifted in his seat and I could hear the leather creak and give, and then he was turned toward me and I tried to smile because I didn't know what else to do, and I realized that it would be a long way to walk to get back to where I was supposed to be, and even farther if I had to run.

"Don't be afraid," Kentucky Mike said, and again I thought of movies and how that's what the person most likely to kill someone always said. "I just thought we could spend a little time watching the sunset."

I looked out the windshield but the sun was behind us and I had to crane my neck to look through the tiny back window in order to watch it begin its greasy slide behind the hills and turn off the light so that night could crash down like a curtain with a broken string, but out of the windshield I could already see stars flung above us and I was amazed at how bright they were now that we were far away from the neon and the flash and the buildings blocking out the sky.

"Okay," I said.

The thing about being a kid and being alone with someone who can hurt you is that you are afraid but not afraid, because deep down you feel like you can trust him because that's what you have been brought up to believe ever since you could climb your way out of a crib—that you have to trust adults—and I guess in a way it's part of our survival instinct, that trust, and even when it gets broken over and over again, you forget it each time, you bury it, and you go back into the same situation again as if nothing bad is going to happen, and even if it does, you'll just bury it again and your first instinct will always be that adults aren't going to hurt you—you need them to survive—and I guess that's how some of them get the chance to kill you.

Kentucky Mike reached into the pocket of the driver's door and pulled out a little vial, and he opened it and then he pulled a handkerchief from his pocket and I knew that he was going to drug me then, with whatever it was that they used to knock you out, and he would probably rape me before he gutted me and left me torn inside-out in the scrub so that I could watch the stars as the last of my blood pulsed weakly into the sand.

"You like poppers?" Kentucky Mike asked.

I didn't know what he was talking about, and at first I thought he meant Pop Rocks, which in fact I did like, but they didn't come in a bottle, and I was thinking maybe the next thing he'd pull out of the door pocket was a packet, and I hoped it was the cherry kind because they were the best.

"I don't know," I said.

"You're gonna love it," he said, and he tipped the bottle into his handkerchief and he breathed it in fast, in a quick gulp like his lungs were aching for air, and he held his breath, and then his eyes rolled back a little bit and I thought that I could see his heart pounding through his chest and then he exhaled and his pupils were as big as plates, and he leaned back in his seat—pushed himself into the leather—and then he gripped the steering wheel and I saw his knuckles turn white and then he looked at me and said, "Fuck," and he passed me the bottle and the handkerchief and I held it up to my nose and I could smell something sharp, but not quite antiseptic and not like medicine, and then Brad said, "no like this," and he tipped the bottle into the cotton and then he held it toward me and he told me to inhale, hard, and I did, and it was like someone had shot me in the lungs with a twelve-gauge and the pellets sprayed into my chest and each one was soaked in adrenaline and I wanted to take a breath but I had gone numb in the lungs and everything was frozen and I could hear my heart in my head and I could feel the blood in my veins and my skin felt like it was swelling—like I might split and explode—and just when I thought that I would never breathe again, that I couldn't ever open my mouth and pull in the air, I did, suddenly, in one long gasp, and it was the best feeling I had ever had—the loss and the breath and the feeling that in one more second I would be dead—and everything inside of me tingled, as if it had been deprived of circulation and had been strangled on need and then given it all back again, and my head had turned to white noise, and then there was a rush, and it all happened in two lines of music, and then it was over and gone.

"It's good, huh?" Kentucky Mike said.

I couldn't talk yet because my tongue had lost coordination so I nodded and looked at him.

"You know what's better?"

I shook my head.

"Hit that just when you come. It's the best you will ever feel. I promise you."

I just looked at him.

He started rubbing at the front of his jeans, and then he unzipped them and dipped his hand inside, and his hand was moving up and down, and I just watched him as I remembered how to breathe again.

"Do it with me," Kentucky Mike said, and he reached out with his right hand and took my left and moved it toward my lap and pushed it against what wasn't there. "I want to watch you," he said, but I didn't unzip my jeans, and I just kept up the show of pretending to rub where something more should have been, but it was just the lump in the fabric where the pistol and the money bunched in a knot, and I watched him as he leaned his head back against the seat, and the Cars kept saying how tough it was to get up, so tough to live up, and Kentucky Mike was breathing through his teeth in a quiet whistle, and I closed my eyes because even though I wasn't really touching myself, everything inside of me had gone electric, and then Kentucky Mike's hand moved over to my lap, past my own pretending, and I could feel him squeezing at me, and his right hand slid over the front of my jeans and his other hand was still moving in his lap, and then he found the pistol in my pants, but he didn't seem to notice what it was that he was really touching, and he was rubbing it with his hand, moving up and over it, squeezing and releasing, and I opened my eyes and out of the windshield the purple had dissolved and the pink had flamed out and the sky had gone darker and there were a million stars above us, straining against the confines of their orbit, and Kentucky Mike's feet shifted on the floorboards and Side One of the cassette came to a close and there was the lag of silence as the last of the tape spun from one reel and filled up the other, and then the click and whir of Side Two, and he started to pant a little bit, and I could feel the friction turning into heat against my thigh and I thought that if his hand moved any faster he was going to make my jeans burst into flames, and then his eyelids fluttered a little bit, and I saw Orion above us, with his belt lined up against the horizon and his shoulders arched so that he could pull back on his bow.

"You're so fucking hard," Kentucky Mike whispered.

And out of the windshield the sky was crushed velvet and everything shimmered like glitter dumped into a water glass, and I was a lightning rod pointed toward the clouds that bulked and divided and scraped by in the scattered catch of short-breathed wind, and my body went tight until I was live as a wire, and I waited for the electricity to hit.

Chapter 17
The Comic In the Bubblegum

The "Do Not Disturb" sign was still on Amber's room and the curtains were pulled, and I stood in front of the door and thought about knocking before I actually did, but I hadn't seen any of them since the night we had stayed up until the sun came through the windows and blinded us to the day and I had walked back out to the parking lot with my jaw tight and my head full of buzzing and feeling like my spine had been picked up and gripped and twisted into a new shape that didn't seem to fit right into my body, and I had gone back to my room and Jerry's bed was still made, and I had stuffed the money into the bible and laid down and tried to sleep but every time that I started to drift, I couldn't break through the surface, and I was bored and lonely and it was dark out now, and Kentucky Mike had dropped me off at the corner and sped away in his metallic car, and I needed something more than company.

I put my fist to the door and tapped it, and I didn't hear anyone move inside, and then I did it again, with more pressure this time, and I thought I heard someone, and then the curtains parted a little bit and I thought I saw a pair of eyes that were nothing but whites, and I heard the lock on the door pull back and then Hurley opened it enough to put his face to the gap, and he said, "yeah?" and I didn't know what to say back so I just cleared my throat, and said, "it's me—I was wondering what you guys were doing," and he looked over his shoulder, and then the door shut and I heard the latch pull free, and he opened the door all of the way and grabbed me by the shirt and pulled me inside.

The room smelled bad—like sweat and men, and Amber was stretched out on the floor with a bottle of nail polish and she was painting her toes, and Reece was on the bed with his shirt off and there was a movie on the TV but the sound was too low to hear the words.

"Where you been?" Amber said and she looked up at me, and her eyes were big and there were dark circles around them, and I pulled out a chair and sat down at the little table, and I could see a pile of powder and Hurley's driver's license with the edge dug in, and Hurley was still leaning over me, looking through the curtains and I could smell him above me and I wanted to pull away but there was no place left to go.

"Just doing the same stuff," I said.

"Yeah, like how much do you think? Like how much do you think Jerry has?" Amber put the brush back into the bottle and twisted it closed and the room smelled like polish and it was better than when I had walked in.

"You guys have been in here a long time," I said.

"No, we go out. We go out at night, right, Hurley?" and Hurley dropped the curtain and walked back over to the bed and laid down next to Reece.

"Always stuff to do at night," he said, and Amber got off the floor and went over and kissed him and then she pulled out the chair opposite from me and took a seat.

"So me and Hurley and Reece have been talking," Amber said. "We know how to make it all work."

"Make what work?" I said.

"Our plan, dummy," and she reached out to tap my arm but she saw the pile of powder and pulled back and said, "hey, you want some?" and I thought about saying no but I already felt like I was playing at two chords lower than the rest of them and I wanted to move to a higher string.

"Okay," I said, and Amber did what Hurley had done, cutting out the lines, and then she handed me a Bic pen that had been gutted and was no more than a hollow tube, and I put it to my nose and inhaled hard, and it hit the back of my throat and I felt the gag come up again, but I swallowed it down and there was a burn and the taste that was worse than chewing on a Tylenol, and I wished that I had something to drink but didn't feel like asking, and then Amber cut out a line for herself and she hit it, too, and we both sat there squeezing our noses and rubbing at our faces, and I could feel my heart pounding through my shirts and I had to concentrate to take another breath because it felt like everything had frozen in my lungs.

"So our plan, we have it all figured out," Amber said. "We think we should just kill Jerry, you know, and take what he has and take the money and everything and then we head out of town and we're on our way."

I looked over at her and the dark circles had gone bright. "That's probably not a good idea," I said.

"Yeah? Why not?" Hurley said from the bed. "Jerry ain't shit."

"He's got a gun," I said. "I told you that."

"So we'll get a gun. A bigger gun," Hurley said.

When I told them everything the night we had stayed high and talked until dawn, I had told them most of it, but not really everything, and I didn't tell them that I was a girl in boy's clothes, and I didn't tell them my real name, and I almost had but at the last minute something had cleared in my head and I had skipped over that part, and I was glad about that now even though they hadn't been listening to me at all.

"You can't kill Jerry," I said. "It's just gonna make it all more complicated," I said.

"Complicated?" Amber said. "What's complicated?"

"The whole thing," I said.

"You're just scared," Amber said, and Hurley laughed from the bed, and Reece looked over at me but his eyes were in the dark and I couldn't read them.

"I'm not scared," I said. "I'm just not stupid."

"What's that supposed to mean?" Hurley said.

Amber picked up a little, brown paper bag from the floor and dug into it and pulled out a handful of Bazooka Joe gum, and she tossed me over a piece and I unwrapped it and licked the powdery sugar from my fingers and peeled the comic loose and put the wrappers on the table and put the gum into my mouth, and it was hard as a rock and my mouth had gone dry and it took me a little while to work it warm and soft, but then it let go and I started chewing it and it was tight against my teeth, but it made my spit taste better for a little while.

"I think we should buy in," Amber said. I hadn't really been thinking about the plan—I had just skipped ahead to being in Portland, and the part about how we got there and had the money to live was just a detail I hadn't quite worked over yet but I could tell that they had, and it wasn't going to work the way that they thought that it would.

"What do you mean 'buy in,'" Hurley said.

"I mean we pay for our own share and then sell it," Amber said.

Amber looked over at Hurley. "Yeah, but like how much is that?" he asked.

"Well," I said, "it's three hundred bucks an envelope."

"That's an eight ball," Hurley said.

"A what?"

"An eight ball. Eight eighths, you know?"

I didn't, but I nodded my head anyway.

"So we figure out how many we can afford," Amber said.

Hurley raised his hand. "No, fuck that. We're not paying retail for wholesale."

"Yeah," Reece said. "Not retail for wholesale."

"What do you mean?" I asked.

Hurley sat up on the bed and faced us in the chairs. "Look, Jerry gets his piece and he sells it for $300 an eight ball, and an eight ball is an ounce, and there's what? Sixteen ounces in a pound? So that's sixteen times three hundred bucks, which is what?"

"A lot of money," Amber said.

"Yeah—exactly," and he snapped his fingers and pointed at Amber. "It's a lot of money," Hurley said.

"It's $4,800," Reece said, and Hurley turned to look at him.

"Okay Mr. Math Teacher," Amber said.

"I knew that," Hurley said.

"So, $4,800 is what he's getting from a pound, selling it for ounces," Hurley said. "So that's all profit."

"Yeah, a lot of profit," Amber said.

"But there's no way it costs $4,800 for that. We ain't gonna pay the sales price," Hurley said. "We're gonna pay the buying price."

"What's the buying price?" I said.

"Look, let me explain it, okay?" Hurley said. "You know that place, Price Club? You ever been to one of those?"

There was one in Chico and my mom and her boyfriend Chris had taken us to it a couple of times and we had spent a lot of money and stocked up on a lot of things that we hadn't really needed, and they had a book area there where I bought a *Truly Tasteless* joke book that had a blank page inside that was called "Jokes For the Blind," and it had made me laugh when I saw it.

"Yeah, I know what you're talking about," I said.

"So, you don't go there and pay regular store prices, right? I mean, they don't sell regular store stuff. They sell big packs of stuff, right?"

I nodded and could remember the bag of chips that we'd bought that had twenty-four little bags inside.

"It's all cheaper because you're buying more," Hurley said. "It's wholesale. And that's what we are gonna pay for our own pound. We don't want an ounce. We want the whole thing," Hurley said, and then he looked at us to see if we understood, and I could see what he was saying but I didn't imagine that Jerry or the guys in Susanville would see it the same way.

"So we go to Jerry and we offer him a wholesale price," Hurley said.

"Like what?" I asked.

"That's what we have to figure out," Hurley said. "How much do we have?"

Amber started biting at her fingernails, and I picked up my gum wrappers from the table and started shredding them into small pieces, and I almost tore into the comic but instead I unfolded it and looked at what it was, and Bazooka Joe was talking to Mort, who had his red sweater over his mouth, and Mort was telling Joe about how his mom wanted to sew three socks for his brother who was in the Army, and when Joe asked why three, Mort told him it was because his brother had written a letter and told them that he had already grown a foot, and it was stupid and I almost tore it in half, but then I saw the ad for the telescope, and it said for two-hundred comics or forty cents, you could get a close-up view of distant planes or buildings, and it opened to seven inches, and I wondered if it really worked, and I shoved the comic into my pocket and Hurley got up and stretched and came over to the table and cut himself a line from the shrinking pile of white, and when he was done, Amber looked at me and said, "You didn't answer my question—how much can you put in?" and I thought about my sock in my backpack and how the money was shoved to the bottom and rolled up tight, and I had counted it every day since I had left home and there was almost $700 inside.

"I've got a little bit," I said.

"Okay, so we all put in and we figure out how much we can come up with," Amber said.

"I have my winnings from the weekend," Hurley said, "and Reece has some, too, and Reece is gonna pawn his belt buckle, right?" He looked over at Reece and Reece reached down and tipped the shiny gold and silver and green jade plate toward him.

"Maybe," he said.

"No fucking maybe," Hurley said. "You have to come up with your end."

"What about Amber?" I said.

"What about me?"

"You have any money?"

154

She laughed. "You don't know shit about me," she said.

"So how much do you think we have if we put it all together?" I asked.

Hurley looked at each of us in turn and he was moving his lips as if he was adding up some numbers. "A few thousand," he said. "Maybe more." He looked over at Reece. "Maybe less."

"I don't know," I said. "I don't know about this."

"You don't know about what?" Hurley said. "You seem to be forgetting a very important thing."

"What?"

"Money talks," Hurley said.

"And what do we do if none of this works," I said. "If Jerry won't go along with any of this?"

"Then we kill him," Hurley said, and he lifted his hand from his lap and pointed his index finger toward the room and curled the rest of his fingers into his palm and he sighted down the line. "Right, Reece?"

Reece dug into his front pocket and pulled out a buck knife and opened the blade and raised his hand and slammed the point into the wall until it disappeared up to the hilt, and it hung there, buried into the plaster.

"Here piggy piggy," Hurley said, and Amber laughed, and I spit my gum into my hand because I didn't have any spit left and it hurt my jaw to keep chewing.

Chapter 18
The Buckle

I had pulled my share of the money out of my sock, and I had brought most of it to Hurley and Amber and Reece, but I kept a little back for myself—but not much—and they stayed closed up in the room, but sometimes I saw that Hurley's truck was gone from the lot, and I knew they were pooling what they had together, and on the second day after Amber presented the plan, I hung out with them for a little while and they were sitting in lawn chairs in front of the open door and the sun was just settling on the hills and there was neon in the sky, and Hurley said they had everything together, and it was time to make a deal, and Amber was wound tight and ready to spring so I left the room and decided to go back and talk to Jerry and told Amber and Hurley and Reece to stay gone for a while until I had a chance to test the waters and see what the temperature was, and I was heading up the stairs when I heard a door swing open on the walkway and I thought it might be Jerry, but really I knew it wouldn't be, and I could hear the noise from TVs and people talking and then I heard two voices that were louder than the rest and I jogged into the hallway and ducked next to the soda machine and stood still and made myself small before I even knew why I was doing it, and I peered around the edge of it so that I could still see who might walk past, and then I could hear them, heavy-footed and leather creaking, and I pulled myself into the shadows against the wall and waited.

"We shouldn't have let that motherfucker come out here again," I could hear one say, and then the voice had a body, and it was a big man with a beard and long hair, and he was wearing a vest, like the one that Lalo had been wearing in Susanville, and then Lalo himself walked by, and they had sunglasses pushed up on their heads, and I could hear chains swinging against their hips, and the one who wasn't Lalo was wiping his hands on a white towel that looked like it belonged to a room, and even though it was dark, I could tell that what he was smearing against the white wasn't chocolate, and he was wiping blood off of his hands, and next to me the soda machine hummed and cycled, and I listened to them and I could hear their feet stop on the walkway, and then I heard Lalo say, "hey, twenty-four hours and then it won't matter anymore," and the other one said, "we should have just finished it all right now," and then Lalo said, "yeah, you're probably right," and the other one said, "it ain't too late to go back and just cut the son of a bitch loose. I got my knife," and Lalo laughed and said, "give him the time to make it right, man. I ain't in the mood to get blood all over and fuck up my boots."

They stood in the walkway and I could hear their voices drop, and I wished the soda machine would kick itself quiet so I could listen better, and I leaned forward a little bit so that I could get a look, and they were standing with their backs to the hall, facing the parking lot, and the big one was still rubbing at his hands. "He ain't gonna make it up," he said.

Lalo shoved his hands in his front pocket. "I figure," he said. "But I know Jerry. He'll get something together. I told him, man. I told him not to piss on this."

"He didn't piss on this. He shit the fucking bed."

"We can sell his car tomorrow. That's worth something."

"Nah, I wanna keep it for Wendy and the kids. Might as well."

They turned around, and I pressed myself back into the dark again. "Hey, you want a root beer, man?" Lalo said. I could hear their footsteps enter the hall and move toward the machine, and something heavy hit the trash can, and I could feel the stucco pressing through my shirts and digging into my back.

"A fucking root beer?"

"Been forever since I had one, man." I heard him digging in his pockets. "You got any change?"

"I ain't got shit. That son of a bitch has all my money." He laughed and the sound bounced off the walls. "Last time."

"Hey, Frank has a guy he says is solid," Lalo said. He was still going through his pockets and I could hear snaps popping and keys shifting and I waited.

"I don't wanna bring Fresno into this," the big one said. "Get stuck running on the I-5 and this is a hell of a lot more consistent."

"Was consistent," Lalo said. "Not no more."

"You're the one who brought in Jerry. This is your fucking mess."

"And I'm handling it. It's getting handled." He exhaled hard and I thought I could smell his breath from where I was hiding. "Something told me it wasn't right out here, man. Could have been worse."

"Fuck that root beer. I want to get back and finish that cook tonight. We're gonna be in the fucking weeds on this one, thanks to that son of a bitch."

I heard them shift around and one of them knocked into the soda machine and it rocked a little bit, and then I could hear them walking away and they hit the stairs and I could hear their footsteps thundering on the cement, and I stayed where I was, and the soda machine was warm, and it felt good to press against it, and I could feel something in my knees that made my legs feel achy and I knew that I didn't want to go back to our room, but I didn't have a choice, and if nothing else, I at least knew that Jerry wasn't dead.

I waited until I heard the sputter of motorcycle engines kicking to life and then the roar as they sucked down fuel and air and their sound echoed off the buildings, and I waited for them to push the bikes around until they pointed back toward the entrance, and then I waited for them to cruise back to the street, and I was surprised that I hadn't heard them come in but I had been so caught up in plans and schemes and the future and dreams that I probably wouldn't have heard the motel office explode if someone had filled it full of Molotov cocktails and I was sorry that I didn't keep a better watch, and if they had been looking for me, I would have never seen them coming, and when I heard their motorcycles turn onto the street and gun and stutter exhaust into the fast-approaching night, I pulled myself loose from the soda machine and walked down to our room, and the door was closed but not all the way, and all I had to do was push on it and it swung wide, and it was as if a tornado had touched down on the second floor of The Slipper and everything in the room had been tossed and pulled loose and piled and kicked and stripped, and even the vent on the wall had been yanked from the screws, and I could see my backpack lying near my bed, turned inside-out and gutted, and I was glad that there wasn't anything left to take, and Jerry was standing in the bathroom, spitting in the sink, and he picked up a towel and put it to his face and his nose was bleeding, and there was a long cut above his eye, and his shirt had been ripped at the buttons, and everything looked bad and wrong and as if it might never get put right again.

Jerry saw me walk in and he moved slowly toward his bed with the towel wadded up and pressed against his face and he sat down and lit a cigarette, and when he pulled the towel back, it was full of blood, but whatever had been bleeding was starting to trickle out and dry, and I just stood in the doorway as if my feet wouldn't move, and I wanted to say something to him but all the spit had been sucked out of my mouth and I couldn't force my tongue to move any more than I could force my feet, and I just stood there looking at the mess and the blood and the way that the shade on the lamp on the nightstand was bent sideways, and then Jerry looked over at me and gave me a smile, and he took another drag off of his cigarette and I licked my lips, and I said, "Jesus, Jerry, what happened?" and it felt stupid to ask the question but I didn't know what else to say.

"You wanna get me some ice?" Jerry said, and I moved into the room and waded through the clothes and the sheets and the beds that had been tossed, and the chairs were knocked over and the TV was on the floor, and there was static on the screen, and I kicked at things and made it to the bathroom and found the ice bucket that was on the counter top, and I picked it up and went back down the hall and I stood scooping ice until my fingers went numb, and when the bucket was full, I went back to the room and I handed it to Jerry, and he took the bloody towel and put a handful of ice in it and pressed it against his nose, and I went into the bathroom and tried to find him a clean towel, but the racks had been cleared, and I did the next best thing and got a T-shirt off the floor, and I took my own handful of ice and filled it up and folded it thick and then I passed it over to Jerry and he put it against his mouth for a second, and then he wiped at his face and said, "thanks, kid," and I went over to my bed and sat down and the mattress was bare and stained and naked under the light, and I rubbed my hands together and tried to think of something to say but I had never seen anyone get beat up before in the way that Jerry had, and I was scared, but not in a fear way, but more like a powerless way where there was nothing that I could do and it had already happened—was still happening—and I felt frozen on the inside and I couldn't have run even though I wanted to.

"Looks pretty bad, huh?" Jerry said. He moved the T-shirt so he could smoke, and he wiped at his face again, and the blood moved around and dissolved, and he looked bad, but not as bad as I thought, and once his nose stopped bleeding, my heart stopped pounding and I could breathe a little bit then.

"It's bad," I said. "What happened?"

Jerry coughed and cleared his throat and then coughed again, and he got up and spit in the sink and I didn't watch him, and then I heard the tap turn on and the water run, and when he came out again, his face was washed, and he looked swollen and red, and the cut above his eye didn't look very good, but everything had stopped bleeding and was pulling back in on itself, and he took his comb out of his back pocket and slicked his hair back, and even though his first cigarette was still smoldering in the ashtray on the nightstand, he lit another one, and I thought his hands might be shaking but they weren't.

"Just part of the job," Jerry said.

"Was that Lalo?" I asked. "I saw him walk by."

Jerry looked up at me and I could see his eye twitch and he put the T-shirt with ice to his face. "He didn't see you, did he?" Jerry said.

"Nah, he didn't see me," I said. "Who was that other guy?"

"That was Chuck," Jerry said.

I knew better than to keep asking questions, and instead I just looked down at the mess of the room and I thought about getting up and putting things right again, but my knees still felt loose, and I wished I could just pull the covers back onto my bed and curl up and go to sleep, and I probably would have if I hadn't been up for a day and a night and a day, and sleep seemed like something that was meant for other people.

"I heard them say something about twenty-four hours," I said, and I didn't mean to keep talking, but it was like I couldn't stop, and I kicked at a pair of jeans that were under my feet, and then I finally got my knees to go tight and I stood up and picked up the chairs and set them upright against the table, and I picked up the TV and put it back on the little stand against the wall, and the snow was sputtering and there was the hum of static down low inside of it, and I wished that I could find the remote and put on something that held together and made sense.

"Just a misunderstanding, is all," Jerry said. "Nothing to worry about." He got up again and dumped the ice from the T-shirt into the sink and then he went back to his bed and filled it again from the bucket, and his face was starting to settle down and arrange itself into the picture that I was familiar with.

"They looked mad," I said.

"They're always mad," Jerry laughed. "Just the way it is."

"But what did they mean by twenty-four hours?" I asked, and I could hear my voice getting that tight whine that I hated and couldn't help, and

I knew that it would be better if I just kept picking things up from the floor and putting them right again, and I started wadding my clothes back into the backpack, and then I pulled the sheets off the floor and started putting them back onto my bed, and I was relieved to cover up the stains and the yellow and the brown that made inkblot patterns on the ticking, and when the bottom sheet was tight, I shook out the flat sheet, and I let it hold the air and float before it sunk down to join the other one, and then I did the same with the blanket, and I stuffed the pillows back into their cases, and I picked up the comforter and folded it at the end of my bed, and I kicked the trash back toward the can and I pushed all the drawers shut again, and with every item I set right, it helped to make the room feel less wrong, and I was trying to put the vent back onto the wall when there was a knock at the door and Jerry crouched down and said, "give me your gun," and I stood in the doorway of the bathroom and looked at him, and he was waving his arm toward me as he stayed low and walked toward the window so he could pull back the curtain and look out at the hall, and I dug into the front of my jeans and pulled out the pistol and he clapped his hands together and I tossed it to him and I could hear him click the safety and then he had it up and pointed at the door, and in the sharp light of the bent lampshade, I could see the doorknob twisting and Jerry put his finger over his lips in the universal sign to shush, and then he motioned at me to get down, too, and I did, and we were both near the carpet, and I could smell it then, full of spills and dirt and a million pairs of shoes that had dragged themselves across the shag, and then the knob turned all the way over and the door pushed in and I heard Jerry rack the slide that send the first bullet into the chamber and I waited for the sound of the trigger pull and to feel the kick.

Amber walked in barefoot, and I could hear Hurley and Reece in the hallway, shuffling behind her, pushing at each other and screwing around, and Amber swung the door wide so that everything in the room was exposed to the hallway, and I could feel the outside light knock in and there were bugs beating themselves against the bulbs and the sound of the street echoed off the wall and Jerry had the gun raised and his arm straight and Amber was lined up with the barrel and she didn't even flinch.

"Jesus, Jerry, don't freak the fuck out," she said.

Jerry rolled back on his heels and stood up and he shoved the gun into the back of his pants and he reached out and grabbed the edge of the bed and pulled himself over, and he sat down and I could see his bare mattress sink in where he sat and Amber took one of the chairs from the table and sat down and I could see her taking in the room, and I was glad she hadn't seen everything, but by the look on her face, I could tell that she had seen enough.

"What the fuck happened?" she asked. "You redecorating or something?" and she laughed and Hurley and Reece stood behind her in the doorway, and I could tell that they were debating about coming in or not, and I was glad that whatever silent votes they had cast had been decided in favor of not walking in and they were keeping to the hall.

"I haven't got time for you right now," Jerry said, and he waved her away with his arm and went back to putting the ice to his face, and I was leaning against the wall near the bathroom and I wished there was a way that I could send Amber some telepathy so she would just get up and go because what she had come here to do wasn't meant for this time or this place.

"So did Joey tell you?" Amber said.

"Tell me what?" Jerry said, and he put his feet up on the mattress and leaned back against the headboard, and I wanted to get his pillows for him and put them back into their cases, but I felt like the only thing holding up the room was my back to the wall so I stayed where I was and stared down at my feet.

"It's nothing," I said. "It's nothing," and I raised my eyes and shot Amber a look.

"No, it is," Amber said. "It's a lot more than nothing."

"Just go," Jerry said. "Go on back to your little cave and call it a night."

I could hear Hurley and Reece on the walkway and their feet were moving as if they were horses pacing and digging in at the chute, and I knew it was just a matter of time before the gates in their heads swung open and they came storming in like it was an arena.

"Don't," I said to Amber.

She raised her hand to me and I knew that there was nothing I could do unless I walked over and pushed her out the door.

"We want a brick," Amber said.

"You want a what?" Jerry said.

"You know what I mean. A brick. A pound. Or whatever it is. We want one."

"Oh, you want one? I don't know what you're talking about." Jerry looked at me then, and I could see his jaw tightening.

"Look, Jerry, we don't have to pretend, okay? Joey told us everything, so we're not stupid."

Jerry didn't take his eyes off of me.

"Who's *we*?" he said.

"Me. And my boyfriend Hurley. And Reece, his brother," and it was as if by hearing their names they suddenly broke from their freeze on the walkway, and they both walked into the room, and I saw Jerry raise up on his hip a little bit so that he could reach around behind him and pull my gun from his pants.

"It's all cool, Jerry," Amber said. "I mean, it's not like I didn't know."

Jerry stayed with his right arm behind his back, and Hurley and Reece crowded in front of the door, and now that they were inside, they didn't know what to do with themselves, and neither of them were wearing shoes, either, and Hurley's lip was tight with chew, and Reece was in an undershirt that had a hole in the middle of the chest, and Jerry sat up straighter in the bed but he didn't bring his arm around to his lap again.

"Shut the door," Jerry said.

Hurley and Reece squeezed together so that they could step all of the way into the room, and Reece turned and pulled the door, and the bugs and the light cut out and there was no more sound from the street, and I could still hear the TV buzzing down low.

"We have money, Jerry," Amber said. "Don't we Hurley?"

Hurley nodded and reached into his front pocket.

"Not yet, baby," Amber said. And Hurley looked embarrassed and he jerked his hand and pretended to be wiping something off the front of his jeans.

"Get the fuck out of the room," Jerry said. "I'm too tired for this bullshit and I'm not in the mood at all."

Hurley cleared his throat. "We want an end," Hurley said. "We want our own piece."

Jerry laughed but his face was still swollen and it looked as if his smile hurt. "I don't know what you're talking about," he said.

"Jesus, Jerry, stop fucking around. We're going into business for ourselves," Amber said.

"Yeah, we just need quantity," Hurley said, and it was as if the more that Amber talked, the more that he found his voice, and he had squared his shoulders and was facing the bed, and I could see a vein standing out in his neck.

"Yeah? What do you want with quantity?" Jerry asked. "I'm not supplying to a bunch of dropouts."

Amber made a face. "I'm not a dropout Jerry. I'm taking my GED this fall."

"Good for you," Jerry said. He lit another cigarette and the room was already hazy despite the door having been opened, and I wanted to fix the lampshade because the bent light was driving me crazy.

"We want to sell it," Amber said.

"Yeah," Hurley said. "See, I've got a bunch of people who would take this right off our hands."

"Hurley's in the rodeo," Amber said. "He knows everybody."

"Lots of people do speed," Hurley said. "Especially when it comes time to move to another town. Everybody has to drive at night and shit, and most of us are pretty busted up, and everybody's looking for something to ... "

Amber raised her hand toward Hurley. "What he's trying to say is that there's a market for it and we want to do our own business. That's all."

Jerry laughed and then he picked up the T-shirt that was dripping melted ice, and he wiped off his lip. "So you think I'm going to just get you started in your, what? Business?"

"We said we'll pay, Jerry. We ain't asking for it for free."

"Honey, I don't think you have that kind of money," Jerry said.

"We have over three grand, Jerry. Almost $3500, to be exact. I'd say that's enough." Amber got up and walked over to the nightstand, and I watched her bare feet sink into the carpeting, and the light caught her tan so that her skin lit up golden like her hair, and she took Jerry's pack of cigarettes and shook one loose and she held out her hand for Jerry's lighter, and I thought maybe he might grab her and pull her to the bed and beat her with the gun, and I was kind of waiting for it, and even the hair on the back of my neck was standing up straight then, and I could already see it happening, and then Jerry reached into his front pocket and took out his lighter and handed it over to Amber and she flicked it over and pulled the cigarette to life.

"How'd you get that kind of money?" Jerry said.

"How'd you get your money, Jerry?" Amber said.

Jerry laughed and looked over at me. "You a part of this?" he asked.

I wanted to sink down until I was so small that I could fit under the bed, but I looked over at Hurley and Reece and they were both staring at me, and Amber blew a long drag toward the ceiling and the smoke banked and clung to the walls, and I said, "yeah, I guess I am," and I went back to looking at the fibers in the carpet underneath my shoes, and Jerry laughed.

"So you want to give me what? Three grand, and you are all gonna be rodeo dope slingers, huh? Wild fucking west."

"We're just gonna make money," Amber said. "It's a free country."

"You don't know the first thing about anything," Jerry said. "You wouldn't know how to hit dirt even if I gave you the shovels." He laughed again. "You got the money, though?"

"We've got it," Hurley said.

"All of it?"

"All of it."

"Show it to me," Jerry said.

Hurley looked at Amber and she nodded to him, and he dug into his front pocket and pulled out a roll of bills he had rubber-banded together and he tossed it forward onto the naked mattress and Jerry picked it up and pulled it loose and he thumbed through it, and I counted with him, and when he was finished, he rolled it all tight and fastened it back again and tossed it back to Hurley.

Jerry went quiet for a minute, and I could hear my heart beating and I felt light inside, like I had been filled up with helium and I was only tethered by the weight of my shoes, and I could feel sweat starting to bead up on my upper lip like it did when I was nervous.

"Then we've got to take a ride," Jerry said. "I don't have that kind of weight here right now."

"We?"

"Me and the money," Jerry said.

"Nah. We ain't handing this over," Hurley said.

Amber sat down on the bed next to Jerry, and I thought for a second that she might put her arm around him, but she didn't.

"A ride where?" Amber said.

"Gotta go to Susanville," Jerry said. "Pick it up."

It felt like all of the bugs that had been beating themselves senseless against the bulbs in the hallway had somehow found a way to drop into my stomach, and I could feel everything inside go jittery and loose.

"We can go to Susanville with you," Hurley said. "Follow you up. We're ready."

Jerry smiled and sat up on the bed. "Nah, that won't work," he said. "This isn't a fucking caravan."

"We can ride with you, then. It's no big deal. You've got that big Ford in the parking lot, right?"

Jerry looked at Hurley. "This isn't a little family trip to go get a fucking Christmas tree." Jerry smoothed the crease in his pants and tried to pull his shirt together and button it, but there weren't enough buttons to meet the holes and he let it hang loose over his T-shirt.

"She goes," Jerry said, pointing at Amber. "And Joey goes. That's it."

"Nah, that ain't gonna work for us," Hurley said. "It's our money. We all go."

"Then nobody goes."

"Fine. Forget it then."

Amber got off the bed and she went over to Hurley and put her arms around his neck and whispered into his ear, and I could see him shaking his head back and forth, and then she said something else and he looked over at me, and Jerry stood up and brushed the loose ash from the front of his pants, and he picked up some clothes from the floor until he found a shirt and then he swapped out his broken one for the one in his hand, and Amber kissed Hurley and turned around.

"Okay," she said. "You've got a deal Jerry," she said. "Me and Joey will go."

Jerry buttoned his shirt and walked past me toward the bathroom, and he gave me a look as he passed but I couldn't tell what it meant, and then he ran water in the sink again and splashed his face and dried it off with the shirt he'd changed out of, and when he was done he put the shirt over the shower rod and his face was clean and there was still the gash over his eye and a split in his lip, but he didn't look as bad as he should have, and when he came out of the bathroom I tried to look him in the eyes, but he didn't even notice me.

"Okay then, you'd better get some shoes on," Jerry said.

"You want to go right now?" Hurley said.

"Unless you want to put it on layaway," Jerry said. "You guys could be in business by breakfast. That's what you want, right? Get the ball rolling before the circus leaves town?"

Hurley looked at Amber and she shrugged. "I'm fine with now," she said.

"Then give me a little while to get some things in order," Jerry said. "Gotta send word up the mountain," and he smiled but it didn't reach all the way to his eyes, and he checked his watch and I could see him

166

figuring out time, and I knew that Lalo and Chuck had left maybe an hour ago and it would take them a while to get back to the woods, and that was what Jerry was waiting for, I figured, and I almost said as much, but instead I said, "we can just go tomorrow, Jerry," and he looked over at me and he stubbed his cigarette out in the ashtray and didn't say anything, and he dusted off his hands and flicked some carpet fuzz off of his shirt and then he reached over and picked up his tie from the floor and put it on and he took a minute to wrap it and knot it and pull it tight.

"Nah, we're taking care of this tonight. No time like the present. Sooner and better, right? Don't want to make your people wait."

"Can I get a cigarette to go?" Amber asked, and she walked toward the nightstand, and Jerry picked up the pack and shook one loose, and then he shook out another one.

"Take as many as you want," he said. "Help yourself," and then he bent down and untangled the phone from itself and picked it up from the floor, and he put the receiver back in the cradle and waited a few seconds and then he lifted up the receiver to check for a dial tone and I could hear it pounding in the room, and then he put it back to rest again, and Reece pulled the door open and the air was cooler outside and it cut into the room and there was the sound of crickets in the grass somewhere, and I could hear them rubbing their legs together in the shadows where the streetlights didn't reach, and Amber helped herself to Jerry's cigarettes and Hurley walked out of the room with Amber close behind him, and she pulled the door shut behind her and I heard it close with a soft click, and the curtains lifted and went still, and it was quiet in the room again, and everything inside of me felt as churned and scattered and torn apart as everything outside of me had looked, and before I could say anything, Jerry pulled my gun from his waistband and tossed it onto my bed, and he looked at me then, and I tried to read what he was thinking, but his eyes were as hard and dark and blank as the table behind him where everything had been swept free and put to ground.

Chapter 19
No Quarters

Jerry was walking around the room, wearing out the stained carpet, and I was wishing I had clean sheets and a way to call Amber so I could see what she was doing and whether or not she was sure about all the balls that were rolling, but I couldn't get off my bed even though it smelled like fat Gordo despite the fact that his presence was nothing more than a ghost, and I could smell my sweat and his sweat and the faint tang of cologne and spilled beer and cigarette ash that had been rubbed out until it left a gray streak of reminder, and I was more tired than I thought was possible, but I knew that even if the lights were off, I couldn't sleep, and it was as if my body had given up sleep as a fast, like my stomach had when I forgot to eat, and then didn't want to eat, and then couldn't eat, and the TV was a blank screen in front of us after Jerry had finally pushed the button, and I forgot how much better the room sounded when there was the crack of a bat and announcers and the warm, wet hit of a ball smacking into a glove, and I thought maybe I would stay on my bed for the rest of the night, and maybe Jerry would forget about what had happened with Amber and Hurley and Reece in the room and the roll of money and the big reveal, but I could tell that his thoughts were churning and as restless as the muscles in my legs when I stretched them out in front of me, and I didn't want to look at him with his face broken up with dried blood and split skin, but I couldn't help it, and he was doing a great job of ignoring me, and then he finally lit a cigarette and sat down on his bed and smoothed his hair back from his forehead, and I could see sweat around his face, and there were lines beneath his eyes and he looked like he needed to sleep as much as I did, and I thought maybe he'd kick off his shoes and settle in until tomorrow and forget about Susanville and leaving tonight, but he said, "okay kid, let's go," and I just looked at him and he stood up and kicked the edge of my bed so that the headboard bounced against the wall and the mattress shook me loose and I stood up and we both filled the small space in front of the nightstand.

"Go where?" I asked.

"We're gonna make a phone call," he said, and I looked down at the phone between us, and he saw where my eyes landed, and he shook his head, and he said, "no, at the phone booth," and I thought maybe he would hand me another piece of paper and we could go back to the way that things had been before they hadn't been that way anymore, but instead he dug into his pocket and I could hear him fingering through change, and he pulled out his money clip and moved it from the left side to his right, and then he started tossing quarters onto the dirty sheets that were still warm from where I had been laying.

"Who am I calling?" I asked.

He didn't say anything—just kept counting out the quarters, and there were a lot of them—and when he was finished, he told me to scoop them up and put them into my own pocket, and I did—raked them off the bed in a swoop of my sweaty palm—and then he turned toward the door and pulled it open and the air conditioner in the window kicked on and blew cold, and I felt the strong blast of air as it spread through the room, and when the door was open, I realized how much better it felt inside than out and I didn't want to leave.

"Let's go," he said.

"Both of us?" I asked.

"Yeah, what the fuck do you think I'm doing? Giving you an escort to the door? We're both going," and he walked out to the landing and waited for me to follow him, and I did, and then he reached past me and pulled the door shut and rattled the doorknob to make sure that it was locked, and when he was satisfied, he turned and walked down the narrow hallway and we passed the soda machine, and suddenly I was thirsty and I could hear all of the quarters knocking around in my pocket and I wanted to stop and pump one in, but I could tell by the way that his shoulders were bent forward that it would be a bad thing for me to fall behind, so I tried to match my steps with his, and I kept pace right behind him, and we filed down the stairs and then we were walking through the parking lot, and we rounded the corner and I could see that Hurley's truck was in front of Amber's room, and the lights were on inside, and I wished that I could give a bird whistle or a signal that I was moving past them, but Jerry was clipping back the pavement, and I realized that this was the first time that I had seen him like this—walking out in the parking lot, and I felt the sweat on my forehead bunch up and creep toward my upper lip and I knew that my palms were already greasy and I wanted so badly to wash my hands, and the sky above us was clear and full of stars and I could hear cars on the streets and the ringing of bells, and over the tops of buildings there was the red flash of neon that lit up the dark until it looked as if the sun was rising in the west.

We passed the office, and I could hear the hollow click of Jerry's shoes as the parking lot narrowed in front of the building, and I tried to look through the window to see if Dee was behind the counter, but the thin gauzy curtains were pulled and all I could see was light and the dance of TV, and then Jerry made a right onto the sidewalk, and I kept behind him, and I could hear his lighter click over again, and then there was a quick burst of flame, and I could hear him smoking and I wondered if he missed the weight of a gun as it shifted with his footsteps in the small of his back, and I wondered where his gun was since it wasn't like him to leave without it, and I had gotten used to seeing it as an outlined bulk underneath his jacket, and I missed the feel of my own gun, slung forward in the elastic pocket, when my jeans were pulled tight over the rub, and I felt naked now without it, and I wondered if I'd ever get it back again, and my shoes slapped the sidewalk and I could hear the small crush of rocks as I hit them and they rolled, and then there was the dim light of the phone and I followed Jerry until we were standing in front of it and he motioned me toward the receiver with his hand, and I picked it up and I could hear the dial tone pulsing against my chest but it could not keep time with the beating of my heart, and I waited for Jerry to hand me a piece of paper, but he just stood there for a second, and then he said, "I want you to call your mom," and I took the receiver and hung it back up and turned around to face him.

"No," I said. "I told you. She's dead."

"She ain't dead, kid. She's as alive as my mother—living in Phoenix and sucking on her social security check. So call your mom."

"Right now?"

"Now. Make your call," he said.

"I can't do that."

I tried to step past him, but he had planted both feet, and I could see the scruff of his beard underneath the light and the way that each individual hair was coated in a sliver of blue and white from the booth, and he looked hollow and solid at the same time, and I wanted him to go back to the room and I didn't want him here, and I didn't want to call my mom, and I wouldn't do it even if he forced me to.

"I'm not calling her," I said.

Jerry ran a hand through his hair and it spread out across his head, and he ashed his cigarette onto the sidewalk and I watched his face change a little bit, and I knew that he was already prepared for everything I was going to tell him even if he didn't have a dog in this fight, and I wondered what he would do if I just didn't call her, and I wondered how far I could push him, and I wondered if he could grab me before I could disappear into the shadows if I took off running down the street, but I wouldn't run, and he knew that, and he knew that I knew, so he just stood there and looked at me and tried to wear me down with his eyes.

"Why do you want me to call her?"

He exhaled and looked up and down the street in both directions, and then he pulled a piece of loose tobacco from his bottom lip and spit toward the ground.

"Because she's worried about you. Because she's your mom. Tell her you'll be home soon. Tell her you're okay."

I kicked my feet against the loose rocks on the cement and I could feel them stick into the rubber of my soles, and I liked the rough sound of rock on pavement and I wished there was a way to scrape them hard enough together so that they would make a spark like flint against steel.

"She doesn't care what I'm doing," I said. "I'm not going home soon."

"Yeah? What makes you think this is gonna keep going?"

"Because me and Amber and Hurley and Reece are gonna make a lot of money and move to Portland."

Jerry smiled and shook his head. "Yeah, I'm sure you are. So let your mom know you've got your life figured out. She's your mom, kid. You owe her that much."

I cleared my throat a little bit and I was surprised at how dry my tongue had become at the thought of punching in the numbers to home, and then I realized that I didn't have a home anymore because my mom was moving in with her boyfriend and I couldn't remember that number even if Jerry reached back and could loosen his pistol and put it to my head.

"I don't know her number anymore," I said. "That's the truth."

Jerry looked down at me, and there was something in his eyes that was wet and made the light slide off like water on wax, and he shifted his feet but didn't move from blocking me into the booth.

"Look, kid. She's your mom. Make the call, okay."

"I'm not going home," I said. "No matter what. I'm going to Portland with Amber and Hurley and Reece," and I didn't drop my eyes when I said it.

"Oh yeah. I know. You're gonna load up and get gone like the Beverly Hillbillies. Get that white gold. Reno tea." Jerry laughed and the light that had bounced off his eyes started to settle and I could see the sweat drying on his face, and on the Strip there were people yelling, and Jerry looked that direction, and the stars above us closed against each other and disappeared.

"I want to go with them," I said.

"So call home and tell your mom," Jerry said. "Tell her you're okay. And tell her good-bye."

I hadn't thought about the fact that I hadn't really told that to my mom—hadn't said good-bye and hadn't closed the door that separated us and that was still hanging open like everything between us was hung on a loose hinge, and for a second I wanted to hear her voice again, and I wanted to hear her be sad or angry or happy or afraid, and I wanted to feel that emotion wash across the phone line and I wanted to be wrapped in her even if it was over all of these miles, and my stomach knotted up a little bit, and I dug my hand into my pocket and I could feel the quarters settled there, warm and loose, and I pulled one out and held it in my palm but I kept my fingers closed so that Jerry couldn't see it.

"Tell her that you love her. Tell her that everything is okay," Jerry said. He stepped back a little bit and I could feel the air pass between us and there was a coolness underneath the heat that was radiating from the sidewalk, and I wanted to put the quarter into the slot and dial home, and Jerry knew it, and I leaned back against the receiver and waited for him to give me enough space to step past him and run.

"Look, kid," Jerry said, and then he looked away from me so that I couldn't see his face. "You owe it to her, okay? Tell her you'll be home soon." He exhaled and took a long drag off his cigarette and then flicked it into the street, and I didn't turn to look at it, but I knew that it was rolling there, in a glow of red ember, and it was fading into dust, and even if I wanted to turn my head to watch it die, it would be out before I could see it.

"And if you're not going home, then tell her good-bye," he said. "Just tell her good-bye."

"Fine," I said. "I'll tell her good-bye."

"Good," he said. "So call her."

I walked over to the phone and picked up the receiver and it was cool in the evening air, and I could hear the dial tone buzzing, and I dug out a quarter and lifted it toward the slot, and it hung there, between my fingers, like air I wanted to suck in, and it would be easy enough to drop it and punch in some numbers, but I couldn't, and the sound in the receiver sounded like somebody shrilling out "don't don't don't" over and over again. I kept my back to Jerry and I put the receiver to my ear and I looked out onto the street and I could hear him behind me, shuffling, and I watched a car pass, slow with the exhaust glass-packed and loud, and I thought about my sister and how I was supposed to rescue her, and how I had missed so many meals and I thought about my mom's boyfriend, Chris, with his slick eyes and the way he liked to grip me in the small hollows under my chin, and how those eyes told me that he wanted to grip me in the small hollows of my hips, and I thought about my mom sleeping in bed while he did it, and how she looked down at her plate when he hadn't, and it was just a matter of time. I put the receiver back on the hook and walked back over to Jerry.

"I can't," I said. "I've got nothing to say."

Jerry leaned his weight into the cement wall behind him and he pulled his cigarettes from his pocket, shook one loose, and then tipped the pack toward me. I took one, and he lit it before he lit his own.

"What's so bad about home?" he asked. "Your mom miss a dance rehearsal? Really piss you off? Made you feel unloved?"

"There was never anything for her to miss," I said. "But yeah. The rest is pretty true." I leaned back against the wall next to Jerry.

"That's the way home works," Jerry says. "Makes you stronger."

"You sound like my stepdad."

I could hear Jerry smile. "Stepdad, huh? So I'm guessing that's why you took the powder? Just like in the movies, huh? The bad stepdad."

I hesitated for a second. "Yeah, he was bad."

"Like to watch you get undressed? Caught you coming out of the shower? Maybe had a hard grab and a long reach?"

I looked down at my shoes. "He never did that. He had friends who did."

"Rough," Jerry said.

"He was bad, but now my mom has a boyfriend she's moving us in with, and I think he's gonna be worse." I paused for a second. "He's always looking at me, but in a way that makes me want to wrap up in a blanket, you know? He comes into my room at night, after everyone is asleep, and he uh," I paused for a second, "hits me for a while, you know? For whatever reason. Not eating all my dinner. Once for having my shoes laced left over right. He likes to pretend it's the Army."

Jerry whistled softly, and I looked over at him. He was staring out at the street in front of us but there was nothing to see. "You ever hit him back? Like a good little soldier?" Jerry asked.

I remembered once when I was eight years old and my mom asked me what I would do if my stepdad Dale ever hit her, and I had a BB gun then, and I told her I would shoot him, and she hugged me then, but maybe she didn't know how much I meant it.

"I couldn't," I said.

"Should have given it a try. Feels better than you think."

"You ever hit your dad?"

"I wasn't much different than you are, kid. In fact, you remind me of myself when I was your age."

"You left home? I thought you said your parents were dead." I laughed at the lie.

"Dead to me," Jerry said.

"My stepfather died," I said.

"You help him with that?"

I smiled before I could help myself. "Nah, he was drunk. Wrecked his car and died."

"So if he was dead, why did you leave home?"

"Because my mom was still alive and moving us in with Chris." I had forgotten about the cigarette and I held it up a little bit and could see the ash crawling from the ember like a snake.

"I left home when I wasn't much older than you. But I got the last word before I did."

"What did you say?"

"Say? I didn't say nothing. Just gave my father a little kiss. That's all."

"You kissed him good bye?"

"Kissed him with a hammer."

"You hit your dad with a hammer?" I looked up at him, but he was still staring out at the nothing.

"He went out to his shed to drink, and I'd used some of his tools that day, you know, building some shit with my friends out in the alley, and I had put everything away, but I forgot to hang the hammer up on the rack—just put it in the toolbox with the rest—got busy. Got distracted. And he called me out there, and I could feel it in my stomach, you know?"

I nodded but Jerry didn't look at me, and I did know that feeling—like everything binds into a knot and you know that trouble is coming and it's going to get you no matter if you hide or ignore or deny—it's coming down no matter if you're right or if you're wrong, and it's just a matter of what form it's going to take and whether or not you can outlast it.

"So I go out there and he's drunk, and he's got the hammer in his hand and he waves it in my face, you know, all pissed off with spit coming out of his mouth while he's yelling at me about disrespect and touching his shit, and it's a speech I'd heard about a million times, and he starts pulling his belt from his work pants, you know, but he's drunk and it keeps getting hung up on the loops, and I don't know why I did it, but I just picked the hammer up off the workbench, you know, and I'll never forget how heavy it was in my hand, and I had held that fucking thing about a million times before that, but it felt foreign, you know, like I had never held one in my hand, and he had just about got the belt free, and he's looking at me and his eyes are all bloodshot under the light, but I see something in them, and I don't think he thought I had the balls to do anything but hunch up when he started wailing on me, but I reached back with that hammer, all the way to the next state over, and I was strong then—wasn't much older than you, but had been playing baseball for the high school and had a pretty good swing back then, was batting .357—and when that hammer got to its highest point, you know, my head just emptied, it was the strangest thing, it just went blank, like somebody had cut the power, and I brought that round end down on him, and I wasn't that tall—he was still bigger than me—so I caught him in the shoulder—the right one—and I heard his collarbone snap, and he went down to his knees—just dropped, you know?—and he looked at me, and I'll never forget his eyes, it was like his face had been swallowed by them, he looked so surprised, and I reached back and swung again, and I clipped him just above the ear, and he slumped over, and there was blood then, and I reached back to do it again, but the lights came back on in my head, and I looked down at him bleeding on the dirt floor, and his mouth was opening and closing so I knew he was still alive, and I just dropped the hammer then, and I walked into the house and got the few bucks I had shoved in a dresser drawer, and my mom was in the kitchen, still washing dishes from dinner, and she yelled to me that I needed to get my homework done, and I didn't say anything to her—just walked out the front door and hit the sidewalk and just kept going, and I never went back." He took a drag from his cigarette but it was down to filter and had gone out in his hand, and he looked at it, like he didn't even remember that he'd been smoking it.

"Jesus Jerry."

Jerry made a noise that sounded like a laugh but I wasn't sure. "Wasn't no Jesus involved. Kick a dog often enough and one of those days it's not going to tuck tail and run."

"You never talked to your mom after that?"

"Never talked to either of them. He was the one who swung the belt, but she was the one who looked the other way."

I cleared my throat. "My mom never stopped my stepdad, either. And she's not stopping Chris."

"That part hurts as much as the belt, don't it?"

"More, I think. At least you can see the belt coming, and then it's over. Her pretending it wasn't happening just hurts on and on."

"Like a toothache."

I thought about my mom and how she had to hear him get up in the night, had to feel the weight lift from the bed and know he was up, and I knew she could hear me crying through the thin walls, and she never walked in, never put her herself between me and him.

"Where did you go?" I asked. "After you left."

Jerry ran a hand through his hair and spit onto the sidewalk. "Went north for a while. Made it to Canada, but never crossed over. Went south for a while. Made it to Mexico, but never went over that line either."

"Why not?"

"Everybody has their borders, I guess. Holds them in. Gives them a sense of containment. Keeps them from leaking out into everything."

"I'd go to Mexico," I said.

"Nothing would be different," Jerry said.

"I'd be in Mexico. It would all be different."

"Nah, kid. Wherever you go, there you are."

"What does that mean?"

"You'll figure it out someday. The past has a way of stamping itself onto you. Sews itself onto you from the inside until you learn to cut the stitches."

"But then you grow up, right?"

Jerry laughed. "Yeah, you grow up. All that shit grows right up with you. And you'll do anything to stop that pain for a little while—quiet the voices, scrub the pictures in your head. Drinking helps for a while. Then it's drugs. Sometimes it's fucking. Money on cards."

"Baseball?" I asked.

"Baseball. Football. Basketball. The ponies. The fights. A dream for every season." Jerry exhaled, and I looked at the side of his face again and could see that it was swelling underneath his eye.

"So why don't you quit?"

Jerry leaned his weight deeper into the wall behind us. "At first, it's about the rush, you know? That high of winning that you keep on chasing. And then it becomes about the money because you owe everybody and you're fucked, and the more you get desperate for the money, the easier it goes. You're always chasing something just so you don't have to stand still too long. You burn through them, one after the other, and then you start all over again, and by the time you want to stop running, it's too late and you can't anymore. That's why."

I thought about how it felt to get high with Amber and Hurley and Reece, and how for a little while, I didn't feel anything except good, and I didn't think about the past and I didn't care about the future, and I just wanted that feeling forever, and I would do anything to make it last.

"You still think about what happened to your dad, Jerry?"

Jerry didn't say anything for a minute and then he took a deep breath. "Every goddamn day, kid. It was thirty years ago and I can still smell the lawnmower seeping gas in the corner of the shed just before I reached for that hammer." Jerry looked up at the sky, and I looked with him, but there was nothing but darkness where the streetlights couldn't reach.

"Rain is coming," Jerry said. "Gonna be a shitty drive."

"Jerry, I've got that feeling in my stomach that something bad is going to happen. You know that feeling—like when you heard your dad calling you out to the shed."

He dug into his pocket and then he handed me something and I realized it was the gun from under my mattress that I'd handed over to him before I didn't use the phone. "Here, kid. Put this where it goes."

I didn't think to ask why and I just turned away from him and shoved it down into the pocket between my skin and my jeans.

"It feels heavier," I said.

"Because it's loaded now," Jerry said.

I looked up at him. "You mean it hasn't been loaded? Why'd you even bother to let me have it? That's stupid."

"It's not stupid," he ran a hand through his hair and looked down at me. "An unloaded gun is for you. A loaded gun is for them."

"I don't get it," I said.

Jerry pushed himself off the wall and I could feel his hand on my shoulder, and he started walking and I fell into stride with him.

"You're covered now," he said. "Remember what you're carrying. Can't nobody reach far enough to touch you. And remember what I taught you—take a deep breath and squeeze steady on the exhale. And don't stop pulling until it clicks." He knocked another cigarette loose and lit it while we were walking. "Besides—nothing bad is going to happen, kid. It already has."

Chapter 20
Snitches In Ditches

I stood in the parking lot while Amber finished getting ready, and Jerry went back to the room, and Hurley stayed with Amber, and Reece came outside and stood with me in the sodium glow of streetlights, and it was warm out but the sky was clouded over and the air felt sticky and I slapped at mosquitoes the bit into my neck, and Reece leaned up against Hurley's truck and I joined him.

"You sure about this?" he said.

I scuffed at the asphalt and started chewing on my thumb and the skin there was already ragged and raw and it hurt to sink my teeth into it, but I did anyway, and I pressed the thin tissue between my front teeth and gnawed on it until I could bite all the way through the strip and I spit it onto the ground.

"I guess it's gonna happen no matter what," I said.

Reece adjusted the top of his pants, and it was strange seeing him without a belt buckle shining in the light to hold up his jeans. "Not too late to quit," he said.

The door to Amber's room pulled open and Hurley came out and lit a cigarette, and then Amber followed him, and the four of us stood next to the truck and did the best that we could to avoid each other's eyes.

"Jesus," Amber said finally. "You are all acting like a bunch of pussies, and I'm sorry to say that, but it's true."

Hurley flicked his cigarette toward the chain link fence on the other side of the lot, and I watched the ember arc and hit the pavement, and then it disappeared, and I slapped another mosquito from my neck and this time my palm came back with a smear of blood.

"Not being a pussy. Just thinking," Hurley said. He jumped up on the side of his truck and used the back wheel for a step so that he had some footing, and he started digging around in the bed and I could hear things move around, and then he hopped down from the side and he had a long-handled wrench in his hand. "Let's go over to Jerry's car," he

179

said. "But be quiet about it," and then he started walking down the row of cars and we followed him, and when he got to the end of the building, he rounded the corner, and Jerry's car was parked against the fence, and Hurley walked over and started looking at the trunk.

"What're you doing?" Reece asked, and he walked over to where Hurley was standing with the wrench in his hand.

"I've got an idea," Hurley said. "We're gonna follow you in my truck—make sure everything stays right."

Something in my stomach tightened, and I could feel the little hairs on my arms stand up and stretch against the fabric of my shirts. "I don't think that's a good idea," I said.

"Yeah? You got a better idea?" Hurley said.

"This isn't a big deal," Amber said. "We're just going to Susanville, pay the money, get the shit and come back."

"I don't trust that fuck," Hurley said. "You trust him?" He looked at me.

I cleared my throat. "Sure," I said. "It's no big deal."

"Well I think it's a big fucking deal," Hurley said. "I'm not sending you two off with all the money we have between us and just sitting here licking my dick while you're gone."

"Jesus, Hurley," Amber said. "It's just for a little while. Then we're gonna make more money than any of us have ever seen. Ain't that right?"

"Maybe," Hurley said. "And maybe he just fucks all of us over."

"Jerry wouldn't do that," I said.

"You *know* this or you just *think* this?" Hurley said.

"I'm pretty sure," I said.

"Well, let me just say one thing. You know what they make us have when we're out there rodeoing? I mean—every damn one of us?"

"A cute ass?" Amber said, and she laughed, and I could tell that she was high and she was pulling at her shorts and knotting her fingers back and forth and she couldn't stand in one place without shifting around on her feet.

Hurley smiled at her. "Yeah that helps," he said. "But the one thing they make all of us have no matter what? It's insurance. You have to sign all this paperwork before they'll ever let you sit in a chute. That way if your head gets stomped on and that bull is just tossing you up and over like you're a dirty piece of laundry—you got a way to get sewn back together and their ass is covered."

Amber was licking her lips and looking up and down the parking lot as if she was expecting someone.

"So I'm just gonna call this a little insurance," Hurley said, and he took the wrench and swung back and busted out the tail light on the passenger's side of Jerry's car, and I could hear the plastic cave in and shatter and then fall to the ground in a bunch of pieces.

"What the hell, Hurley?" I said.

Hurley started kicking the broken pieces toward the fence so that the little pile underneath the light scattered.

"This way I can follow you guys," Hurley said. "I'll be able to know which car you are on the highway, and I can keep my distance, but I'll be back there just the same."

"Insurance," Reece said, and he started scraping his boot against the ground to get the last of the plastic out from under, and when he was finished, he bent down and picked up the smaller pieces by hand.

"And this," Hurley said. He lifted the bottom of his T-shirt and I could see the wink of light on metal and the curve of a pistol grip sticking from the waistband of his jeans.

"Holy shit," Amber said. "That's fucking sweet! Let me see it." She reached toward Hurley but he stepped away from her grip.

"Uh-uh, baby. Look but don't touch."

"You're gonna shoot your dick off," Reece said.

"Yeah? But there'd still be nine inches. What's your excuse?"

"Fuck you," Reece said.

"Where'd you get it?" Amber asked.

"I got connections."

"Don't do anything stupid, Hurley," I said. "Seriously. This isn't right."

"Hey, it's not my fault you aren't smart enough to think of this. You think we're gonna carry a bunch of dope and money and not have a piece? What isn't right is you think this shit isn't serious."

I heard a door open on the second floor, and I looked up and Jerry was coming out of the room, and I heard him walking on the landing, and Hurley and Reece bent over and started moving out of the light, and before they rounded the corner of the building and headed back toward Hurley's truck, Hurley said, "we'll be right behind you," and then they dissolved into the shadows, and I could hear Jerry coming down the stairs, and then a pair of headlights lit up the parking lot and a car pulled in behind us and the engine gunned once and went quiet, and then the door opened and fat Gordo stepped out.

"You ready?" Jerry said.

"He's not going with us, is he?" I asked and I nodded my head toward fat Gordo, who was pulling a short bottle out of his jacket pocket and walking to the back of his car.

"Yeah, he's going," Jerry said. "You two and me and him. Sounds fair to me," and Jerry unlocked his car and told me and Amber to get in, and I stood for a minute on the blacktop without moving, and I could see fat Gordo opening the trunk of his car, and Jerry walked over to him and they stood there, moving things around.

"Get in the car," Jerry said, and Amber started walking and she grabbed me by the arm and I let her pull me toward the open rear door, and then I got in and slid across the seat and Amber sat down but she didn't pull the door closed, and we could hear Jerry and fat Gordo talking low, and I turned my head so that I could see out the back window but they were blocked behind fat Gordo's car.

"What do you think they're doing?" Amber said.

"I don't know."

"You think they'll notice the busted light?"

"Maybe," I said.

I heard metal on metal and I tried to see what they were doing, but Jerry was walking back to his car then, and then he stopped at his trunk, and I heard him pop the lock, and then my view was blocked completely, and then fat Gordo pulled the passenger door open and sat down and the car shifted and groaned on the shocks, and Jerry fired the engine to life, and I could feel everything in my stomach sliding lower until I thought that it might all just spill out over my knees and onto the floor, and then Amber leaned forward and asked Jerry for a cigarette, and he passed one back to her, and fat Gordo gave her his lighter, and we were on the street that ran parallel to the Strip, and there were people walking and not many cars, and Jerry rolled his window down and the air had cooled off and I could finally smell the rain building up somewhere, and then we crossed past where the casinos trickled out for the highway and Jerry moved over in the lane and Amber lit her cigarette, and there was no sound except for the wind coming through the window and the tires slapping pavement, and then Jerry got on the freeway and I looked over my shoulder to see if Hurley and Reece were behind us, but there were too many pairs of headlights and there was no way I could tell the difference.

We drove for a while like that—in silence—with Amber smoking and fat Gordo with his arm draped across the back of the seat, and then he reached forward and started tuning the stations on the radio, and he put on a baseball game, and Jerry told him to turn it up a little bit, and they both lit up cigarettes, and then fat Gordo passed his bottle over to Jerry and Jerry took a drink.

"Took a hell of a beating, Jerry," fat Gordo said.

"It'll even out," Jerry said. "It's the turn before the river."

Fat Gordo ran a hand through his hair, and I looked over at Amber but she was picking at the threads on her shorts and lining up the fray into straight and even lines.

"What are you short?" fat Gordo asked.

"A dime. Maybe two."

Fat Gordo whistled through his teeth. "*Maybe* two?"

"Okay, three. Three. I had some carryover." Jerry was quiet for a minute. "Maybe you should put in a call to Nicky."

"Nicky Little?"

"Nah. Nicky Dago."

"He bounced out of here about six months ago. Or he was bounced. One or the other."

"What about Kentucky Mike? That son of a bitch owes me a string."

"I don't have any pull with him anymore. I haven't seen him in months."

I thought about the shiny Datsun and the desert and losing my breath when fat Gordo had promised that I was only gonna take a quick ride.

I leaned over the front seat. "I was just with Kentucky Mike," I said. "Gordo made me go with him. He called me 'Vig.'"

"He called you what?" Jerry asked.

"Vig. Or something like that."

Jerry was quiet for a minute, and I could see his face in profile and there was a muscle jumping in his jaw.

He turned toward fat Gordo. "You fucking used her to cover your vig?"

Gordo smiled. "She's full of shit Jerry. She's making shit up."

I snapped my head around and Amber had stopped pulling at her shorts and she was staring at me and I could feel her eyes gripping me in the darkness.

"Stop saying 'she'," I said. "Stop calling me a girl."

Gordo turned his head toward me. "Get over yourself," he said. "This whole fucking show is over."

183

"I don't know what he's talking about," I said to Amber.

Amber smiled. "I already knew," she said. "I've known the whole time."

"I don't know what you're talking about," I said.

"Gordo's right. The whole fucking show is over. Right, *dad*?" She moved her eyes off of me and put them into the back of Jerry's head.

"Wait," I said.

"C'mon, Joey," Amber said. "Don't play dumb."

"I'm not playing dumb. Why are you calling Jerry 'dad'?"

"Because he's my dad," Amber said. "*Uncle* Gordo can vouch for that."

"*Uncle* Gordo? Are you serious?"

"Well, more *like* an uncle. Not blood, but basically, yeah," Amber said. She turned her head and was looking out the window.

I sat back in the seat and my stomach felt as if it had crawled into the upholstery underneath me.

"You could have squeezed those shitkickers for more," Jerry said, and I could see his eyes in the rearview mirror and he was looking at Amber.

"But what about Portland?" I said.

Amber laughed. "Yeah," she said. "Sure."

"But what about Hurley? What about the money—what about them follow—"

Amber reached over and slammed her closed fist into my thigh. "You're babbling," she said.

Everything felt as if it had been tipped sideways, and I was trying to set it right but the floor underneath me was slanted and I couldn't get my balance, and I had a feeling like I was stumbling and falling forward but I was still sitting upright in the seat.

"You knew?" I said to Amber.

"It was my dad's plan," she said. "I knew you were coming before you even got there."

"Everything's a lie?"

"Not everything," Amber said.

"Anyway," fat Gordo said from the front seat. "Now that everybody has been introduced, what's the plan, Jerry?"

Jerry was quiet. "You fucked me for your own vig," he said quietly.

"Jesus, Jerry. Move on. You got too much dip on your chip as it is."

"Was it Kentucky Mike?"

Fat Gordo lit a cigarette. "Yeah. I needed a week. He hit me for double points in a series, and I was trying to buy time. We just had a disagreement with the fee structure. You would have done the same thing."

Jerry cleared his throat. "This was my thing. Not yours. All of this is mine."

"Look, Jerry, I've been under a little too much pressure to stroke anybody off and make them feel better about me."

"Can you turn up the radio, Jerry?" Amber asked.

"Hey, honey, the adults are talking now." Gordo said.

"I wasn't talking to you, you fat fuck."

Jerry laughed, but his voice sounded funny. "She got you there, Gordo."

"Yeah, she's got a mouth on her." Gordo turned so he was facing over the seat. "I bet I can stuff something in your mouth to shut you up for a little while."

"Oh, you mean your dick?" Amber asked.

"I wasn't talking about a fucking sandwich."

"You don't look like you'd be quick to give up a sandwich, so I didn't figure it. But go ahead. Shove your dick in my mouth. I bite," Amber said. "But why don't you try it."

"Honey, I got a dick like cement. You could hang a wet bedspread on it. I'd break your fucking teeth."

Gordo reached forward and twisted the knob on the radio and whatever Amber said next was lost in the music pumping through the speakers behind us. I took a deep breath and could taste the air churning around me and I felt like I wanted to puke but there was nothing in my stomach, and I wanted to jump out of the car, but I knew I'd never make it out of the door.

I pressed my cheek against the cool glass of the window and there were lights everywhere and the highway was just a stream of white and red, and I checked behind us every few minutes but I didn't want to look obvious, and Jerry stayed tucked in the fast lane and the minutes were eaten up with the miles, and it was impossible to tell if there was anybody keeping up with us, and I didn't even know anymore if there was supposed to be—if Hurley and Reece were coming at all—and as we climbed toward Susanville, rain started falling and the sound outside of the car changed to wet, and I watched the wipers come on and smear the windshield, and Jerry snapped off the radio and fat Gordo lit another cigarette and the car was quiet.

"I love the smell of rain," Amber said suddenly, and she pressed her

185

face against her own window, and I wanted to ask her a million questions but knew I didn't really want to know the answers.

"You still awake back there girls?" fat Gordo said and I wanted to punch my knees into the back of the seat so that they hit him in the kidneys, but I didn't.

"I'm always awake," Amber said.

I didn't say anything. Everything had been smoke and mirrors, and I had lost the ability to see what was real.

The highway grew steeper in the headlights and Jerry stayed tight to the fast lane, and the rain came down in a light curtain that clung to the windshield for a second before being wiped away, and it felt as if it had taken forever to come out of Susanville on the day that Jerry had picked me up and we had stopped off at Lalo's, and I had to think back on how long ago it had been, and I counted the days on my fingers, and it had only been ten, and now I could see the signs for Susanville glowing white on green as the headlights scraped across them, and it had taken a finger snap to come out of the desert and break into the pine trees again.

I could feel the car slowing beneath us, and then Jerry moved over in the lane and he hit the turn signal and we exited the highway and took a short off ramp that crested at the top of a small hill, and at the stop sign Jerry went right, and I recognized the road, and then there were more turns, and I looked behind us to see if Hurley was following, but there were no lights, and there were so many lies that maybe he was telling his own when he said he'd follow us, and maybe he hadn't intended to come at all, and it had felt better to think that he and Reece were back there somewhere—just in case—but maybe the truth was that I was really alone.

We left the pavement and turned onto a dirt road, and we kept climbing, and I could smell forest through the window that Jerry had rolled back down now that we were off the highway, and I could hear the rain drops pelting into the dirt, and the car bounced over the narrow ruts of tire tracks that had been carved into a road, and I could hear rocks pinging beneath us, and I looked over at Amber and she didn't seem afraid about anything at all, and we took a short bend in the road and then there were lights in front of us, and we dropped down into a narrow ravine and climbed up the other side, and then we were on a small patch of gravel, just like we had parked on before, and there were a couple of motorcycles parked close to the house and a car to the side, and fat Gordo cleared his throat and then rolled down his window and spit a flash of white into the dark, and Jerry brought the car to a stop and we were dropped into silence, and all I could hear was the engine ticking as it cooled.

I expected Jerry to say that he would be right back, or that we had to wait there, but instead he flung his door open and said, "c'mon," and I could see the rain hitting him as he stood between the car and the house.

"We can wait here, Jerry," I said.

Fat Gordo opened his door and got out and stretched and then he pulled his bottle out of his pocket and took another drink, and he leaned against the front fender of the car and stared out into the darkness.

"Nah, let's go," Jerry said. "Everybody's coming in," and then Amber was pulling her legs underneath her and climbing out of the car, and I followed her, and there was a wind that was picking up, and I could hear it pushing at the trees.

"Give me the cash," Jerry said, and he held his hand out to Amber. "Let's have it."

Amber dug into her pocket and pulled out the wad. "It was the best I could do," she said, and I heard the front door open and a circle of light spilled onto the porch that was still covered in tarps, and I saw a shadow move and then it took shape, and I could tell that it was Lalo, and Jerry started walking that direction and he raised his hand and said, "hey," and then he crossed the gravel and walked up the front steps, and fat Gordo followed him, and I was trying to get my feet to keep moving forward.

The inside of the house was lit up bright, and we followed Lalo into the kitchen where there was a table in the center of the room and chairs around it, and Chuck was leaning against the counter, drinking a beer, and Lalo motioned us to the table and Jerry pulled out a chair and sat down and so did fat Gordo, and Amber stood for a minute, looking at the room, and then she took a seat, and I did the same, and there was a woman in the corner, with long, black hair and pretty eyes, and she opened the refrigerator and took out more beer and passed it around the table and Jerry popped his can open and Lalo took a chair that was pushed against the wall and sat down in it, and I could see him out of the corner of my eye, and he picked up a shotgun from the floor and put it across his lap.

"So what's new, Jerry?" Chuck said, and then he laughed, and he took a long drink from his can and crushed the sides and tossed the empty into the sink. The room smelled like food, and there were dishes stacked on a towel to dry, and it was clean and there was a too-bright bulb above the table, and I could hear bugs knocking themselves around to get closer to the light.

"Like I told you on the phone, this is what I've got. If you float me another piece, I can step on it, farm it out, make everything up," Jerry said, and he reached into his shirt pocket and pulled out his cigarettes and shook one loose, and I thought that his hand was shaking but it could have just been the way the bugs made shadows in the room.

"A piece of what?" Chuck said, and he looked at Amber.

"Look, Chuck. You know I can make up what I owe. I'm close to even right now."

"Is that right?" Chuck said. He ran a hand through his hair and looked down at his boots. "Wendy, hand me another one of those beers, would you?" And Wendy opened the refrigerator and passed him over a can and he snapped the top and it foamed over onto his hand but he didn't seem to notice.

"I see you brought your bagman with you, Jerry," Chuck said, and he nodded toward fat Gordo who was tipped back in his chair and sucking on his beer. "Could have left your puppy in the car."

"He just came for the ride," Jerry said.

Chuck looked at the money on the table. "That's it? You really fucked this up, Jerry," Chuck said, and Jerry didn't drop his eyes. Chuck stepped forward and grabbed the money off of the table, and when his arm crossed beside me, I could feel myself flinch. He unwound the rubber band and then he lined up the bills and started counting them, one after the next, and we sat there quietly and waited for him to finish, and when he was done, he looked over at Jerry. "You're still short," he said.

"I think I made myself clear on the phone," Jerry said.

"You sure about that?" Chuck said.

"Jesus, they're just a couple of kids," Wendy said, and she stepped out from the corner. "Why'd you bring them up here, Jerry?"

"Ask Chuck," Jerry said, and Chuck smiled and took a drink from his beer and set the can back on the counter, and I could hear the bugs above me against the glass.

"I don't like to clean up messes," Chuck said. "Ain't my style."

"They're just kids," Wendy said again. "Just take them back with you, Jerry, and get your shit together."

"Too late for that," Chuck said. "You know that, Wendy."

"Look, I told you. I leave them here for two days, I unload, and then I'm back. Gordo has a guy in Sparks that will take it all and he's got the cash and we're even," Jerry said.

"Wait, I'm not fucking staying here," Amber said.

I looked over at her. I could feel my heart in my head.

"That wasn't part of the deal," Amber yelled.

"You boys need to settle down and figure this shit out some other way," Wendy said. "You were a couple of kids once, too. You can't do it like this."

Chuck laughed. "I don't know about you, Jerry, but I was born old. I wasn't never a kid."

"I don't want any part of this," Wendy said, and I thought she would leave then, but she stepped back into the corner and started combing her fingers through the ends of her hair, and I wanted to stand up and move out the door but my legs had gone numb.

Chuck sighed and he rubbed his hands on the front of his pants. "Had us a good thing going, Jerry," Chuck said, and he nodded toward Lalo who was still in his chair against the wall, and I had been on enough hunting trips and target practice weekends to know the unmistakable sound of a shotgun racking—the pull of the slide and the seat of a shell into the chamber—and I tried to get my feet underneath me to push out of my chair, but then someone grabbed the side of the table and flipped it and I heard chairs scraping loose, and then there was a lot of commotion in the room, and I felt my chair tip backward and I tried to put my hand out to catch myself, but it was too late and the light above me seemed to trade places with the floor and I felt my neck roll backward and my head went into a row of cupboards beneath the countertop and I felt it hit, and my teeth snapped together hard enough to make my ears pop, and my chin hit my chest, and I heard somebody scream but I was pretty sure that it wasn't me, and I thought that I saw legs coming toward me but they could have just been more shadows that crept into the room before the light caved in behind my eyes and then everything went black.

Chapter 21
In the Pines

I came to with rain pelting me in the face and my throat wrapped in a thick fold of arm, and I wasn't walking, I could feel myself being dragged into the darkness, and I wanted to dig my feet in and try to stop the momentum, but I couldn't seem to get my legs to obey what I was thinking, and my teeth hurt from where I had locked my jaw when the table flipped and my chair went backward, and I thought that I could feel blood on my head but it was probably my imagination, and up above me the trees shifted and bent and I stared up at them even as the water filled my eyes and I could not see.

I yanked my head forward and it didn't loosen the grip on my neck, and I could smell sweat and wet dirt, and I was trying to stand on my own, but my feet always seemed to be about two inches too short for the ground, and I knew that whoever had me, had me alone, and I thought maybe it was Jerry, but then I heard whoever had ahold of me cough and I could smell his breath, and I could feel sweat wrapping me up even as I choked to swallow, and I looked up as far as I could see, and I knew that it was fat Gordo that had me and I felt better about that, and I thought that if I could just dig in and cut myself loose, I'd be free.

"Quit fucking moving around," he said, and I jerked against him and he pulled me upright by the throat again, and this time I coughed even though I didn't want to, and I was able to see the house in the distance, with its lights still spitting out a warm glow, and I wondered where Amber was, and I didn't want to think too much about her, but I couldn't help it, and I wondered if Hurley and Reece were somewhere hunkered down and waiting to sight in and make the perfect shot and I could almost see them, with a rifle and a scope, and me ducking down just in time for them to line up the crosshairs and pull the trigger on fat Gordo, but I felt like I had been getting dragged by him for a long time and maybe Hurley and Reece had never shown up, and if they did, maybe they were saving their one shot to get Amber free.

"Please," I said to fat Gordo, and I choked on the vowels, and he either didn't hear me or didn't care because he kept dragging me into the darkness, and the rain had pulled up for a while, but now it was cutting loose, and it was finding its way through the canopy of trees so that it could fill our faces and drown us, and I could hear fat Gordo spit and wheeze, and I was still struggling to put my toes to the ground, and then the house went out of view, and it was nothing more than a bright arc over the top of a hill, and we had gone down and over and were away from its reach, and I didn't know what was going to happen next, and maybe fat Gordo didn't either because he whispered, "shut the fuck up," into my ear, and I let him drag me even though he was choking me and I couldn't breathe.

We made it over the embankment from the house, and I couldn't see lights or the cars anymore, and fat Gordo was wheezing against me and I tried to time it so that I could pick up and run with his next breath, but it was so hard to anticipate when he was going to breathe next, and I counted to myself even though I couldn't even mouth out the words anymore because fat Gordo was crushing my throat, and then I heard sticks cracking and branches snapping in front of us, and I knew that it was either Chuck or Lalo, but I thought that I could hear Amber screaming, and maybe she was, but the sound was far away and muffled, and I knew that the next thing that I saw would tell me everything, like someone had taken the axe off the raw stump that we'd seen when we'd pulled in, and had swung it into the earth and cracked it open, and I wanted to shut my eyes and even though they were filling with dirty rain, I couldn't.

"Let her loose," someone said, and I tried to jerk my head toward the voice, but fat Gordo caught my neck and locked it up tighter in his arm, and I coughed and then gagged a little bit.

"Nah, nah, just go back up there," fat Gordo said, and I wanted to see where the other voice came from, but I couldn't get my head around, and fat Gordo had buried my face into his arm and all that I could feel was slick cotton and weak skin underneath.

"It's over," the voice said, and I had been around that voice enough to know that it was Jerry, and he was the one who had been crashing through the branches and bending the sticks, and I spit the rain out of my mouth and called over to him.

"Jerry," I said, and I couldn't think of anything more to say and it didn't matter anyway because fat Gordo's arm had found the sweet spot in my throat and was back to choking off breath and sound, and I couldn't turn my head around to see Jerry, and all I could see was dark and trees and the rain coming down in a curtain, and then fat Gordo jerked me around so that my feet brushed the pine needles and I could feel the rubber in my toes strain toward the ground, and then I was looking at Jerry, and his hair was matted down from the rain, and he was breathing hard, and over his shoulder there was only more darkness and the sound of somebody crying.

Jerry put his hand up toward fat Gordo, like he was warding off a spell, and I would have laughed if I hadn't been the one between them.

"Just let her loose," Jerry said. I kicked at the dirt with my shoes as if to punctuate his sentence, but there was nothing for me to grab but wet air and cold.

"I can't, Jerry," fat Gordo said. "It can't be that way."

"It doesn't have to be any way," Jerry said. "Just let her go and we can figure out another plan. Me and you. Just let her go and cut her loose. That's all I'm asking."

"Can't do it, Jerry. I'm sorry, but I can't."

"You can," Jerry said.

"Jesus fucking Christ you've gone soft. I mean, I saw it coming, but not like this. What happened to you? You got all fucking soft on this."

"I'm not soft. Just being reasonable."

"No, fuck you, Jerry. You got soft. And I covered you. And I was the one who was reasonable. And you just fucking let me."

Jerry was still speaking with his voice low, and I tried to meet his eyes, but he wouldn't look at me, and he was focused on fat Gordo, and I could hear something breaking over the top of the hill that Gordo had dragged me down, and I knew that Amber was putting up a fight, so I dug my feet in and swung them against fat Gordo's leg, and he may have been fat, but he was quick, and he separated his legs before I could make contact with him and take him out at the knees.

"Settle the fuck down," he said to me. "Or I won't keep playing nice."

"Just let her go and me and you can fix this," Jerry said to fat Gordo.

Fat Gordo laughed, and I could feel his chest vibrate against the back of my head. "Fix this? You're fucked up, Jerry. I ain't got nothing to fix. This is all you."

"Exactly," Jerry said. "So just hand her over to me. Let me take care of it."

"You had your chance, Jerry," fat Gordo said. "You blew it, man. Got soft."

Jerry ran a hand through his hair, and fat Gordo loosened his grip on me enough to drop my toes back to the ground and when I tried to pull myself forward, he yanked me back and up so that I was off my feet again, and I could feel my windpipe getting crushed in the hard angle of his elbow.

I looked over at Jerry, and he still had his hands up and I wanted him to grab onto me and yank me free, but I knew that it wouldn't happen like that, and I had my hands loose at my sides, and I had already tried beating at fat Gordo, but it was like I was hitting wet bags of cement, and I had tried to grab and pinch and squeeze and scratch, but then he would just tighten his grip around my neck and choke the fight out of me.

"So what do you want to do, Gordo? Huh?" Jerry asked. "You've got her. So now what?"

Fat Gordo laughed again and I wanted to struggle against him but I was tired and giving up. "I'd say we could have had a lot of fun out here if you wanted to man up about it. I mean, I would have held her down so you could go first."

Jerry smiled at me. "You think that's what I picked her out for?"

"I don't give a shit. I'm just saying I would have held her. And now I don't trust you to hold her down for me."

Jerry stepped forward, and I could feel Gordo grab me by the top of my head and my neck snapped backward and I yelled a little bit, and the rain kept coming down so that everything shone wet and black underneath the moonlight that was still straining to get control through the clouds.

"You go first then," Jerry said to fat Gordo. "Go ahead."

Fat Gordo yanked me backward and we slid a little bit down the embankment, and I could smell the pine needles breaking underneath of us.

"I don't trust you," Gordo said. "I was gonna cover your end, Jerry. I fucking covered you. And this is what I get?"

"You're the just bagman, Gordo. What more do you want?"

"I'm not the fucking bagman, Jerry."

Jerry looked at me then, and I could see his eyes in the dark, and his pupils were just shadows in the whites of eyes and I wanted to send him a signal, but he was the one who was hitting my eyes, and then dropping them, and then raising them back up to my face again, and I screamed then, for Amber, and then fat Gordo slapped a thick hand over my mouth and I tried to bite him but he pulled his palm flat and my teeth couldn't get any traction.

"I'll hold her," Jerry said. "Why not?"

I could feel fat Gordo looking at Jerry over my shoulder. "You owe me, Jerry."

"Yeah, I owe you. So hand her over to me. You can go first."

I could feel fat Gordo loosen his grip on my throat and I thought about yanking my head free from his arm, but I knew that Jerry didn't want me to, and more than anything I was listening to Jerry.

"Fuck you," fat Gordo said, and he pulled me against him again, and I could smell his sweat underneath the rain and the damp ground and I would have held my breath if I could move my lungs and pull in air.

"She ain't worth this," Jerry said, and he reached out toward me, but not with his hands, and then I figured out what he was looking at.

"She doesn't belong to you, Jerry," fat Gordo said. "I get this one. Go get your fucking daughter." And with that, I swung my legs up so that my feet pulled higher than my knees and I pushed them back with everything I had, and I could feel them slam into fat Gordo's legs, and he stumbled backward for a second, and he loosened his arm on my neck, and I could get a quick breath, and then my hands were all of the way free, and I reached down into my underwear and pulled out the gun that Jerry had given to me, and I threw it forward and Jerry had to take a couple of steps to catch it, but then he did, and fat Gordo grabbed me by the hair and pulled my head backward, and I went from looking at Jerry to looking at sky, and I could see the clouds racing above us, like they had someplace better to go.

I heard the round chamber, and then Jerry said, "Let her go," again, and I felt like I was in a movie, and I felt sort of happy about that because in the movies, all the people who are supposed to live always do, and fat Gordo yanked me backward so that I slammed into him again, and I could feel my teeth rattle and my tongue pull back from the strain, and then he was moving down the hill, slipping in his slick shoes, and then I heard the sound from the gun before I even saw the short flash from the barrel, and there was a burst like lightning, but it was only a .22 bullet breaking loose, and Jerry shot fat Gordo in the leg, and fat Gordo went down on his knee and he dropped his arms from around me and I dug in and started to run, and then Jerry caught me, and I had only made it through three steps before I went from frying pan to fire.

"You fucking shot me," fat Gordo said, and he was on his knees in the dirt and I could hear him trying to stand up again.

"It's just a fucking flesh wound," Jerry said. "You can handle it."

"Fuck you, Jerry. You're gonna pay for that."

I could feel Jerry holding onto me, and even though his grip was strong, he wasn't using it to bite into me, and I could have bolted free and taken off, but I didn't, and then Jerry pulled me next to him, and he put his mouth to my ear and I could feel his breath on me and it was warm, and he said, "Run, kid. And don't fucking stop," and then I was out of his grip and at first I just stood there while Jerry pointed the pistol down at fat Gordo, and I realized just how small the gun really was, and I didn't know which way to go—up or down the hillside—and beyond Jerry I could hear Amber yelling and I could hear voices, and I knew that what I should really do was go back up the embankment and into the circle of light from the cabin and find Amber and pull her with me into the dark down the hill, but Jerry had the gun on fat Gordo and he waved it toward me and said, "Run," again, and I did, and I could barely keep up with my legs, and I tried to lean into them, and I was going down the hillside, and I slid in a break of pine needles, and the rain kept coming down and everything felt wet and green, and branches snapped at my face, and I heard the gun go off behind me, and then fat Gordo was saying, "You shot me, Jerry, you motherfucker," and there was something thick in his voice, and I kept running, and I could hear fat Gordo saying something that sounded a lot like begging or praying, or maybe a combination of both, but I couldn't see anything under the darkness of the clouds and the angle of the rain, and I fell, and I could feel my palms pull through dirt and rub across red rocks, and I got up again and kept running even though I was having a hard time keeping up with my feet, and I kept my head down and the passing branches reached for my eyes, but I wouldn't give them up, and then I saw a shadow below me, and it was big and dark and I could hear the rain bouncing off metal, and I tripped again and caught myself before I landed head-first in a lanky growth of manzanita, and then the rain pulled back and let up and I could see the shadow clearly and it took on more shape, and I ran toward it with my tennis shoes slick-bottomed and wet, and then Hurley's truck came out of the shadow and I was running into it, and I was running past it, and I slowed up enough to grab the door handle and pull myself to a stop, and somewhere up the hillside, from the direction that I had run, I heard another gunshot, and the woods went quiet, and the wind caught its breath long enough for me to hear Amber's voice in the distance, and even though I was far away from her, I could hear what she said carrying over the soft hills and the standing water and the trees that had bent down to trip me up and catch me, and I knew that in the darkness, even though she couldn't see me, that she was calling my name.

Chapter 22
Pulling Off the Wings

Reece moved over in the seat and got behind the wheel and I could see the keys still hanging from the ignition, and there was no light outside except for the moon passing through the trees, and in the darkness I couldn't see anything moving and I strained my eyes to separate shapes from the shadows, but there was nobody out there, and the driver's side window was cracked open and I could hear a million insects calling into the night, and the woods smelled like rain and wet and damp and green, and I could hear the drops still falling from the trees and the windshield was streaked, but the heavy downpour had lifted, and I should have been cold but I wasn't, and then we both heard a gunshot from somewhere not too far away and to the left, and Reece started chewing on his bottom lip and his hand froze between the steering wheel and the keys, and I reached over and pounded on his leg and said, "Start the truck—we've gotta go."

"I can't," he said, and I watched his hand go limp against the seat, and he was staring straight ahead, and I tried to follow where his eyes were looking but there was nothing to see, and then we heard another gunshot, and it was a little further away, and I said, "Please, Reece, just start the truck and go," and I could tell that he wanted to, but he was afraid of what that wanting might mean, and when I had left Amber in the dim spread of light from the cabin, Chuck had her in his arm and was dragging her toward darkness, and Lalo was standing in the doorway and Wendy was behind him, and Amber was thrashing around and digging her shoes into the dirt, and all she needed was to create enough slick traction to slip out and run.

"Everybody's gonna be okay," I said. "Everything's gonna be alright," and I reached out and touched his leg, gently this time, and I could feel him flinch underneath his jeans, and there was a flash in the distance of lightning touching down somewhere, and it was a long bright streak in the sky, and when I was little I had learned to count until I heard the thunder so I would know how far away the storm was moving, but I couldn't do anything but hold my breath and hope that Reece would break the ice that was holding him hostage and keeping him from turning the key and getting us in motion and setting us free.

"I've gotta go find Hurley," he said, and outside his window a bird called, and it was high-pitched and loud, and it startled me a little bit, and there was a wind up high that was bending the tops of trees, and all I wanted was to hear the sound of the engine gun to life and to feel the tires bite into the ground and pull us back toward the road, and I was still damp from the rain and I could feel it soaking into me suddenly, and my teeth started to chatter, and I wanted to touch Reece again but I knew that it wouldn't do any good, and I searched around in my head for something to say that might undo the spell that was keeping him tight to the seat, but I didn't know the magic words, and outside the windshield something moved in the distance and I sucked in my breath, and I waited for what was coming for me.

"Just start the truck, Reece," I said, and I tried to keep my voice low, and all I wanted was for him to look at me, but he wouldn't, and I said it again, "Start the truck, Reece," and I could see his fingers stretching and wanting to reach for the keys, but it was as if his arm wouldn't follow, and I thought I heard the sound of branches breaking outside of the truck but it could have been the wind, or it could have been Jerry, or it could have been Chuck, or it could have been nothing at all.

"I can't," Reece said.

"You can," I said. "Turn the key and take me to the bottom of the hill. Drop me at the road and then you can come back," I said.

He ran a shaky hand through his hair and then he wiped it on his jeans, and there was a roll of thunder in the distance that grew like a slow wave until it crested and peaked on the mountainside so that I could feel it come up through the floorboards, and then there was another crack of lightning, and the rain started to pelt the windshield again in fat drops that clung to the glass and refused to slide the distance to the hood.

"I can't leave Hurley," he said.

"You can come back for him if you want," I said. "Or he can find us. But we can't stay here. You know that."

"I want to go home," he said, and for a second I could hear his voice break and I thought that he might be crying and I knew that if he started crying, I was gonna start, too, so I reached out and hit him in the arm, hard, but not too, hard, and he jerked his head around and looked at me, and his eyes were wide.

"What the fuck did you do that for?"

"You have to wake up," I said. "Wake the fuck up and start the truck and drive."

He reached for the keys and there was the sound of another gunshot—or maybe it was thunder—and the sound was starting to distort itself and it was hard to get a sense of the direction, and all of the insects that had been humming and thumping themselves into the routine of the call had all gone quiet, and all I could hear was the sound of rain hitting the trees from up high, and the wind came in a long burst that bent the tops and they sighed as if they were waiting for us to get gone.

Reece turned the key and the truck sputtered and the engine turned over, and I could see his leg flexing as he pumped the gas, and then the engine coughed and died, and he turned the key again and I could hear the starter grind, and the engine coughed again as if it was choking on its own fumes, and I could tell that Reece was going to flood it, and I reached out and put my hand on his leg and this time he didn't flinch and didn't pull away, and I could feel him take his foot off of the pedal, and he turned the key again and there was an attempt at a spark, and then he turned it again and this time the engine rolled over as if it were a tired dog that was taking up some sun, and instead of falling back into quiet, it sucked in a long breath of fuel and air, and it didn't cut out, and Reece feathered the gas pedal, and then the engine was running and he pumped the clutch and put the truck into gear, and he rolled us backwards and I told him not to turn on the lights, and he listened to me, and he turned his head to look over his shoulder so that he could see out the back window, and the reverse lights lit up the ground, and he jerked the wheel back and forth so that the tires slipped and grabbed ahold again, and I could feel them slipping through the pine needles, and then he hit a log that was sitting upright in the dirt, and I could hear the crack of something breaking and we slammed forward in a hard stop, and then he put the clutch down again and popped us into first gear and the truck lurched and slid sideways, and Reece twisted the wheel and caught us from going into the deep, wet silt from the trees, and I rolled my window down so that I could listen for the sound of motorcycles gunning to life and spitting exhaust so they could grip ground and take up after us.

We didn't hear anything else as Reece moved through the gears, and he was going fast down the hillside and it was hard to see without the lights, and I saw the flash of eyes pass in front of us and then cut to the bank and climb the hill, and I knew it was a deer, and Reece kept punching the gas and pulling his foot free and twisting the wheel and we slipped and slid back down the mountain, and I could see the highway in the distance, between a low clip of bushes and brush, and then Reece hit the brakes and the truck locked up and came to a stop, and he was breathing hard, and I realized that my nails were biting into the armrest, and I had to will myself to pry them loose when everything finally stopped moving.

"Now what?" Reece said, and in the distance, I could hear cars cruising over the 395 and I could see the headlights splashing, and I had only known that we had to get out of there but I didn't know anything about what we'd do once we did. "I gotta go back," Reece said.

I took a deep breath and the air tasted like wet asphalt, and I swallowed it in mouthfuls, and I counted to ten in my head and then I pulled the door handle and the dome light came on and I swung the door open and I could hear the woods again but they were quieter now in the wake of our escaping, and the clouds were still holding a tight fist above us and letting the rain out in a gentle squeeze.

"Go back," I said, and I tried to drop to the ground, but I couldn't feel my legs and I was afraid that they wouldn't hold me, and I tried to scoot over on the seat and push them to the edge of the floorboards, but they wouldn't go, and then I got tired of trying and flung myself out of the truck and I landed on my feet, and I turned and grabbed the door and looked at Reece. "I'm going to wait in the bushes," I said. "I'll look for you."

Reece looked at me under the soft, yellow light, and he seemed a lot older than he was, and I figured that I did, too, and over the crest of the soft hill another car passed on the highway, and there was a weak flash of light, and I knew that if I was somebody else maybe I would have said that I would go back with him, or I would get back into the truck and tell him that we just had to drive back to Reno and get what we could and go on to someplace else, but it was his brother that was running through the woods, and I knew that I couldn't make Reece leave him, and I knew that if Reece went back there, he had no choice but to leave me instead.

"Just wait for me," Reece said.

"Be careful," I said, and he nodded at me, and I pushed the door shut, and then I heard the gears grind and the truck was rolling in reverse and Reece swung the tail end around and then got it going forward again, and I watched him climb back up the road, and he still didn't have the lights on and the truck was just a dark shape moving through the trees, and I watched it until I couldn't see it anymore, and then I listened for it until the sounds of the highway buried it under the pounding of its own wheels.

I stood in the dark for a little while, and I was cold suddenly, and I shook the rain out of my hair, and I reached up and touched the back of my head where I had hit it on the counter, and there was a lump under the skin and I could feel that everything was matted around it, but when I looked at my fingers, they didn't come away with anything that looked like blood, and then the big drops that had been falling had split and divided and the rain was coming down in tiny drops that barely stung my skin, and I turned toward the highway and climbed the small embankment and pulled myself through the bushes, and I sat in the darkness so that I could watch the cars on the road, and I tried to listen for sounds on the mountainside but there was nothing, and the lightning had grown bored and moved on to the west, and there was no more thunder, and my stomach growled and I dug my shoes into the soft dirt, and I watched the highway and counted the cars, and I didn't have a watch and I didn't know how much time had passed, and I was in a place where ten minutes could be four hours, and I stood up and brushed the packed dirt from my wet jeans, and I walked out to the edge of the asphalt and I could hear rocks breaking loose underneath the rubber of my shoes, and when I saw headlights round the bend in the distance, I stuck my thumb out and kept my head down, and I waited.

To the east there was a big rig slapping eighteen wheels against the pavement, pulling through the low gears as it made the climb, and I had already felt the blowby of a half dozen cars as I stood there on the side of the road, and I figured it was a sign that I should just give up and go back to the bushes and wait for Reece, and then the big rig passed me by in a stream of lights, and I pulled my thumb back in and turned toward the embankment, but I heard the pumping of air brakes and I could hear them squealing and I saw the emergency flashers come on and it had pulled to the side of the road, and I saw the passenger door fling open and I heard a voice say, "come on," and I walked toward where it had pulled to the edge of the highway, and I had never been in a big truck like that before, and there was a step and a silver handle to grab, and I could feel the warmth seeping from the cab, and it was full of soft, yellow lights, and I could hear country music playing, and then a man's voice said, "Let me give you a ride," and I dug my shoes into the step and my grip slipped and I fell back to the road so I tried again and it took me a long time to climb in.

The first thing I noticed about the driver was that he had long hair pulled back from his shoulders in a low rubber band, and a thin beard that ran all the way up his cheeks, and he was an older guy, though it wasn't easy to tell age in the dark, and his eyes were deep set and wrinkled as if he had a spent a lifetime staring into the sun, and he was wearing a hat that had a patch on the front that said "Shepherd's Trucking," and I settled down in the seat and it held me like a blanket, and I pulled the door shut with the last of what I had to give, and he reached between us and he offered me a thermos of coffee, but I told him that I was okay, and then he asked me what I was doing out there in the middle of nowhere at this time of night, and I told him that my car had broken down, and my teeth were chattering and everything inside of me was shaking loose, and he looked over at me, and I could tell that he was doing the math on my age, and I let him, and the truck was warm, and the inside smelled like cinnamon and vanilla and I breathed it all in, and he reached behind him and pulled a towel from behind the curtain that led to the sleeper, and he handed it to me and I ran it over my head and across my face, and it came away with dirt and leaves and a little bit of dried blood, and he put the truck back in gear and I felt the wheels rolling forward before they picked up speed, and then we were moving faster, and he turned the fan up on the heater and pointed the vents my direction and I let the hot air blow across me until my skin went tight and it got hard to breathe.

"I'm going as far as Redding," he said. "Then I'm headed north to Portland."

I thought about Portland and how me and Amber and Hurley and Reece had the dream that we would end up there next, and I could still imagine our apartment in some building that had a store underneath, and I could see myself standing at the window on a Saturday morning and watching the people on the street, and we would be playing music, and Amber would be cooking breakfast in the kitchen, and we would all live like a family, and then I remembered Amber sitting under the light in the house, just before the chairs scraped away from the table and I went backward and the center fell in.

"You want me to call for a tow?" he asked, and he pointed toward a CB that was mounted below the dash with a spotted trout on a keychain dangling from a knob.

"I just need a ride," I said. I had thirty dollars in my pocket, and I'd left everything else behind.

He nodded and reached over and turned up the radio.

"You don't mind, do you?"

I shook my head. "No, I like it," I said. "It's pretty."

"Barbara Mandrell. She has a voice like an angel."

I smiled and looked out the window, and I could see streaks of trees, but I couldn't hold on to the smile, and I started crying then, and once I started, I knew that I couldn't stop, and part of me felt as if I had just been watching everything go down and the worst parts had happened to somebody else.

"Hey, you okay?" the driver asked, and I wanted to tell him that I wasn't okay, would probably never be okay again, but I didn't even know what that meant yet, and I couldn't stop crying to use my voice to speak. I knew that I had gone out beyond where I could touch bottom, and I wasn't a strong swimmer, and I had tried to make it back to shore but I had drowned.

Jerry would be ashamed of me if he saw me like this—he had taught me better. I could almost hear him—"Grow the fuck up, kid"—so I wiped my face with the back of my hand and sucked in my crying, but I couldn't think about what was behind me—what had happened in those woods, and I didn't know what was in front of me, but part of me was missing home for the first time in a long time, but deep down I didn't even know what *home* meant. I could feel the trucker looking at me, and I turned my head so I could see him better, and he gave me a smile that showed he was missing some teeth.

"You don't look like much of a boy," he said, and I could see his thumbs rubbing on the steering wheel while he drove. I didn't say anything to him—just tried to feel the vents in front of me blowing heat.

I could feel the bench seat move underneath me as he shifted his weight, and I could feel him taking quick glances between me and the highway that was taking shape in front of us in the weak and unsure light. It was quiet for a while, and then he turned toward me again and cleared his throat.

"You wanna make some money?" he said. "There's a rest stop not too far up the road."

I could hear Jerry in my head again, *Hey, it's your deal. Lots of truckers out there. Gets lonely on the road. I'm sure there'd be a few who didn't mind getting a girl up in the cab, all alone,* and for a second I was standing in that gas station bathroom again with the scissors snapping close to my right ear and Jerry waiting on me to make a decision to stop and quit or to keep going forward with him, and I reached up and touched the short ends of my hair that had gone soft with so much distance from the blades, and I ignored the driver and tried to think about nothing at all because everything felt like it wanted to come at me all at once, and maybe he would leave me alone if I just faded into the seat, but then he cleared his throat again and said, "You know what a happy ending is?" and I looked over at him then and there was a smirk on his face because he knew that I knew exactly what he meant, and somewhere in the distance I could hear Amber laughing.

"Yeah," I said. "It's the end of a story when the bad guys get what they deserved and the good guys get everything that they wanted." I looked over at him. "It's when everything turns out for the best."

He laughed then and dropped his right hand to the seat between us and it moved toward me, clumsy and thick, and I could see that there was a scar on the back of his knuckles, and he leaned sideways and reached toward my thigh. "That's not what I—" and he was still laughing when I slapped my hand over his and grabbed his middle finger and pulled up as fast and hard as I could, and even when I felt something give underneath the skin, I did not let go, and he made a noise that filled the cab like the mixture of surprise and a scream, and the truck swerved over the center line and came back to the lane, and I could feel the tires hit the warning bumps between us and the ditch, and I loosened my fingers so that he could yank his arm back and then he shook his hand out and held it up against his chest like a bird with a busted wing.

"You don't want to be touching me," I said. "I'm stronger than I look," and I rubbed my own hand over the leg of my jeans where the gun that I had never used had once sat in my pocket, and I didn't look away from him as the highway cut a hard line between the trees and the rocks and everything out the windows was a streak of dark green, and I saw boulders stacked in unsteady piles and flagged with orange paint, and the forest thinned around us, and then the engine dropped down to a deeper growl blowing diesel, and neither of us spoke, and he didn't so much as glance over at me, and after what could have been five minutes or an hour, we finally climbed above the tree line and burst out into the sun.

Acknowledgments

There are many people who stood behind me and helped me to push this boulder up a hill, and I would like to thank them for the support and the guidance that they gave to me. Thank you, Jan Haag, Daniel Rounds, Maureen Wanket, and Carrie Marks, for being patient with early drafts and asking good questions. Thank you to Christian Kiefer for going above and beyond—always. Thank you to Michael Spurgeon for always being a solid voice of reason and advice. And finally, thank you to my longtime agent, Danielle Svetcov, who never gives up on me, and still, after over a decade of working with me, returns my emails without delay, dusts me off, and points me in all the right directions.

About the Author

Jodi Angel is the author of two story collections, The History of Vegas and You Only Get Letters from Jail, which was named as a Best Book of 2013 by Esquire. Her work has appeared in Esquire, Tin House, One Story, Zoetrope: All-Story, Electric Literature Recommended Reading, and Byliner, among other publications and anthologies. Her short story, "Snuff," was selected for inclusion in The Best American Mystery Stories 2014. She grew up in a small town in Northern California—in a family of girls.

CPSIA information can be obtained
at www.ICGtesting.com
Printed in the USA
JSHW082012250123
36837JS00003B/15